ROY STRONG

LOST TREASURES OF BRITAIN

VIKING

Published in association with *The Sunday Times*

VIKING

Published by the Penguin Group
27 Wrights Lane, London W8 5TZ, England
Viking Penguin, a division of Penguin Books USA Inc.,
375 Hudson Street, New York, New York 10014, USA
Penguin Books Australia Ltd, Ringwood, Victoria, Australia
Penguin Books Canada Ltd, 2801 John Street, Markham, Ontario, Canada L3R 1B4
Penguin Books (NZ) Ltd, 182–190 Wairau Road, Auckland 10, New Zealand

Penguin Books Ltd, Registered Offices: Harmondsworth, Middlesex, England

First published 1990
1 3 5 7 9 10 8 6 4 2

Typeset in 12/15 pt Linotype Garamond 3 by Wyvern Typesetting Limited, Bristol
Printed and bound in Italy by Amilcare Pizzi SpA
Colour origination by Colorlito Rigogliosi s.r.l. Italy

A CIP catalogue record for this book is available from the British Library

ISBN 0–670–83383–5
LCCN: 90–70967

Frontispiece: *Detail from a copy of the mural behind the high altar in St Stephen's chapel, Westminster Palace, showing the Adoration of the Magi.*

Contents

Picture Acknowledgements

James Austin: 61, 95; Ashmolean Museum, Oxford: 81, 113, 138, 146, 168 (above), 183; Bayerische Verwaltung der Staatlichen Schlösser, Gärten und Seen: 78; Berkeley Castle: 126, 152 (photos Central Photographic Services); Tom Brett: 60; British Library: 18, 20, 28, 66, 69, 71, 224; British Museum: 30, 39, 64, 83, 94, 168 (below), 186, 199, 204, 206; John Britton, *Graphical and Literary Illustrations of Fonthill Abbey*, 1823: 193; S & N Buck, *A Collection of Engravings of Castles*, 1726–52: 35; Burrell Collection, Glasgow Museums and Art Galleries: 25; Cambridge University, Collection of Air Photographs: 40, 41; Cambridge University Library: 20, 68; Castle Museum, City of Nottingham: 148; Issac de Caus, *Wilton Garden*, 1645: 170 (above), 174 (below), 175 (right), 177, 178 (above); Christie, Manson & Woods International Inc., New York: 180; Clore Gallery (for the Turner Collection): 197; Country Life: 115; Courtauld Institute, Conway Library: 100; Christopher Dalton: 36; William Dugdale, *The History of St Pauls*, 1658: 22, 135 (above), 136; John Fox, *Acts and Monuments*, 2nd edition 1576: 52; GGS Photography: 55; Mark Girouard: 114; The Worshipful Company of Goldsmiths: 82; Guildhall Library, City of London: 130, 135 (below), 151; Simon Gunton, *The History of the Church of Peterburgh*, 1686: 97; George Hall: 58, 154; Sonia Halliday and Laura Lushington: i, 90; Historical Museum, University of Bergen: 14; Historisches Museum, Basel: 85; A F Kersting: 99; Koninklijk Museum voor Schone Kunsten, Antwerp: 107; Kunsthistorisches Museum, Vienna: 102; Musée du Louvre: 62 (photo Giraudon), 63 (photo Giraudon), 108 (above) (photo Giraudon), 145 (Cabinet des Dessins); Frederick Mackenzie, *The Architectrual Antiquities of the Collegiate Church of St Stephen's*, 1844: 205; Eric de Mare: 159; Mas: 106, 108 (below); Metropolitan Museum of Art, New York, Fletcher Fund: 59; Major More-Molyneux: 140 (photo Jeremy Whitaker); Musée Royal des Beaux Arts, Antwerp: 107; Museum of London: 132, 133, 143; National Portrait Gallery: viii, 51, 120, 121, 161; Nationalmuseum Stockholm (photograph Statens Konstmuseer): 84 (below); National Trust Photographic Library: 190; Öffentliche Kunstsammlung, Basel: 80, 167; The Earl of Pembroke: 170 (below), 173 (photos Jeremy Whitaker); Philadelphia Museum of Art, the John H McFadden Collection: 214; Pierpont Morgan Library, New York: 123; John Pine, *Tapestry Hangings of the House of Lords*, 1739: 212, 213 (photos British Library Map Room); Private Collection: 92 (photo A C Cooper); by gracious permission of Her Majesty the Queen: 112 (left), 118, 153, 160, 202; RIBA Drawings Collection: 104, 105, 112 (right); John Rutter, *Delineations on Fonthill and its Abbey*, 1823: 188, 191, 194 (courtesy Salisbury & South Wiltshire Museum), 195, 198; Eddie Ryle-Hodges: 33; St John's College, Cambridge: 87; Lord St Oswald: 166; St Thomas's Church Salisbury: 56 (photo Roy Reed); by courtesy of the Marquess of Salisbury: 74, 84 (above); F Sandford, *A geneological History of the Kings of England*, 1677: 93; by courtesy of the trustees of the Earl of Scarbrough's Settlement: 141 (below), 142 (photos Victoria & Albert Museum); Scottish National Portrait Gallery: 86; Edwin Smith: 42, 43; by courtesy of the trustees of Sir John Soane's Museum: 184; Society of Antiquaries: 23, 162, 207, 208, 209, 210, 211; John Speed, *Theatre of the Empire of Great Britaine*, 1611: 141 (above); John Summerson, *Architecture in Britain 1530–1830*, 3rd edition 1958: 116 (drawing Malcolm Higgs); Sunday Times: 178 (below) (photo Clive Boursnell); Julia Trevelyan Oman: 175 (left), 176; Trinity College, Dublin: 72; Trinity Hall, Cambridge: 27; University Museum, Trondheim: 46; University Museum of National Antiquities, Oslo: 54; by courtesy of the Board of Trustees of the Victoria & Albert Museum: 164, 166; Isaac Ware, *Designs of Inigo Jones and others*, 1743: 182; by courtesy of the Dean and Chapter of Westminster: 49, 124; Westminster Public Library: 156–157; Provost and Fellows of Worcester College, Oxford: 174 (above).

Preface

This essay on the *Lost Treasures of Britain* arose out of the threatened sale of the Hereford Cathedral *Mappa Mundi*. Julian Browne of *The Sunday Times* asked me whether I would write a piece on treasures which had not, for one reason or another, survived into this century. Initially we considered an international and timeless approach, but quickly realized how amorphous the result would be. By confining it to the British Isles it gained both coherence and an intellectual point which perhaps needs to be made, reminding a heritage-fixated public about the interrelationship of creativity and destruction.

The basis of that article, which appeared in *The Sunday Times Magazine* in November 1989, has been enormously expanded. I am fully aware that such a survey could never be written without drawing very fully on the work of scholars in many fields, but no one, as far as I know, has ever attempted to draw this material together in one book. In doing so I have been enormously helped by the enthusiasm and critical acumen of my editor, Tessa Strickland, and her team, in particular the designer, Wilf Dickie, and Susan Rose-Smith, who chased the abundant illustrative material.

Roy Strong
January 1990

Introduction

Lost treasures of Britain may seem a melancholy subject for a day dream. There is so much to throw us into a reverie of enchantment: the wonders of Nonsuch Palace, the legendary Tudor royal plate and jewels, the glittering shrine of St Cuthbert at Durham Cathedral, the spectacle of Wilton's great pre-Civil-War garden. The choice is a dazzling one. It is a list open to arbitrary expansion – and yet not quite, for glories which vanished before the age of scientific verisimilitude must remain a feast for the imagination alone. This is why my narrative begins in the Tudor age. No literary description – which, almost without exception, is the most we have of treasures lost in earlier periods of Britain's history – can ever replace the impact of even the crudest of visual images. From the reign of Henry VIII onwards the material, although uneven, becomes substantial. In the following chapters the reader will find a pot-pourri of pictorial evidence – paintings, drawings, designs, fragmentary remains – to indicate losses. Some are more evocative than others but all of them recapture something of the magic and importance of the lost originals.

Inevitably the selection has the character of a personal anthology. In making that selection I was anxious not to swamp the narrative with lost buildings about which we tend to hear all too much but rather to remind the reader of the transitory nature of such items as jewels or tapestries or the contents of a palace. The book ends with the fire of 1834 which consumed

Opposite: *A detail from a painting of Edward VI and the Pope of c. 1548–49 showing the destruction of holy images. Two men haul down a statue of a female saint from a column while another smashes an image to pieces. In the background huge buildings crash to the ground amidst an inferno, perhaps casting the fate of papal Rome as a Fall of Babylon.*

Westminster Palace, three years before the accession of Queen Victoria, for a number of reasons. The first was that the Victorian age created the idea of national treasures and their conservation as part of an inalienable heritage belonging to everyone. Another was the advent of the camera and hence a massive increase in the recording of what has since disappeared. A third factor was that over the last two decades a number of books have covered nineteenth-century losses, which are almost wholly architectural. Finally, we are still part of that Victorian continuum, whereas what happened before belongs to a different age with a totally different attitude towards the past. No one has ever brought together those earlier losses or compared the attitudes that governed then with our own quite different ideas about what is and what is not of worth. Perhaps, I thought, we can learn something from the pre-heritage centuries.

My search through the archives of the past made me turn my thoughts towards the future, and the context in which Britain is moving towards the next century. Why should we think in terms of treasures or, as we now define them, heritage, at all? We are, I believe, at the end of a series of complex changes of attitude to the artefacts of the past. That attitude evolved over four centuries into the almost universal belief that what is old is *de facto* worthy of preservation. We now accept this belief unquestioningly. But should we? The changing ideological framework through which the British have viewed their past became, as I worked on this book, the most fascinating aspect of my research.

In the sixteenth century on the eve of the Reformation the British Isles was criss-crossed with a network of shrines, relics, images and a thousand varieties of ecclesiastical artefact to remind people of their place as members of Holy Mother Church. They paid their devotions to those sacred shrines and images as objects of worship, not as works of art, wending their way in their thousands to the great places of pilgrimage. This was the iconography of medieval Britain as part of the Church Universal. In that sense the country was not nearly so insular as it was to become in later ages. After the Reformation came the ascendancy of a newly powerful monarchy. The ritual and imagery that had been the prerogative of the Church was transferred to the Crown and used to emphasize its territorial integrity over the 'Empire of Great Britain' against the claims of Rome.

This insularity was heightened further by the nineteenth-century cult of British history, whose tangible form was the preservation of old buildings and of artefacts in museums and galleries. Preservation on such an unprecedented scale made visible and accessible to the ordinary citizen a common national mythology necessary to an age of universal suffrage. That attitude, which is as remarkable for its introspective as for its retrospective aspect, became increasingly sacrosanct in our century until, in the 1970s, we witnessed the emergence of 'heritage', a concept locked exclusively into things past. This essay on our lost treasures is both a dream and a nightmare, for it should, if read aright, make us question what seems to be an exaggerated fixation with the past.

The idea of treasures and heritage is dependent upon a sense of history and a sense of aesthetics. In Britain the former came first, although the two inevitably intertwine. History springs from a sense of human beings placed in time. It is a concept which is essentially Renaissance in spirit, for it was during that period that man framed himself within a continuum which was not theological but based on the civilization of classical antiquity, its loss in the Dark and Middle Ages, and its recovery in the present. In England, as in many other nascent European states in the sixteenth century, this concept served the new dynasty that had come to power. The Welsh Tudors were *nouveaux* and court historians were ever anxious to reinforce their right to rule through their descent from Brutus, the mythical Trojan king of Britain, and from King Arthur. This need for the sanction of the past was intensified by the Reformation, when the English Church broke with Rome and argued, along with the monarchy, that the *Ecclesia Anglicana* pre-dated St Augustine and his monks and went back via the Celtic Church to St Joseph of Arimathea, who was believed to have come to Britain direct from the Holy Land, and to Lucius, the first Christian king of Britain.

The past was scoured for artefacts – manuscripts, inscriptions and coins – in order to concoct arguments for the new Tudor *status quo*. This process began with the antiquary John Leland, and culminated in the figure of William Camden, whose *Britannia*, published from 1586 onwards, contained the first topographical description of England, Wales and Ireland and was also notable for its interest in artefacts reverenced as evidence: the stained glass at Peterborough containing the history of its abbots, or King John's Cup at King's Lynn. The initial focus of this antiquarian stream was monuments and muniments which revealed land rights, coats of arms and all aspects of genealogy. Aesthetic criteria did not exist. In Elizabethan England, to show any interest in the ruined abbeys from the dissolution was to attract the stigma of recusancy, and indeed the earliest laments for their loss came from those who remained loyal to the old faith.

With hindsight one can argue that the Tudor monarchy, having destroyed a centuries-old network of holy relics and images, began to create another, wholly secular one through the work of its antiquaries. The Elizabethan Society of Antiquaries, which was founded in the mid-1580s, flourished for only some twenty years. Its impulse was partly nationalistic, reinforcing the legends of the island kingdom, and limited to a small circle, although this did not prevent the antiquary as a type from being satirized for an educated audience. Such eccentric figures were recorded in the well-known portrayal by Earle in his *Microcosmography* of 1628:

He is a man strangely thrifty of time past ... A great admirer he is of old monuments ... He will go forty miles to see a saint's well, or a ruined Abbey; and there be but a Cross or stone footstool in the way, he'll be considering it so long till he forget his journey ...

In this sketch we have the precursor of the modern tourist of historic sites, museums and galleries.

By the accession of Elizabeth I the tide of destruction left by the Reformation was seen as a possible threat to public order. In 1560 a royal proclamation was issued 'against breaking or defacing Monumentes of Antiquitie set up in Churches, or other publike places, for memory, and not for superstition'. This was particularly aimed at preserving the tombs of the aristocracy and gentry. It associates the preservation of old artefacts with the preservation of established society and its motive was in no way aesthetic.

The proclamation is the first evidence we have of official action taken to preserve something old. It was followed by an indenture by the queen's successor, James I, in 1605 to set aside a select group of 'Roiall and Princely Ornaments and Jewells to be indyvidually and inseparably for euer hereafter annexed to the Kingdome of this Realme'. The list included items such as 'The Imperiall Crowne of this Realme of Gould', which the Commonwealth melted down, and jewels such as the legendary Three Brothers and the more recent 'great riche Jewell of Goulde called the Mirror of Greate Brittaine', which James's son was to pawn and then consign to destruction. What the indenture describes as 'this his royal and religious Resolution' was in fact startlingly original. It implied not only the preservation in perpetuity of such jewels but that they should perhaps remain unaltered. Like the Elizabethan intervention, it establishes a connection between specific artefacts and a given social structure, in this case the sanctity of the Crown. For the first time royal jewels assumed the status of those that had adorned the medieval shrines before the Reformation: they were to be revered as untouchable.

After the demise of the Elizabethan Society of Antiquaries in the early seventeenth century, the movement was revived with a new fervour after 1660. The trauma of the Civil War, which swept away what seemed a God-ordained society, contributed greatly to the British obsession with the past; after the Restoration attempts were made to put the clock back and eradicate any trace of the Commonwealth. When the monarchy returned, antiquarian heralds had to re-create the crown jewels, the coronation ceremony, the rituals of the Order of the Garter and the lost world of pre-1642. This was also the great era of the county histories, with their emphasis on the stability of England through the old aristocratic and gentry families, their lands and houses. Sir William Dugdale, Robert Plot, Sir Henry Chauncy and others took advantage of the advent of the topographical draughtsman and engraver to publish their treasuries of views of towns, cathedrals, churches, monastic ruins, country houses and gardens. It need hardly be added that as antiquarians their mental stance was essentially backward-looking.

At the opening of the seventeenth century the antiquarian was joined by a new figure, the aesthete. Had he existed a century earlier, the aesthete would at least have attempted to save some works of medieval religious art from the holocaust of destruction that attended the Reformation. However, it was not until the very last years of Elizabeth I's reign that picture collections were formed. This interest in art reached its apogee in the circle of connoisseurs centred on Charles I. This is the period in English history when certain objects – whether pictures, sculpture or *objets d'art* – came to be looked upon as supreme expressions of the human genius. A Roman statue of Venus or Apollo, for instance, was admired not only as the embodiment of a civilization the viewer wished to revive, but also as art. It was no longer a pagan idol. A Madonna and Child by a master of the Italian Renaissance was also prized, although in Protestant England the majority of the population would have viewed such a picture as a limb of the Antichrist of Rome and defaced it. For the first time, to be a gentleman required some knowledge of art, a trend we catch in a popular handbook of the day, Henry Peacham's *Compleat Gentleman* (1634), which includes long sections on antique statues, coins and painting. 'Such as are skilled in them,' he writes, 'are by the *Italians* tearmed *Virtuosi*, as if others that either neglect or despise them, were idiots or rakehels.' And that virtuosity embraced not only classical antiquities and old master paintings but the work of contemporary artists both foreign and English. Over the next two centuries the aristocrat and gentleman responded to this new requirement by assembling in the country houses of Britain some of the finest concentrations of European art in the world and by commissioning on a massive scale works from the greatest artists of the day. In this way altarpieces wrenched from Italian churches or views of Venice by Canaletto were to become naturalized as part of a British heritage. However, the context into which they were put was modern, the latest in terms of architecture, interior design and furnishing. As time went by this became as important as their original setting, if not more important, or so conservationists were to argue. What had started life as old art in a strictly modern setting acquired an immutable patina, as though conceived as a unity from the outset.

Ordinary travellers in Stuart England, however, focused their attention firmly on contemporary achievements. Before the advent of a decent road system in the late seventeenth century, travel was undertaken out of necessity rather than pleasure. Apart from foreigners, who pursued a set route embracing the royal palaces and universities, only topographers and antiquarians travelled. When other people made a journey what they looked for was anything new. Lieutenant Hammond, who journeyed through twenty-six counties of England in 1633–4, noted above all the tremendous changes inside churches as a result of the Laudian movement. He was not interested in a church or cathedral as an ancient building but in the new altar rails, the introduction of canopies, embroidered cushions and copes, and of candlesticks on the altar. Hammond also keenly observed industrial sites, fortifications and anything that might be categorized as a curiosity. This way of looking at the world continued into the first half of the eighteenth century, and is epitomized in the tours of two very dissimilar people, Celia Fiennes and Daniel Defoe. What binds them is their passion for the *contemporary*. Old buildings were seen as mean. The sight of burgeoning industry – coal or tin mining, weaving, papermaking – always excited them, even though industry then was no more picturesque than it is now. Fiennes and Defoe set out to portray a rich, populous and prosperous country. Their progress was the total reverse of our own itineraries – we move from one monument to the past to the next, usually bewailing anything modern that impinges upon the nostalgic scene – yet they are not devoid of admiration, on occasion, for things past. 'King's College Chapple is the finest building I ever heard of,' Celia Fiennes somewhat ineptly records, but the now famous Rows in Chester are condemned as darkening the streets and spoiling the city.

Celia Fiennes travelled between 1685 and 1705 and Daniel Defoe began his series of descriptive letters in 1725. By that date the antiquarian eye was beginning to exert its influence over a wide section of the educated classes. There had been, however, isolated instances of the deliberate preservation of an old building for its own sake; indeed, the earliest reference we have is the account by the antiquarian John Aubrey of how Inigo Jones preserved the 'Holbein Porch' at Wilton, Wiltshire, on the grounds that it was 'as good architecture as any was in England'. This was during the 1630s, when Philip, Earl of Pembroke, embarked on replacing the mid-Tudor house with a vast Palladian villa. The impulse behind Jones's recommendation was a unique mixture of the aesthetic and the antiquarian, for the architect was both, writing a disquisition on the origins of Stonehenge as well as advising Charles I on his picture collection. Jones had a clear idea, as we know from his other work, of some kind of historic schema into which architecture fitted. This schema moved from ancient British classical through 'the ignorant Goths' to the gradual restoration of classicism in his own age. The 'Holbein Porch', which showed some stirrings of that revival, was therefore worthy of preservation.

Sir John Vanbrugh represents a radical change in attitude to the buildings of the past, evident in his famous exchange with Sarah, Duchess of Marlborough, over the medieval royal palace of Woodstock. In 1709 the duchess ordered the architect to demolish it, but he argued for its retention as 'one of the Most Agreable Objects that the best Landskip Painters can invent', and because of its associational value: 'it was rais'd by One of the Bravest and most warlike of the English Kings; And tho' it has not been Fam'd, as a Monument of his Arms; it has been tenderly regarded as the Scene of his Affections'. The duchess, however, had no time for what she regarded as 'an old Building that Stood awry and Spoiled the view'. And so Woodstock went. Vanbrugh had greater success in 1719 in saving the 'Holbein gate' of Whitehall Palace when it was threatened with demolition for road widening. He was astonished that anyone should consider the destruction of 'one of the Greatest Curiositys there is in London', and gained it a thirty-year reprieve.

Vanbrugh was not alone in heralding a radical shift in attitude to the buildings of the past. In 1718 Stephen Switzer in his book, *Ichnographia Rustica*, anticipated the picturesque movement of fifty years later by writing that 'to Noble and Ingenuous Natures a Piece of Ruin is more entertaining than the most beautiful Edifice; and the sorrowful Reflection they draw from the Soul ascend the very Heav'ns'. Such sentiments are partly derived from the literary tradition of the lamentation over ruins, but are also linked with the revival of the Gothick in the early eighteenth century. What is so striking about the initial phase of that stylistic revival is that it was in no way concerned with surviving Gothic buildings and their preservation, but with the erection of new ones in a version of the old style. In the long run, of course, this prompted a change of attitude to the genuine artefacts, for the fashion began as a celebration of the heroic British past and the struggles for constitutional liberties against the claims of the Crown.

The earliest Gothick garden building went up at Shotover, Oxfordshire, around 1717 and was an emphatic statement of the Whig allegiances of its builder, James Tyrrell. This was the beginning of a steady stream of garden buildings in the Gothick manner by William Kent, Thomas Wright, 'Capability' Brown and Sanderson Miller. All of these Gothick pavilions and ruined baronial castles set as eye-catchers on the horizon refocused attention on the ruined abbeys of England. For two centuries used as quarries for local house building and regarded as the remnants of dens of iniquity, they now began to be viewed as objects of great romance, evoking the halcyon days of bygone chivalry. In such a vein Horace Walpole wrote to Richard Bentley in 1755 describing the ruins of Netley, Hampshire:

The ruins are vast, and retain fragments of beautiful fretted roofs pendant in the air, with all the variety of Gothic patterns of windows wrapped round and round with ivy – many trees are sprouted up against the walls, and only want to be increased by cypresses ... In short, they are not the ruins of Netley, but of Paradise. Oh! the purple Abbots, what a spot they had chosen to slumber in!

Such a radical revision in the reading of the landscape led, for instance, in 1768 to Fountains Abbey being brought into the garden of Studley Royal, Yorkshire. In 1774 'Capability' Brown was to do the same at Sandbeck in the same county when he drew in as part of his composition the remains of Roche Abbey.

The result of a widening admiration for the artefacts of the past was that such ruins were now to be not just visited but *preserved*. A very early call for legislation to ensure preservation of such monuments was made in a paper to the Society of Antiquaries of 1776. The Gothic revival of the eighteenth century was certainly responsible for the survival of untold numbers of medieval buildings. There are several early instances of their rescue and re-erection. In 1765 Henry Hoare secured the Bristol High Cross and St Peter's pump and sited them in his great garden at Stourhead. At Nuneham Courtney Lord and Lady Harcourt seized the opportunity to re-erect the Carfax Conduit from Oxford as part of one of 'Capability' Brown's schemes for their garden.

These are early stirrings, for the eighteenth century was not backward-looking. When the Georgians toured their own country, which they now did in large numbers, to view country houses and visit the spas, like their Stuart forebears it was everything new which pleased them. At the top of the list came Houghton, Holkham and Blenheim, with Castle Howard, Kedleston and, more surprisingly, Hardwick Hall in the second eleven. Medieval buildings and artefacts attracted as little appreciation as did Elizabethan and Jacobean. The Tudor seat of the Petre family at Ingestre was dismissed as 'both inconvenient and inelegant'. Horace Walpole considered Haddon Hall simply barbaric: 'It is low & can never have been a tolerable House, the gallery is the only good room. Within the court is a strange confusion of half arches & beams, that imply the greatest ignorance in the art.'

The forces which were to change those viewpoints were gaining momentum. At the opening of the century the Society of Antiquaries had been founded. The society still exists but it is now entirely peripheral to the mainstream of contemporary culture. During the first century of its existence virtually everyone who was of any importance in the world of learning and the creative arts among the establishment classes was a member. The extent of their influence was due to the antiquarian William Stukeley's belief in the importance of making visual records of old pictures and artefacts as well as of archaeological items. Through their long series of publications in *Archaeologia* and *Vetusta Monumenta* every aspect of the past was recorded, from ancient furniture to medieval silver. All of this provided the material necessary for any artist or individual who wished to dwell permanently in the past.

The result of this recovery during the eighteenth century gave us two streams, both of which are alive today. One was to build and decorate in a style of the past, the other to fill one's house with old things, i.e. antiques. Eventually the appreciation of old things would lead to the reassessment of old houses, which ceased to be dismissed as 'inconvenient and inelegant' and became instead places of all-consuming mystery and romance, an attitude which is almost universal today. In 1800, by contrast, those who indulged in what has been categorized as the Romantic Interior – people like Horace Walpole at Strawberry Hill,

10

William Beckford at Fonthill Abbey, or Sir Walter Scott at Abbotsford – were considered odd, quirky beings. Although they were exceptions, they must bear quite a heavy blame for the British obsession with anything old, for it was they who transmuted what had been the tradition of the Renaissance museum or cabinet of curiosities (such as John Tradescant's Ark, still in the Ashmolean Museum) into a species of sophisticated interior decoration. Before then old furnishings had been either thrown away or relegated to the servants' rooms or attics.

Strawberry Hill, Twickenham, is perhaps the most famous instance of this new genre which was to have such a profound influence. Horace Walpole purchased it in 1747 and went on building and embellishing it for over half a century. As a master of self-promotion in matters of taste, he had innumerable prints made to ensure that his message was broadcast for others to follow. The house itself was in the new Gothick style, irregular and rambling, its interior an innovative mish-mash of modern chimneypieces based on medieval tombs, chairs with backs derived from the tracery of lancet windows, ancient Tudor and Stuart portraits in the picture gallery, old stained glass in the windows and a scattering of historical relics such as Cardinal Wolsey's hat or a clock Henry VIII had given Anne Boleyn. Walpole was obsessed by old things and the possibilities that they offered for the voyage of the mind. 'I am deeper than ever in Gothic antiquities,' he wrote in 1759; 'I have bought a monk of Glastonbury's chair ... I pass all my mornings in the thirteenth century, and my evenings with the century that is coming on.'

The attitudes of Walpole and the creators of the Romantic Interior were to affect the way in which old houses were viewed by the populace at large. This movement was helped by something else, the idealization of medieval society; the cult of the manor house as epitomizing a lost, benign paternalism still finds its adherents amongst today's country-house visitors. That strand, described as 'The Return to Camelot', was heralded in an article in the *Gentleman's Magazine* in 1739:

I own I am always griev'd to see the venerable Paternal Castle of a Gentleman of an ancient Family, and a competent Fortune, *tasted* and dwindled down into an imperfect Imitation of an *Italian villa*, ... Methinks there was something respectable in those old hospitable *Gothick* Halls, hung round with the Helmets, Breast-plates and Swords of our Ancestors; I entered them with a Constitutional Sort of Reverence.

Such devotion to Old England and her ancient houses was not to gain universal momentum until the close of the eighteenth century, under the impact of the romantic movement, with its cult of the picturesque, and the French Revolution, which shook the old aristocratic classes and made them turn back to the ideals of medieval chivalry to justify an unchanged social structure. There was a new, idealized climate of courteous mutual obligation between the classes and the sexes, between lord and tenant and knight and lady. As had occurred after 1660 (and was to be repeated after 1937) the monarchy reasserted its antiquity. James Wyatt redecorated Windsor Castle in the Gothic style and George IV's coronation in 1820 was a gigantic pseudo-Elizabethan pageant based on 'old customs'. During the same period there was a boom in castle building, setting the scene for the medieval, Elizabethan and Jacobean revivals which followed through the century.

By the time Queen Victoria came to the throne in 1837 virtually all the elements were in place for the creation of 'the museum society'. Our average traveller through the British Isles was now avoiding the industrial sites and factory chimneys, dwelling instead upon mountains, once looked upon as hideous obstacles, as objects almost worthy of worship, and following an itinerary which was firmly focused on things old. In the Victorian period the iconography of what we call heritage – ancient cathedrals, churches, houses, works of art and relics – was projected, as a result of the various Acts of Parliament extending the franchise, to become a common sacred patrimony of the nation. That move towards embracing everybody into the cult of the physical artefacts of the regal and aristocratic British past, unknown to any previous century, is usefully summed up in one book produced in the 1840s, Charles Knight's *Old England: A Pictorial Museum of Regal, Ecclesiastical, Municipal, Baronial and Popular Antiquities*. It presents the history of England through a tapestry of views of old buildings, old portraits and old artefacts and ran into many editions. Although it projects passion for the past on to a huge middle class, it retains the optimism of the previous periods, for its theme is a triumphant progress to the present:

What we propose . . . is to narrate briefly the rise, progress, and application of the great inventions and discoveries of this latter era, which, themselves the offspring of human necessities, have proved the grand means of social amelioration and advancement – to glance at the progress of art and literature, and the means available for their universal diffusion – and to suggest the connection and correspondence which ever must exist between the progress of science and invention, the spread of letters and the fine arts, and the progress towards the complete civilisation and happiness of the human family.

Here is all the confidence of the mid-Victorian age in social and material improvement. The book is forward-looking. The glories of the past are not deployed for escape or to bemoan the present. Britain has now lost that forward-looking confidence, as pride, once equi-poised between yesterday, today and tomorrow, is firmly locked into antiquity.

Many forces muster today to extend the preservation of even more of the past, widening its range even into language. One is left wondering whether this excessive preoccupation with the past is not detracting from the achievement, opportunities and challenges of the present. In the past when one treasure went, either as a result of revolution or change in fashion, another came to replace it. *Lost Treasures of Britain* bears witness to the unimpeded cycle of creation and destruction before the invention of preservation. Virtually everything we admire most from the past would never have been created if any of the planning procedures, government quangos and protest groups of our own day had existed. We might pause to ask whether this is in fact the reason we have produced so little of distinction in the twentieth century. And would we, for that matter, be so pleased to be saddled with the maintenance of some 800 monastery buildings? It has taken our own century, with its two World Wars and the loss of an empire, to reverse the spirit of our ancestors and see security and achievement only in relics of history.

PART ONE

REVOLUTION AND REFORM
1529–1603

No one who was present at the battle of Bosworth in 1485 could have foreseen that the victor, Henry Tudor, Earl of Richmond, would establish a dynasty which was to rule England for more than a century and preside over the greatest revolution since the Norman conquest. That revolution was the work of his son, Henry VIII. The English Reformation altered the face of the landscape and the physical appearance of thousands of buildings. Over 800 monasteries either vanished totally or were reduced to ruins and convenient quarries for stone. The interiors of parish churches in towns and villages changed beyond recognition as their contents were destroyed. In short, the Tudor period witnessed more destruction of what we would now categorize as British heritage than any other period in the nation's history.

Yet this period is regarded with favour, as the era of the Tudor *pax* that replaced the disastrous fifteenth-century dynastic struggles of York and Lancaster. This attitude shows us to be the victims of the Tudor propagandists, for what is so striking about the Wars of the Roses is how little they affected society in general. The damage caused in no way approaches the scale of the cataclysms brought by the Reformation and the Civil War of the seventeenth century. War was limited to battles between aristocratic factions fought on a seasonal basis by small armies of retainers. Where destruction did occur, as on the march south of Margaret of Anjou's army after the battle of Wakefield in 1460,

Opposite: *A beautiful and rare carving of Christ crucified, believed to be the work of an English sculptor who ran a workshop in west Norway, c.1230–45. The polychrome figure comes from a small rood or altar cross of the kind found in virtually every English church before the Reformation, but no wooden thirteenth-century English crucifix survives to clinch the association.*

it was recorded with horror precisely because it was an exception. The Tudors inherited a country whose visual fabric was virtually intact. In towns and villages the most striking buildings, dominating their surroundings, were the royal palaces, the great monastic churches, the castles and fortified manor houses of the aristocracy and gentry, and the ordinary parish churches. By 1603, when the last Tudor died, much of that had changed irrevocably.

The aesthetic implications of the English Reformation are less appreciated than they should be. For our purposes these events began in 1533 with the Act in Restraint of Appeals. This Act obliterated the sovereignty of the pope over matters ecclesiastical, transferring his powers to the Crown in the person of Henry VIII. Under the aegis of his new chief minister, Thomas Cromwell, the financial and administrative structure of the Catholic Church was dismantled piece by piece in a series of major Acts of Parliament, which included the Dispensations Act, the Act for the Submission of the Clergy, and the Act of Uniformity, which enforced an oath of loyalty recognizing the king as the supreme head of the Church. Parliament then dissolved the monasteries and, in 1538, the translation of the Bible into English was issued under royal auspices. Cromwell's fall from power and execution in 1540 effectively terminated this first phase of the Reformation, for after his death there followed a period of conservative reaction.

However, this was to alter radically with the accession of the boy king Edward VI in 1547. Under the protectorate first of the Duke of Somerset and then of John Dudley, Duke of Northumberland, the pace of the Reformation accelerated. The two prayer books were issued, that of 1549 and the far more reformist one of 1552, while the churches were emptied as officially sanctioned iconoclasm swept the country. In terms of artistic losses, this was as violent and traumatic as the Cultural Revolution in twentieth-century China. The contents of the churches – paintings, sculptures, metalwork and textiles – were either confiscated by the Crown or publicly burnt. Those who owned a missal or a breviary with the old Catholic forms of devotion were bound to surrender them for destruction. And what couldn't be burnt was hacked down or defaced with hammer and chisel. After the brief respite embodied by the five-year reign of Edward's Catholic half-sister, Mary, renewed frenzy broke out on Elizabeth's accession in 1558, when England once more turned Protestant. By 1603, when she died, religious expression and experience were very different from what they had been in 1485.

The effect of that holocaust was, of course, irreparable. The damage was such as virtually to obliterate any true assessment of English medieval art, because nearly everything that wasn't a building simply vanished. The direction of English civilization was also radically affected. Church building ceased. The silversmiths, wood carvers, stone sculptors, embroiderers and painters whose main source of employment was the production of church art almost overnight found themselves without a market.

The Reformation also affected the reception of Renaissance ideals in the visual arts, for the break with Rome meant an end to the visits of Italian sculptors, painters and architects who, during the reign of both Henry VII and Henry VIII, had begun to introduce English artists to new influences. Equally it ruled out any chance of them visiting Italy. As a result, this rupture contributed to making British art provincial, almost retrogressive in character.

The Crown and the aristocracy who shared in the spoils of the medieval Church provided a new focus to replace religious art. By 1603 an account of a journey through England by visiting tourists, in the main German Protestants, reads very differently from one in the previous century. The country's aesthetic splendours were no longer great churches with their glittering, bejewelled shrines, but the new palaces built by Henry VIII – Nonsuch, Hampton Court, Greenwich and Whitehall – and the great houses of the nobility, above all Lord Burghley's Theobalds in Hertfordshire. Likewise for the ordinary citizen, the ritual and colour of the old Latin Mass was now only to be found in the spectacular epiphanies of the Virgin Queen on one of her many progresses or when she presided over the celebrations of her Accession Day. Her semi-divine status was further emphasized in extraordinary icons of her. It is ironic, however, that the destruction of the Reformation should have perpetuated the aesthetic of the Middle Ages, which was not to be dislodged until the succeeding century.

CHAPTER ONE

The Destruction of Shrines and Relics

The earliest onslaught on medieval art was the destruction of the shrines. This was a logical progression from the legislation which severed the English Church from Rome in 1532–3 and set in train the demands of the Protestant reformers. There is no doubt that the suppression of the monasteries and the confiscation of their wealth, of which the shrines formed a substantial part, lay at the back of the minds of both Henry VIII and Thomas Cromwell when they began their struggle with Rome. Through this they would be able to satisfy the demands of the reformers, who condemned the monastic life and the cult of saints, eliminate those loyal to the pope, and fill the royal coffers.

Cromwell, in his new role as the king's vicar-general in things ecclesiastical, had beneath him a set of commissioners of unscrupulous character; in the summer of 1538 they were directed to effect within every region the demolition of all noted shrines. Under the guise of suppressing superstition, they were enjoined to take away 'the shrine and bones with all the ornaments of the said shrine belonging and all other relics, silver, gold and all jewels belonging to the said shrine, and . . . see them safely conveyed unto our Tower of London'. In addition they were 'to see that both the shrine and the place where it was kept be destroyed even to the ground'.

These shrines were places of pilgrimage, such as Chaucer celebrates in his *Canterbury Tales*, attracting visitors from far and

Opposite: *Edmund, King of East Anglia, was martyred at the hands of the Danes in 870. As a royal saint, his shrine at Bury St Edmund had attracted the devotion of virtually every king of England from Canute to Henry VII, yet it was the first to be demolished in 1538. This shrine appears in a series of illuminations in a life of the saint written by John Lydgate and presented to the young Henry VI.*

near, who combined something resembling a holiday with a petition to the saint for his or her prayers. Late medieval England had a network of shrines to its saints, from the most famous – St Thomas à Becket at Canterbury and St Cuthbert at Durham – to lesser ones such as St Richard at Chichester or St Thomas Cantilupe at Hereford. In addition there was the veneration of particular images, such as Our Lady of Caversham, or of the many individual relics, such as the Holy Blood of Hailes. All of this was to be swept away in the first attack on the visual fabric of the medieval Church.

Pilgrimages and the cult of relics were among the first abuses to which the reformers put their minds in the Reformation. In the fifteenth century they had been rejected by the Lollards as false piety. The Lollards' rejection centred on a distaste for symbols. To them God was omnipresent, so no place or image was holier than any other. They were followed by the humanists, epitomized by Erasmus. In *A Pilgrimage for Religion's Sake*, translated into English in 1536–7, Erasmus satirized pilgrimages. He condemned the avarice displayed by such shrines with their amassment of gold and jewels and pointed out that if all the

fragments of the true cross were put together, 'they'd seem a full load for a freighter. And yet the Lord carried his whole cross.'

The settings for the shrines must have made up some of the greatest ensembles of medieval art, so their loss during this first phase of destruction was catastrophic. By 1500 the shrines had developed into the elaborate structures reconstructed in the Victorian period that we see today in many of our greatest cathedrals. Only the shrine of the royal saint, Edward the Confessor, in Westminster Abbey survives reasonably intact, as left, half restored, by Mary Tudor on her death in 1558. The astounding tableau of gold and jewels about the coffin of the saint had been replaced by sober, inexpensive materials, but none the less it shows what the format was for the great shrines before they were swept away. Each had a substructure of stone or marble, often adorned with sculpture or mosaic, which contained niches or recesses where pilgrims crouched to offer their petitions. These 'thrones' were usually of lofty proportions, for upon them rested the *feretrum*, or feretory: a portable coffin or chest which could be lifted down and carried in procession on festival days. The whole or part of the saint's body lay within this coffin or container, which was covered in gold plates, surrounded with golden statues and hung with all the jewels and cameos given to the shrine. The feretory was so precious that a wooden cover on pulleys usually concealed it. An officer in charge of the shrine would raise the cover for a group of pilgrims to spectacular effect. The impact of this theatrical unveiling of the relic was heightened by bells attached to the cover which tinkled as it was elevated.

We can see from secondary evidence that all the skills known to the medieval artist and craftsman were lavished on these holy structures. Wenceslas Hollar, the engraver, provides us with a picture of the feretory of St Erkenwald in Old St Paul's Cathedral. In 1335, three London goldsmiths toiled for a year on the feretory, which was of silver gilt, shaped like a Gothic church with flying buttresses on each side, and covered with small statues (not shown on Hollar's engraving), including the Coronation of the Virgin; they were all studded with precious stones. The feretory of St Thomas Cantilupe at Hereford had 'An image of the Trinity of gold with a diadem on His head with green stones and red ... A child of gold with Jesus and Our Lady ... The salutation of Our Lady ...' St Swithun's

In 1163 the remains of St Edward the Confessor were translated into this shrine in Westminster Abbey, commissioned by Henry II. The illumination shows pilgrims waiting their turn to creep into one of the apertures in the throne to make their petition, while its custodian recites aloud the miracles of the saint. On the throne rests the golden feretory adorned with figures and on the pillars either side are statues of Edward and St John the Baptist, who appeared to him in disguise. This shrine was replaced by Henry III with an even more splendid one.

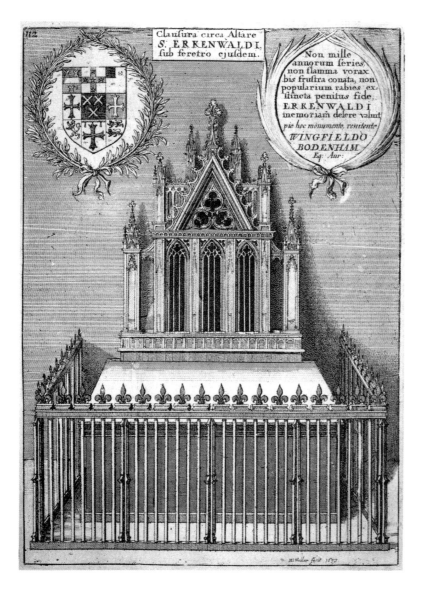

Clausura circa Altare S. ERKENWALDI, sub feretro ejusdem.

Non mille annorum series, non flamma vorax bis frustra conata, non popularium rabies extincta penitus fide ERKENWALDI memoriam delere valunt pie hoc monumento, renitente WINGFIELDO BODENHAM Eq: Aur:

Every cathedral in medieval England had a shrine as a focus for pilgrimage. The shrine was usually sited behind the high altar. Each consisted of an architectural base, or throne, upon which rested the saint's relics in a container, or feretory, which could be lifted off and carried in procession on feast days. These feretories in gold, silver, enamel and precious stones must have exhibited some of the greatest medieval craftsmanship. All of them were melted down and destroyed in 1538 and the 'thrones' razed to the ground.

Left: St Erkenwald was a Saxon bishop of London whose shrine was completed in 1339. Sir William Dugdale's history of Old St Paul's contains this engraving by Wenceslas Hollar, said to be made from the original drawing. The view is of the east end of the feretory with an altar enclosed by iron railings. The drawing omits the jewelled images which stood in every niche.

shrine at Winchester pre-dated the Norman Conquest, having been commissioned by King Edgar, and was 'of plate silver and gilt, and garnished with stones'.

St Edmund's shrine at Bury was destroyed in 1538, the first to go, but we are fortunate in having several fifteenth-century illuminations depicting it. These are part of a life of the saint by John Lydgate, presented to the child-king Henry VI, who can be seen kneeling in the foreground of one of the illuminations. The appearance of the shrine varies, but we can see why it was found to be 'very cumbrous to deface' and yielded 5,000 marks of gold, silver and jewels for the royal coffers. What the

Henry III commissioned a new shrine for St Edward the Confessor which was erected in 1269. It was the work of 'Petrus Romanus' and had twisted columns of mosaic or cosmati work emulating what the then abbot had seen in Rome. The feretory above was of untold splendour. It was destroyed in 1538 but the throne remained in situ. *Mary Tudor returned the saint's body to it and commissioned the present wooden cover in the Renaissance classical manner. Remarkably, it escaped the fresh surge of iconoclasm in 1559 and during the Commonwealth.*

king's commissioners were hacking to pieces was a masterpiece of thirteenth-century art, 'of admirable workmanship', commissioned by King Henry III in 1269. The same monarch was responsible for the even more impressive shrine to St Edward the Confessor in Westminster Abbey. Begun in 1241, work continued until 1270 and we can still see the twisted, mosaic-inlaid columns of the throne. The feretory must have been spectacular, for on it figured 'six gold kings set with precious stones', St Edmund wearing a bejewelled diadem, another 'King, holding in his right hand a flower, with sapphires and emeralds in the middle of the crown, and a great garnet on the breast, and otherwise set with pearls and small stones', five golden angels, a Virgin and Child set with jewels, St Peter trampling Nero underfoot and 'a Majesty' (Christ enthroned in glory) 'with an emerald in the breast'.

Of the two most famous shrines we have only vivid word pictures. St Cuthbert's at Durham had 'most curious workmanshipp of fine and costly marble, all limned and guilted with gold'. The cover of the feretory alone must have been a major piece of medieval painting:

> all gilded over, and on eyther syde was painted fower lively images curious to the beholders; and on the east end was painted the picture of our Saviour sittinge on a rainbowe to geive judgment, very lively to the behoulders; and on the west end of itt was the picture of our Lady and our Saviour on her knees. And on the topp of the cover from end to end was most fyne carved worke, cutt owte with dragons and other beasts, most artificially wrought, and the inside was vernished with a fyne sanguine colour that itt might be more perspicuous to the behoulders ...

This record comes from a fascinating document, *The Rites of Durham*, an account of the vanished pre-Reformation splendours and rituals written by a former monk in the Elizabethan period. He goes on to describe how the cover was lifted to reveal the reliquaries. The total assemblage was considered 'the most sumptuous and richest jewels in all this land'. After pilgrims had said their prayers, they made an offering: 'if it were either gold, silver, or jewels, straightway it was hung on the shrine'. The commissioners were well satisfied with their loot at Durham, for 'they found many worthy and goodly jewels, but especially one precious stone belonging to the shrine which, by the estimate of these three visitors and their skilful lapidaries, was of value sufficient to redeem a prince.' This doubtless would have contributed to one of the royal jewels.

The *Rites of Durham* does not give us an exact description of the feretory. For this we must turn to the writings of a Venetian visitor who saw the shrine of St Thomas at Canterbury in 1500. Over the centuries the shrine of Thomas à Becket, martyred for his loyalty to the Church and the pope against King Henry II in 1170, had attracted lavish gifts of gold and jewels. Beneath a cover with silver bells was a feretory:

Reliquary boxes were placed on a beam above the altar, as seen in the drawing of St Augustine's Abbey. This early-thirteenth-century box is of Limoges enamel and depicts the martyrdom of St Thomas à Becket in Canterbury Cathedral. It may have come from a Kentish church and, at the Reformation, passed into private hands.

all covered with plates of purest gold; yet the gold is scarcely seen because it is covered with various precious stones, as sapphires, ballases, diamonds, rubies and emeralds; and wherever the eye turns, something more beautiful than the rest is observed. Nor, in addition, to these natural beauties, is the skill of art wanting; for in the midst of the gold are the most beautiful sculpted gems, both small and large, as agates, onyxes, cornelians, and cameos; and some cameos are of such a size that I am afraid to name it; but everything is far surpassed by a ruby, not larger than a thumbnail, which is fixed at the right of the altar.

Like so many medieval works of art the shrine was cumulative, although the main part was carried out by Walter de Colchester, sacrist of St Albans, assisted by Elias de Dereham, Canon of Salisbury, in the thirteenth century. We know that three silver gilt finials were added in 1314; the offerings of jewels were secured by a mesh of gold wire. The demolition of this shrine in September 1538 was the grand climax to the government's campaign. Eight men were needed to lift the two coffers into which the gold and jewels were packed and no less than twenty-six carts removed all the other material from Canterbury.

The destruction of the shrines was not the only task occupying the king's commissioners in 1538. All other forms of religious relic were to be seized. Relics might be displayed in simple boxes placed on a beam above the reredos or the altar, or, if there were many, in a reliquary table or tabernacle, whose doors would be opened for the faithful. Canterbury had some 400 relics on the eve of the Reformation. A tour of the cathedral would take in the Altar of the Sword in the north-west transept, where Becket had fallen. Above this, Richard le Breton's sword was suspended in a reliquary together with two golden rings 'of great and wonderful virtue for relieving the eyes of sick persons', which had either belonged to or been worn by St Thomas or St Edmund the Archbishop. In the crypt pilgrims saw a silver head reliquary of St Dunstan and to the north side of the high altar in the choir there was a reliquary tabernacle containing the heads of St Blaise, St Furse and St Austrobert enclosed in silver gilt, eleven arms of saints also enclosed in silver gilt, and fifty-six other relics including pieces of the true cross, a thorn from the crown of thorns encased in crystal, and a chalice and paten in crystal, gold and enamel which had belonged to St Alphege. Many of the hundreds of relics at Canterbury must have been major works of medieval art. The most famous was the *corona*, or head, of St Thomas à Becket, in which there was 'the whole face of the most holy man, gilt and ornamented with many gems'.

Not one important English medieval reliquary is known to have survived. The commissioners' zeal seems to have surpassed even the zest with which they had exposed the private lives and abuses of the inmates of the monastic houses. 'I send you the Vincula of St Petrus [fetter or girdle of St Peter], which women put about them at the time of their delivery', Richard Layton wrote with a certain glee to Thomas Cromwell in August 1535, after his visitation of the Cluniac cell at Lewes. 'Ye shall also receive a great comb called Mary Magdalene's comb, S. Dorothy's comb, S. Margaret's comb the least,' he added. The loss to British heritage is not apparent until we realize that the combs may have been Anglo-Saxon. The insatiable Dr Richard London reported in 1538: 'I have divers other proper things, as two heads of Saint Ursula, which because there is no manner of silver about them, I reserve till I have another head of hers.'

One of the cult images destined for destruction was Our Lady of Caversham, which was in a chapel belonging to the Augustinian Abbey of Notley in Buckinghamshire. London wrote to Thomas Cromwell that it was 'plated all over with silver' but 'I have put it in a chest locked and nailed up . . . I have also pulled down the place she stood in . . . and have defaced the same thoroughly.' Regret is only expressed when the pickings turn out to be meagre. At Winchester the shrine of St Swithun was found to have 'no piece of gold, nor any ring, or true stone, but all great counterfeits'. Yet the haul was not too bad, for they delivered to the king's Jewel-house a cross of emeralds, a cross called Jerusalem, another of gold, two chalices of gold and some silver plate. The story was repeated up and down the country as the purge of the trappings of the late medieval Church took place.

Like the events of any major revolution, the destruction of relics and shrines could be used for propaganda purposes. Some of the most famous relics and images which had attracted veneration and pilgrims were brought to London and exposed to public ridicule and then burnt. These burnings were hailed as bonfires of the artefacts of superstition, but they also served to accustom and excite the public to the defacement and destruction of religious

This early fifteenth-century drawing depicts the arrangement of relics and shrines at the eastern end of St Augustine's Abbey, typical of all the great pilgrimage centres. Over the high altar there is a shelf with a reliquary box containing the relics of St Ethelbert, first Christian king of Kent. The box is flanked by two arm reliquaries with the fingers arranged in benediction, and beyond them two books which Pope Gregory the Great gave to St Augustine. Above the altar is a beam on which two further reliquary boxes stand. The doors on either side of the altar-screen lead through to three chapels with no less than thirteen shrines. The three largest have altars attached, St Augustine being in the place of honour in the middle at the east end.

26

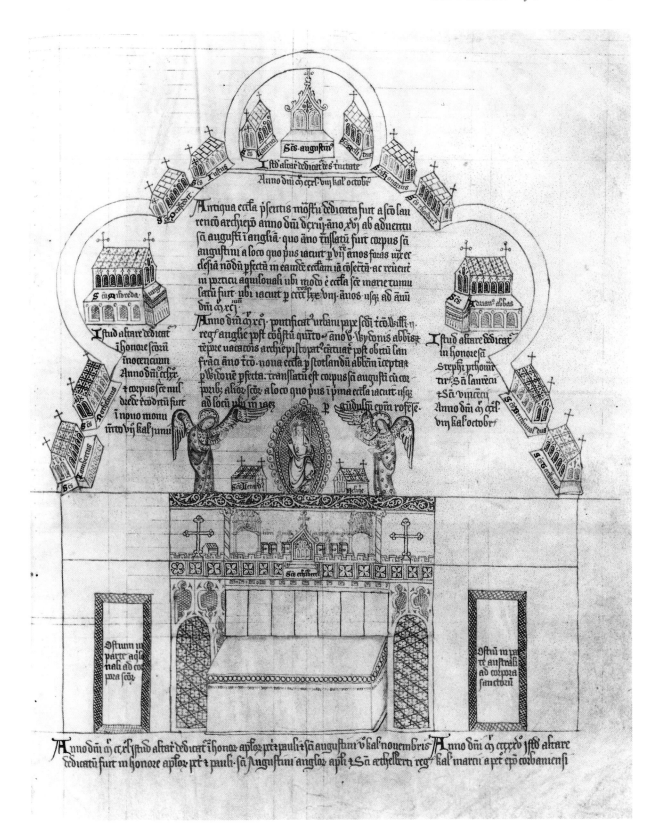

The most famous of all English shrines was that of St Thomas à Becket at Canterbury. The only indication we have of its appearance is this damaged drawing made some time after its destruction from unknown sources. It depicts the throne with the cover over the feretory; three gilt finials appear to protrude through apertures in the cover. They are part of the magnificent jewel-encrusted feretory to which the saint was translated in 1220. Its demolition in September 1538 marked the climax of the campaign against shrines. The cult of Becket, who had been canonized for upholding the pope and Church against the state, was abolished in November and all representations of him were to be 'put down and avoided out of all churches'.

art. This frenzied phase took place under the direction of Thomas Cromwell and lasted throughout 1538 and the early part of 1539. It opened with the public display of the Rood of Grace from Boxley, which was found to have wire mechanisms capable of moving the eyes and lips of Christ on the Cross. The government officer exposed this deception in the marketplace at Maidstone. This must have alerted Cromwell to the potential of such events, for the rood was brought to London and paraded through the streets; at court it was subjected to the jeers and ridicule of the king and courtiers. Shortly afterwards in February 1539 the Bishop of Rochester had the image set up before him and preached at length on its iniquities, while exposing another widely venerated relic, the Holy Blood of Hailes which, he said, was 'but duckes blood'.

Then when the Preacher began to wax warm, and the Word of God to work secretly in the hearts of his hearers, the wooden trunk was hurled down neckover heels among the most crowded of the audience. And now was heard a tremendous clamour of all sorts of people; – he [the Christ figure] is snatched, torn, broken in pieces bit by bit, split up into a thousand fragments, and at last thrown into the fire; and there was an end of him.

This was the first of a series of public burnings. A huge wooden image from Wales, called Darvell Gadarn, was burned at Smithfield in May along with a recalcitrant friar. In July Cromwell himself set light in Chelsea to a bonfire of cult images including Our Lady of Walsingham and Our Lady of Ipswich.

Recent research has shown that far from the cult of images and of relics being in decline, it was as popular and vigorous in the 1530s as it had ever been in the later middle ages. That the first phase of its eradication passed without widespread public unrest is a testimony less to the absence of local grief and anger at their destruction, than to the strength of Tudor government after half a century of rule. By the 1540 the first foray into the destruction of English medieval art had reached its end. Worse was shortly to come.

CHAPTER TWO

The Dissolution of the Monasteries

The destruction of shrines and relics went in tandem with the dissolution of the monasteries. We need only map out the main events of this familiar story before turning to look at what might be described as its aesthetic and antiquarian implications.

By 1500 there were only some 10,000 monks and 2,000 nuns divided among 825 religious houses, a huge decline since the Middle Ages. The monastic life, once both the spiritual and the cultural life-blood of the country, was at a low ebb, yet it seems extraordinary that, apart from the Pilgrimage of Grace, a rebellion in the north, no one tried to stop the dissolution. Indeed, the reverse was true.

Thomas Cromwell was again the key figure. In the service of Cardinal Wolsey he had undertaken a survey of the religious houses which had been suppressed, with papal approval, for the endowment of the cardinal's two colleges at Oxford and Ipswich. Shortly after the cardinal's death Cromwell was made a privy councillor, quickly attracting the attention of the king, who made him chancellor of the exchequer in 1533 and king's secretary the year after. He was the moving force behind the legislation of the Reformation Parliament and in January 1535 was made vicar-general in matters ecclesiastical. This appointment had one end in view: the suppression of the religious houses and the secularization of their property. In that year the *Valor*

Opposite: *The great Cistercian house of Tintern was founded in 1131 but the present building was begun in 1270. It was surrendered to the king's commissioners on 1 September 1537. Turner, who began his career as an architectural draughtsman, did a series of watercolours of the Abbey from studies he made of the ruin in about 1792. The view is across the transepts and reflects the artist's response to the late-eighteenth-century romantic attitude to the Abbey ruins.*

Ecclesiasticus, an assessment of the wealth of the Church, was instigated. Commissioners visited about a third of the houses and produced the inevitable bad report on their condition and morals. At the same time reforming preachers denounced the monks as hypocrites, sorcerers and drones, and told the people that if the abbeys went there would be no need for further taxes. In February 1536 an Act of Parliament suppressing the lesser houses, almost four hundred, was passed and the Court of Augmentations was set up to see the matter through. This precipitated the only movement against the suppression – a rising in Lincolnshire which was quickly put down but led to the more serious Pilgrimage of Grace. This, too, was suppressed with the utmost ferocity, including the execution of the heads of six monastic houses. The remaining greater houses, sensing that the end was near, began 'voluntarily' to surrender.

By the close of 1539 the three brave abbots of Glastonbury, Reading and Colchester, who defied the royal will, had been hanged; with the surrender of the last house, Waltham, on 23 March 1540 the story was brought to its conclusion. By then the Act for the Dissolution of the Greater Houses had gone through Parliament, rounding off the legal process, leaving only the chantries to be dissolved in the first year of Edward VI's reign.

So successful was the government's propaganda campaign against the monasteries that by the Elizabethan period it was accepted as fact that they had been dens of iniquity, which was certainly far from the truth. Of the hundreds of monastic houses dotted across the countryside, a huge number were not only major architectural monuments, but they contained sculpture, stained glass, woodwork, embroidery and metalwork that embodied a large part of what we would now define as English medieval art. Suddenly these works of art vanished.

The fates of the monasteries themselves were various. The Government saved sixteen major churches, eight cathedrals (Canterbury, Rochester, Winchester, Worcester, Ely, Norwich, Durham, and Carlisle), six abbeys (Westminster, Gloucester, Peterborough, Chester, Oxford, and Bristol) and two churches, which were to become colleges (Burton and Thornton). A fair number of other abbeys had their churches purchased by the local community and turned into parish churches. To this we owe the survival of such famous medieval churches as Great Malvern

In some rare instances items were rescued from the monasteries during the dissolution and put to use elsewhere. These mid-fourteenth-century choir stalls, thought to come from Cockersand Abbey, escaped being burnt to melt the lead from the roof and now stand in the late-fourteenth-century chancel of Lancaster Church.

Priory, Hexham, Cartmel Priory, St Alban's, Tewkesbury and Malmesbury. Often, as in the case of Croyland or Binham Priory, the locals could only afford to maintain part of a great church, such as its choir or nave. Statistically, the buildings which survived and were adapted to a new use (something redolent of our own age) were the exception and not the rule, for the Government's initial intent was to wipe them from the face of the landscape; the official instructions were 'to pull down to the ground all the walls of the churches, stepulls, cloysters, fraterys, dorters, chapter housys', so that even the memory of them would be eradicated. Of the 650 houses suppressed between 1536 and 1540 no vestige remains of about one third to indicate that they even existed, and there are substantial remains of less than a third.

What is so extraordinary about this decimation of a thousand years of art and architecture is that those who carried out the work seemed to lack any sense that they were destroying things of untold beauty and craftsmanship. Sir Arthur Darcy's reference in June 1537 to the abbey of Jervaulx as 'one of the fairest churches that I have ever seen' stands out as an anomaly and his reaction in no way impeded its demolition. That those involved in the suppression should have been devoid of any aesthetic sensitivity is perhaps less surprising when it is remembered that the idea of a work of art as a supreme expression of human genius was first formulated by the connoisseurs and collectors of the Jacobean age. Robert Aske, who led the Pilgrimage of Grace, was one of the few who recognized the aesthetic loss, stating that monasteries were 'one of the beauties of this realm to all men and strangers passing through the same'. John Leland, the antiquary, who was unshakeably Protestant, travelled through the country in the 1530s and 1540s and did comment on the beauty of the monasteries. Neath in Glamorgan he found 'the fairest abbay of al Wales' and Malmesbury Abbey, by then a parish church, was 'a right magnificent thing'.

The suppression of every house was seen in strictly business terms. The inmates were pensioned off, jewels, plate or vestments of quality were confiscated and sent to London, and the remaining contents or rather what was left after the locals had made off with what they could, was disposed of in local sales. The lead was then stripped from the roof and the glass from the

In the eighteenth century the monasteries became centres for a very different type of pilgrimage, which was partly antiquarian but mostly romantic and picturesque. This renewal of interest is reflected in the long series A Collection of Engravings of Castles, Abbeys, and Towns, in England and Wales *(1726–52) by Samuel and Nathaniel Buck.*

Opposite, above: The transepts of the Cistercian house of Roche Abbey, Yorkshire, in 1725. An Elizabethan cleric who wrote an account of the dissolution asked his father why he had taken part; 'What should I do, said He: might I not as well as others have some Profit of the Spoil of the Abbey? For I did see all would away; and therefore did as others did.'

Opposite, below: A view of Netley Abbey from the north. Netley, Hampshire, was a Benedictine abbey founded in the mid-thirteenth century. After the dissolution it became a house and then a ruin. It was much admired by the poet Thomas Gray, who typified the new attitude to the ruins, which now were seen to evoke thoughts of romantic melancholy.

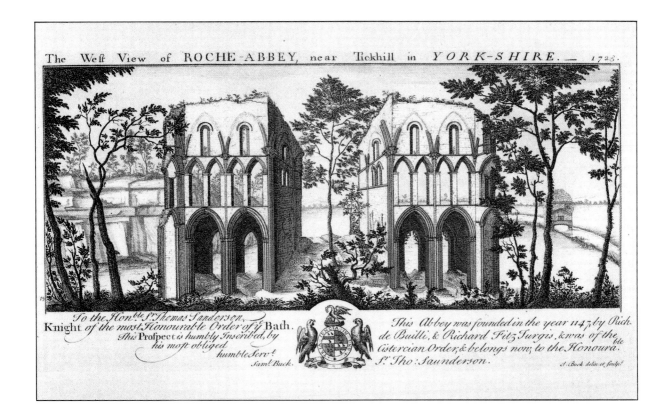

The West View of ROCHE-ABBEY, near Tickhill in *YORK-SHIRE.* — 1723.

To the Hon.ble S.r Thomas Sanderson,
Knight of the most Honourable Order of y.e Bath.
This Prospect is humbly Inscribed, by
his most obliged
humble Serv.t
Sam.l Buck.

This Abbey was founded in the year 1147, by Rich.
de Builli, & Richard Fitz Turgis, & was of the
Cistercian Order, & belongs now, to the Honoura.tle
S.r Tho: Saunderson.

S. Buck delin et sculp.t

THE NORTH VIEW OF NETLEY ABBY, IN HAMPSHIRE.

NETLEY call'd otherwise Lettley-Abby was founded by K.H.III. An. 1239, for Cistercian Monks, & dedicated to S.t Mary & S.t Edward; from
which last it was call'd S.t Edwards Place. He endow'd it with Lands in y.e 35.th Year of his Reign. It was a large Building built in form of a Cross, some
part of which, was desecrated (as Tradition says) by converting y.e West end of the Church into a Kitchen & other Offices; but the East end was kept for a
Chappel. In which State it continued a long time — When y.e then Proprietor had Sold this stately Fabrick, the Roof & a great part of the Walls were pull'd
down, & the principal Undertaker endeavouring to throw down the West Wall, was crush'd to death in his Enterprize. The present Proprietor is — Cliff Esq.r
1. The Sea near Southampton.   An. Val.{ 100: 14: 8. Dug. 160: 2: 9. Speed.}   J. & N. Buck. delin. et sculp. 1733.

The Benedictine priory of Great Malvern was founded in 1085. At the dissolution in 1539 both the Lady Chapel and the south transept had already been pulled down. The people of the town, headed by one John Pope, then came forward and purchased it from the Crown to replace their old parish church.

windows, followed by total demolition and the sale of the materials from the site. All of this was carried out with a ruthless efficiency strangely reminiscent of the more extreme communist regimes in their bid to obliterate all memory of a past society. By 1540 there was already an export market on the Continent for what was being thrown out of the dissolved monasteries. In that year an English priest reported from Holland: 'The Lord of Barrow showed me that there were brought to this town and to Antwerp so many rich and goodly copes out of England to sell these years past that it caused them all no less to marvel than in a manner mourn to see them come to a sale that were prepared to the service of God'.

There is a graphic account of the surrender of the Cistercian house of Roche Abbey by someone who was a boy at the time and whose uncle witnessed what happened. He describes how the government officials deliberately came upon it 'suddenly'. The abbot and officers of the house were assembled and asked to hand over the keys; an inventory was then taken of all their goods, both within doors and without. After that the abbot and inmates, with 'not a little grief', were sent away and the plunder began:

Some took the service books that lay in the church and put them upon their wain 'coppes' to piece them; some took windows of the hay-loft and hid them in their hay, and likewise they did of many other things. Some pulled forth the iron hooks out of the walls that bought none, when the yeomen or gentlemen of the county had bought the timber of the church. The church was the first thing that was put to spoil and then the abbot's lodging, dorter and frater with cloister and all the buildings thereabout within the abbey walls. Nothing was spared but the ox-houses and swine-cots and such other houses of office that stood without the walls ... It would have pitied any heart to see what tearing up of the lead there was, what plucking up of boards and throwing down of spires. And when the lead was torn off and cast down into the church and the tombs in the church all broken ... all things of price, either spoiled, carried away or defaced.

The persons who cast the lead into fodders plucked all the seats in the choir, wherein the monks sat when they said service, which were like the seats in minsters [i.e. misericords], and burned them and melted the lead therewith, although there was wood plenty within a flight shot of them, for the abbey stood among woods and rocks of stone. In these rocks were found pewter vesels that were conveyed away and there hidden, so that it seemeth that every person bent on himself to filch and spoil what he could.

Lewes Priory is another good case history of dismantlement. In February 1538 Henry VIII entrusted its destruction to Cromwell himself. Within a few weeks the dismemberment of the priory church was well in hand under the supervision of one John Portinari. His matter-of-fact account of its demolition can only leave the contemporary reader somewhat chilled:

I told your lordship of a vault on the right side of the high altar, that was borne up with four great pillars, having about it five chapels, which be encompassed in with five walls 70 steps in length, that is 200 feet. All this is down on Thursday and Friday last. Now we are plucking down an higher vault, borne up by four thick and gross pillars . . . This shall [go] down for our second work.

Seventeen tradespeople were brought down from London to dismantle the place. Ten were deployed to pull down the priory walls, while the lead from the roof was melted down in a large furnace. All of this was proceeding apace in March. By April the demolition squad had accomplished its work so thoroughly that Cromwell's son Gregory and his wife were able to take up residence in what was described as the priory house. Such was the fate of the majority of monastic sites as they passed into secular hands: the remaining buildings were incorporated into a great house, or the stone was used for the construction of something new. The architectural punctuation marks of medieval England had been holy places of devotion and prayer; now the prime focus of the landscape became the country house and its surrounding park.

However, some monastic sites were too remote to be turned into houses. Moreover it soon became apparent that the Government's ideal of total eradication was too costly to be achieved. As early as August 1538 John Freeman wrote to Cromwell at some length about the cost:

Sir, there be more of great houses in Lincolnshire than be in England beside suppressed, of their values, with thick walls, and most part of them vaulted, and few buyers of other stone, glass, or slate which might help the charges of plucking down of them . . . therefore, I think it were best to avoid this charge, to take first down the bells and lead . . . and this done, to pull down the roofs, battlements, and stayers and let the walls stand, and charge some of them as a quarry of stone to make sales of as they that have need will fetch.

This indeed proved to be the fate of some abbeys and is the reason why places such as Tintern or Fountains survive as the grandest and most poignant of ruins. Two centuries were to pass before the cult of ruins and their association with things past became part of the make-up of every educated person.

From these ruins we can at least reconstruct what such houses were like in their heyday. What we cannot do is resurrect their vanished contents, the most important of which were shipped up to London to the king's Jewel-house. The commissioners' letters abound in expressions of disappointment if the moveables proved

The abbey of Bury St Edmunds, once a great pilgrimage centre, became a ruin. By the close of the eighteenth century the ruins were converted into a row of dwelling houses each set within an arch.

RUINS OF THE WESTERN FRONT OF THE ABBY CHURCH IN ST EDMUNDS BURY.

This Structure was in the time of its perfection, accounted the largest Church in England, being 240 Feet broad, & 513 Feet in length, it had 5 Aisles, & was exceeding lofty. Its inside was enrich'd with the most beautiful Work in Carving & Gilding; exclusive of the many stately Monuments which were erected over the remains of Royal & Noble Personages, whose Interments in this Church, were numerous, among these were St Edmund, King & Martyr. — Constantia Countess of Richmond, Daughter of K. Wm the Conqueror, by the Lady Matilda Daughter of the Earl of Flanders. Richmond, the Conqueror's Nephew, who landed with William & shar'd the Command in the famous Battle of Hastings. His Brother & Successor Alan Niger, Earl of Britany & Richmond. Thomas Plantagenet Son of King Edward the 1st, by the Lady Margaret Daughter of Phillip King of France, Earl Marshal of England & Earl of Norfolk. Thomas, of Beaufort, Son of John of Gaunt, by the Lady Catherine Swainford. Mary Tudor, Queen of Louis the 12th King of France, & Sister of K. Henry the 8th. John of Lydgate, the famous Poet, Monk of this Abby. Robert the Martyr, who was Crucified by the Jews. St Wm Elmham, St Wm Trussel, St Wm Spencer, &c &c. with most of the Lord Abbots.

Published April 21 1787 by J. Kendall, Cook Row, Bury.

to be poor in quality and value. Such a lament went up over Battle Abbey in Sussex, for 'the vestments are old and so base, worn, and torn as your Lordship would not think'. 'Here', a subsequent letter reported, 'is one cope of crimson velvet embroidered, and two of blue, nasty and soiled'. As for the Austin Friars in Stafford, there were 'no jewels, but one little chalice'; similarly the Grey Friars in Shrewsbury yielded 'no jewels but a plate cross silver, and one little chalice of little value'. These were exceptions, for an immense amount of valuable stuff deemed 'meet for the King's majesty's use' made its way to London.

Aerial photography dramatically catches monastic ruins in the English landscape, reminding us of the careful siting of such places in terms of self-sufficiency and seclusion.

Right: Fountains Abbey, Yorkshire, was a Cistercian house founded in 1132 and dissolved in November 1539. Its abbot was executed for taking part in the Pilgrimage of Grace. In the eighteenth century its ruins were incorporated into a landscape garden.

Opposite, above: Titchfield Abbey, Hampshire, was a Premonstratensian house founded in 1232–3 by Peter des Roches, Bishop of Winchester. It surrendered in December 1537 and was rapidly transformed by Thomas Wriothesley, later Earl of Southampton, into a splendid house.

Opposite, below: Lindisfarne, Northumbria, was founded by St Oswald, King of Northumbria, for St Aidan in 635. It surrendered in 1537.

We are fortunate that Sir John Williams, Master of the Jewel-house, made an inventory of everything that came into his possession. Some of it, especially very grand sets of vestments, was earmarked for use in the chapels royal. For example, from Canons Ashby came an altar frontal of 'cloth of silver worked with fleur-de-lys and angels'; from Winchester 'six copes of blue tissue and one piece of arras, with the image of the Passion'; from Cirencester 'a cope embroidered with the story of Jesse'; and from Westminster Abbey 'Two altar hangings, called frontals, of cloth of gold with lions, fleur-de-lys and arms of the late — Islip, formerly abbot of the monastery' together with 'Five copes of needlework (one called St Peter's cope, one the cope with angels of pearl and three others called Jesses)'.

In Scotland the Dissolution came later and not under government aegis. Instead there was spontaneous destruction at the hands of the followers of John Knox.
Left: Melrose Abbey, Roxburghshire, was founded in the seventh century and refounded in 1136 by the Cistercians. After the Reformation the Earl of Morton made a house for himself out of the ruins.
Opposite: Sweetheart Abbey, Kirkudbrightshire, was the last religious house to be dissolved. The community survived until 1605, when it was finally expelled by force.

Most items, however, were dismantled, the gold and silver sent to the Mint for making into coin and the jewels re-set for the king. It is no coincidence that the late 1530s saw a vast increase in the amount of jewelled plate for use by the crown and Henry's queens were showered with magnificent jewels. Williams's inventory reads like a heart-rending litany of lost medieval metalwork and *opus anglicanum*, the embroidery for which England was famous. Some of the descriptions, however banal, are clearly of major works of medieval craftsmanship whose loss is irreparable: the 'superaltare, garnished with silver and gilte, and parte golde, called the great saphure of Glastonbury', the gospels from St John's Smithfield 'plated upon with a crucifixe, Mary and John of siluer, and a texte of a gospell booke plated vppon with siluer Mary and John'. From Christ Church, Canterbury, came a 'staffe [i.e. crozier] garnished with siluer, called Beckettes staffe', from Ely a folding altar, 'thinner parte therof plated with golde, & garnished with spahures, balaces, small sparckes of emeraldes, and course perles'. From St Augustine's, Canterbury, came magnificent sets of vestments: 'a riche cope of crymsyn veluet, with riche orphrais of golde, embrodered all over with a traile and ffawcons of Venice golde', 'iij olde copes and ij vestementes, called St *Augustynes* coppes, with flowers of fyne golde; a riche cope and a riche vestement, all embroderde with fyne golde, with vij amyces of some woorkes sett with stones'.

One great graphic artist in the Renaissance tradition was in England at this time and recorded some of the lost treasures. In the background of Hans Holbein's portrait of Archbishop Warham there is a splendid processional cross and, on a shelf to the right, a pearl-encrusted mitre. Many such mitres were removed from Canterbury: 'two myters garnisshed with siluer, and sett with course perles & counterfete stones', 'a myter of silver and gilte garnished with counterfeete stones & very small perles, receyved ... which myter was delyuerde amongest other to thoffice of the Jewelhouse, and ther defaced'.

So appalling was this loss that within two generations these ruins were stimulating a consciousness of the past and a new spirit of historical inquiry together with a lament for the barbarity of the deed. And this came not only from those loyal to the old faith but from Anglicans. 'Many do lament the pulling downe of abbayes', wrote Francis Trigge, a Lincolnshire cleric, as early as 1589. 'They say it was never merie world since.' Even more passionate feelings of regret seized the beleaguered Catholics under Elizabeth as in this anonymous recusant verse:

Bitter, bitter oh to behould the grasse to growe,
Where the walls of Walsingham so stately did shew.
Such were the works of Walsingham while shee did stand,
Such are the wrackes as now do shewe of that holy land.
Levell levell with the ground the towres doe lye,
Which with their golden, glitteringe tope pearsed once to the skye.

It was not until the High Church Laudian movement of the early seventeenth century that the lament for what had gone united with a desire to record it and, occasionally, to make reparation. One example was the restoration of the church of the Cistercian Abbey Dore by Lord Scudamore under the influence of Archbishop Laud in the 1630s. In 1611 John Speed in his *History of Great Braitaine* decried the destruction of 'so many beautifull Monasteries'. By 1630 Francis Godwin could write:

And indeed, even they who confesse the rowsing of so many unprofitable Epicures out of their dennes, and the abolition of Superstition, wherewith the Divine Worship had by them beene polluted, to have beene an act of singular Justice and Piety; do notwithstanding complaine of the losse of so many stately Churches dedicated to Gods service.

This reversal is summed up by Sir Henry Spelman in his *History and Fate of Sacrilege*, left unfinished on his death in 1641. To him, the dissolution of the monasteries was a heinous crime not only in devotional terms but also in aesthetic ones: 'the axe and the mattock ruined almost all the chief and most magnificent ornaments of the kingdom'.

CHAPTER THREE

The Reformation of Images

Thomas Cromwell's hold on Henry VIII began to slacken even before the last religious house fell, and his fate was sealed by his part in the king's disastrous marriage to Anne of Cleves. In 1540 he was executed. For seven years no further inroads into the medieval inheritance were made as the king entered a conservative phase in things ecclesiastical. That, however, did not mean that the views of the reformers stopped spreading. Although the devastation of the shrines and images which were centres of pilgrimage had satisfied many, more extreme forms of Protestantism which rejected the whole visual apparatus of late medieval religion were gaining ground. The more reforming bishops, including Thomas Cranmer, Archbishop of Canterbury, wished to sweep away what they saw as accretions to primitive Christianity. Images that once served as the Bible of the illiterate had become objects of worship and when the nine-year-old Edward VI succeeded his father in 1547, Cranmer urged him at his coronation to emulate the kings of the Old Testament by banishing idols and removing all images from churches.

During the six years of his reign under the protectorate of the Duke of Somerset and then of the Duke of Northumberland, the Reformation entered its most iconoclastic phase, which emptied the churches of their heritage of religious art and changed their

---

Opposite: *This life-size polychrome figure of St Michael spearing the dragon, a masterpiece of mid-thirteenth-century English art, comes from a church at Musvik near Trondheim in Norway. It is unlikely to have found its way there as a result of the Reformation and was probably carved by a number of English sculptors who seem to have worked in this area. Although the wings are missing, this piece conjures up more powerfully than any other object what disappeared at the Reformation.*

appearance radically as they ceased to be buildings centred on the mystery of the Mass and became instead preaching boxes.

The principles of reform had taken a strong hold, particularly amongst the urban population, and a week or two after Henry's death the wardens and curates of St Martin's in London took things into their own hands and 'of their own authority pulled down the images of the saints in the church'. They were forced to reinstate them, but they had merely anticipated events. In March 1547 Nicholas Ridley, Bishop of Rochester, openly denounced the use of images in his sermon at Paul's Cross. In May a royal visitation was ordered; among its numerous injunctions issued under the auspices of Cranmer, curates were enjoined to take down all images which were centres of pilgrimage or offering, and all other monuments of idolatry were to be obliterated from the walls and windows of the churches. The text under article 28 of the injunctions reads as follows:

Also, that they shall take away, utterly extinct and destroy all shrines, coverings of shrines, all tables, candlesticks, trindles or rolls of wax, pictures, paintings, and all other monuments of feigned miracles, pilgrimages, idolatry, and superstition: so that there remain no memory of the same in walls, glass-windows, or elsewhere within their churches or houses. And they shall exhort all their parishioners to do the like within their several houses.

Inevitably such an instruction was open to interpretation and where Protestant zeal ran high the destruction was very great. During the autumn and winter of 1547–8 there were frequent outbreaks of mob iconoclasm; by December 1547 it was reported that not only images but crucifixes were being thrown out of the churches. The vagaries of the injunctions were finally clarified in February 1548, with the Privy Council's decision in favour of the total destruction of all holy images and pictures, regardless of whether or not they might be construed as being idolatrous. This culminated in the Act of January 1550 against books and images, whose demand for destruction is categorical:

And be it further enacted by the authority aforesaid, that if any person or persons of what estate, degree, or condition soever he, she or they be, body politic or corporate, that now have or hereafter shall have in his, her, or their

The high altar of Westminster Abbey with the hearse erected in the sanctuary on the occasion of the funeral of Abbot John Islip, who died in 1532. The drawing is one of a series by the Flemish artist, Gerard Hornebolte, and is topographically exact, giving us the only known representation of a high altar in one of the greater abbeys just before the Reformation. Over the altar is a panel painting of the crucifixion, and statues of saints adorn the doors each side that lead to the shrine of St Edward the Confessor. In the gallery above, two statues of saints flank another painting, a triptych with its doors open. A pyx with the Reserved Sacrament hangs from the flat canopy and above that angels flank the rood. All of these artefacts were to be destroyed within twenty years.

custody any books or writings of the sorts aforesaid, or any images of stone, timber, alabaster, or earth, graven, carved or painted, which heretofore have been taken out of any church or chapel, or yet stand in any church or chapel, and do not before the last day of June next ensuing deface and destroy or cause to be defaced and destroyed the same images and every of them ... and be thereof lawfully convict, forfeit and lose to the King our Sovereign Lord for the first offence twenty shillings, and for the second offence shall forfeit and lose being thereof lawfully convict four pounds, and for the third offence shall suffer imprisonment at the King's will.

The story was rounded off with a final act of sheer greed: in March 1551 the Government decreed that all remaining wealth in the churches, in the form of gold or silver plate, vestments and church furniture, should be surrendered to the Crown. Inventories reveal how little was left by that date. Bishop Burnet, the historian of the Reformation, wrote, 'and so the churches were emptied of all those pictures and statues, which had been for divers ages the chief objects of the people's worship'.

What exactly was destroyed? This can only be gauged by considering the interior of a late medieval church, which consisted of a series of rooms culminating in the chancel and the high altar. The chancel was divided from the main body of the church by a carved and painted screen above which there was the great rood or crucifix, flanked by life-size statues of the Virgin and St John. Often this upper tableau was backed by a huge wall-painting of the Last Judgment, the Doom. The walls and windows were covered with imagery in paint, stone and glass, designed to instruct the faithful in the stories of the Bible and the lives of the saints. Certain images, such as those of the Virgin or St Christopher, were accorded cult status thanks to the tradition of venerating the saints as intercessors. Some images might even be dressed in expensive fabrics and adorned with jewels donated in gratitude.

Resplendent with stained glass, gilded and painted walls, woodwork and figure sculpture, on festival days church interiors would be decked with floral and evergreen decorations. In addition the old Catholic liturgy called for vestments, altar frontals, canopies and a range of items needed for the Mass or for rituals associated with feast days such as Corpus Christi: altar crosses, censers, incense boats, candlesticks and staves, processional

Edward VI and the Pope. Henry VIII is depicted, presumably on his deathbed, pointing to his heir, Edward VI, to whom he entrusts the Church of England. The picture must have been painted after February 1548, when Archbishop Cranmer ordered the destruction of all holy images, but before the fall of Edward VI's Protector, the Duke of Somerset (who stands on his left), in October 1549. The Pope lies slumped below Edward, crushed by a Bible inscribed THE WORDE OF THE LORDE ENDVRETH FOREVER. *The infulae of the Pope's tiara are inscribed* IDOLATRY *and* SVPERSTICION. *Friars to the left attempt unsuccessfully to pull down the royal dais. The Council sits around a table, the top row including the Duke of Northumberland, Cranmer and the Earl of Bedford.*

crosses and illuminated service books. Most of these artefacts, had they survived, would today be valued as works of art, but then, of course, they represented an approach to the supernatural through things visible and tangible, a visual form of religious experience condemned by the reformers as false.

We get an exact impression of what was to be swept away from a unique record depicting the high altar and sanctuary of Westminster Abbey on the eve of the Reformation – a roll of pen drawings by Gerard Hornebolte of scenes from the life of the abbot, John of Islip, who died in May 1532. Over the altar we can see a panel painting of the crucifixion, statues of saints standing on columns on either side, above a gallery with a pyx suspended from a canopy; behind this is a painted retable flanked by two carved figures of saints, and above that, supported by the crossbeam, is the rood surrounded by multi-winged angels. A tableau of this kind, although rarely so rich as this, was the norm in every church in the country. 'Above all', a Venetian observer

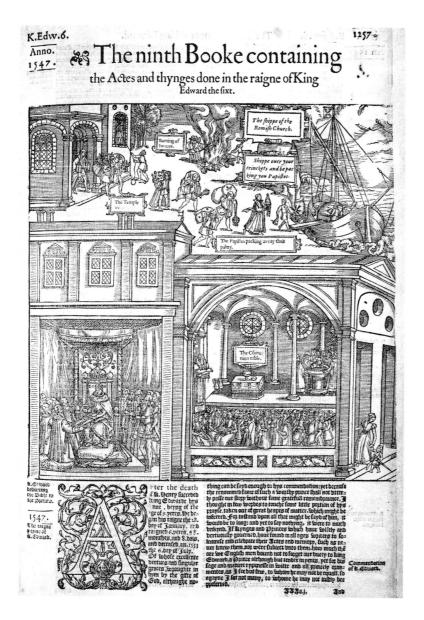

This woodcut appeared in John Foxe's Actes and Monuments, *which, by order of the Government, was placed in every parish church. In pictorial form the woodcut tells the people how their rulers had purged the Church and restored it to its ancient purity. Although symbolic, it graphically records what actually happened. The churches were emptied of all objects used in the old Catholic forms of service and devotion; some were shipped abroad and sold but most were simply taken out into the churchyard and burnt.*

wrote in 1500, 'their riches are displayed in church treasures: for there is not a parish church in the kingdom so mean as not to possess crucifixes, candlesticks, censers, patens and cups of silver.'

To see pictures of the destruction wreaked upon them we should look at the background of the group portrait *Edward VI and the Pope* in the National Portrait Gallery, London. There two men haul down an image of a female saint while nearby another is busy hacking a statue to pieces. We can see the same activity in the woodcut which adorns the 1563 edition of John

Foxe's *Actes and Monuments*. This shows men leaving a church laden with loot and a man pulling down an image from a niche in the exterior wall while a sad posse of 'papistes' bearing a holy water bucket and crozier make for a departing ship.

For the five years of Mary I's reign, from 1553 to 1558, this movement was abruptly reversed and parishes attempted to put the clock back. The accretions of a thousand years are not so easily restored, but, it was recorded, 'the carvers and makers of statues had a quick trade for roods and other images that were to be set up in churches'.

The final outburst of iconoclasm occasioned by the accession of Elizabeth I is vividly described in the diary of an ordinary London citizen called Henry Machyn, a provider of funeral trappings. In August 1560 he records the Lord Mayor witnessing 'ij gret [bonfires] of rodes and Mares and Johns and odur emages, ther thay wher bornyd with gret wondur'. These bonfires took place near St Thomas of Acres, and the ritual was re-enacted at St Botolph's, where books as well as the wooden churchyard cross were burned. In September the same fate was meted out to the rood from St Magnus the Martyr. Machyn lists what was thrown out of the churches in the last round of destruction: 'copes, crosses, sensors, alter-clothes, rod clothes, bokes, baners, bokes, and banerstayes, waynskott, with myche odur gayre'.

The churchwardens' accounts of virtually any parish church will tell roughly the same story. St Martin's at Leicester is a typical example. In 1545–6 the church plate was sold off locally. In response to the injunctions of 1547 the vestments and fittings were sold, together with a more radical stripping of the church interior: 1*s.* 8*d.* was paid to 'Robert Sexton and his fellow ffor takyng downe tabernacles & Images' and 1*s.* 6*d.* to 'John Wynterscale, Robert Sekerston & Roger Johnson for takyng downe the Rode lofte'. What was put back under Mary was disposed of in 1558–9 in a variety of ways: fires were made with the rood lofts, 'which mended ye churche leades', or the wood was used to make seats for the church or sold off. Altar stones were used for bridges, fire-backs, gravestones or sinks. Copes became covers for the new communion table. The old service books were burnt or 'sold to pedlars to lap spice in'. Other textiles – banners, frontals, vestments – were 'defaced, cut to pieces and put to prophane use'.

In the aftermath of Elizabeth I's excommunication by the pope in 1570, Protestant zeal was reactivated in the parish and 1*s.* 8*d.* was expended 'for cutyng downe the ymages hedes in the cherche'. Some things were hidden, awaiting better times. As late as 1567 a case was brought against five of the vicars of Ripon Minster who had taken the keys from the sacristan and one night removed 'all the images and other trumpery ... where it is not known'. They must have buried them, for seven years later the Vicar of Preston explained how 'I digged of late in my own grounds and found a great number of alabaster images, which I destroyed'. There are many other instances of alabaster panels turning up in hiding-places such as church floors at a later date.

Given that some artefacts were sold off and found their way to the Continent, English Gothic religious art in European churches should allow us to gauge the quality of what was destroyed in England, although caution is needed. For instance, there are a remarkable number of Nottingham alabasters scattered through France, the Low Countries, Germany and Spain, but they could have arrived earlier, for it was a trade which boasted an export market. Much more interesting is any carved wooden figure which is clearly English, for very few survived and not one medieval carved rood has been preserved.

Perhaps the most famous wood carving by an English sculptor is that of the Archangel St Michael at Trondheim in Norway. Scholars date this to the middle of the thirteenth century and identify the sculptor as an Englishman who either worked on or influenced two equally fine figures now in the Chapter House of Westminster Abbey. Aesthetic considerations never entered into what should or should not be destroyed; a work of art of such supreme beauty gives us an idea of the enormity of what went up in flames as literally hundreds of such figures were tossed on to churchyard bonfires.

Metalwork vanished apart from the items in museums today, in the main chalices and patens with an exceptionally rare crozier, a censer or an incense boat. The untold masterpieces of medieval metalwork that had been kept in the Royal Jewel-house since the 1530s were destroyed under Edward VI. A list of 'plate molten by order of the king's council', compiled in July 1547, included 'gold coming from defacing 3 books, a mitre, two gloves', a 'ship of mother of pearl and silver', 'three mitres, 2 gold crosses and an

Also from Norway, but likely to have been the work of an English artist, this serene Virgin and Child is a rare example of the exceptionally high standard of medieval wood-carving.

54

ark' and 'a ring of gold called a pontifical having an eagle and in her breast a small ruby'.

Most textiles and the famed *opus anglicanum* suffered the fate described by Peter Heylin in his account of the Reformation written in the next century:

Many private men's parlours were hung with altar-cloths, their tables and beds covered with copes, instead of carpets and cover-lids . . . It was a sorry house, and not worth the naming, which had not somewhat of this furniture in it, though it were only a fair large cushion made of a cope or altar-cloth, to adorn their windows, or make their chairs appear to have somewhat in them of a chair of state.

The survival of the famous Norwich retable was due to its use upside-down as a table top in one of the cathedral's side chapels until its discovery in 1847. Commissioned by Bishop Despencer for the high altar in the late-fourteenth century, it was certainly the work of local craftsmen. As a result of the destruction of virtually all English medieval panel-painting, we are only able to assess the work of the Norwich school from its stained glass.

Images in stone fared slightly better. If they were high up on a church façade they might escape through inaccessibility, but most were removed, decapitated or, in extreme instances, had the whole carved surface hacked off. Many elaborately carved reredoses survive today without a single figure in the niches. Local stories about this mass destruction of statuary must have abounded; in 1579 John Louthe, Archdeacon of Nottingham, recalled the fate of the images in the chapel of Winchester College.

There was many golden images in Wykam's colleage by Wynton. The churche dor was directly agaynste the usher's chamber. Mr. Forde tyed a longe coorde

Wall-paintings vanished beneath layers of whitewash until they began to be painstakingly uncovered in the nineteenth century. The chancel arch of St Thomas's, Salisbury, was decorated with a Doom painting, as was common in the later Middle Ages. Christ sits enthroned in judgment, raising the virtuous up to heaven and consigning the vicious to the jaws of hell. To re-create the scene as it would have been c.1500, we need to add the chancel screen with its rood above.

Overleaf: A Tree of Jesse reredos in the north transept of St Cuthbert's, Wells, Somerset, shows the devastation wreaked by the iconoclasts. The reredos carved by John Stowell in 1470 was polychrome, with the figure of Jesse reclining above where the altar once was. The niches all around the window would have been filled with statues, numerous fragments of which still survive.

to the images, lynkyng them all to one coorde, and, being in his chamber after midnight, he plucked the cordes ende, and at one pulle all the golden godes came downe with heyho Rombelo. It wakened all men with the rushe.

Wall-paintings vanished beneath layers of whitewash and biblical texts. Because they were in distemper, when plaster was stripped off the walls of churches the paintings simply disappeared. Not until this century have the layers of whitewash been painstakingly removed and the surviving medieval wall-paintings restored.

The overall picture which emerges is pretty grim except for one medium, glass. It was an expensive commodity and, if removed, it had to be replaced, otherwise the interior of the church would be exposed to the elements. A saying at the time ran: 'Whiche ben the most profytable sayntes in the chyrche? – They that stonde in the glasse windowes, for they kepe out the wynds for wastynge of the Lyghte'. The position was summed up even more clearly by William Harrison in his *Description of England*, written at the close of the 1570s:

Churches themselves, belles and times of morning & evening praier remain as in time past, saving that all images, shrines, tabernacles, rood loftes and monuments of idolatrie are removed, taken down & defaced: Onlie the stories in glasse windowes excepted, which, for want of sufficient store of new stuffe, & by reason of extreame charge that should grow by the alteration of the same into white panes throughoute the realme, are not altogether abolished in most places at once, but by little and little suffered to decaie that white glass may be set up in their roomes.

We can trace exactly what happened in Norwich, where an inventory of church goods taken in 1547–52 includes such entries as: 'the new glasing of xvij wyndowes wherein were conteyned the lyves of certen prophane histories', 'for glasyng of xxviij[th] wyndows with whyght glasse, wyche war glasyd with faynde storys' or 'for makinge of a glasse wyndow wherein Thomas Beckett was'.

It should not be forgotten as a footnote to this tale of woe that Ireland was, at least ostensibly, subject to the English Crown, although its authority rarely extended beyond the area of English rule known as the Pale, centred on Dublin. In Ireland, too, the

Previous page: *English embroidery, known as* opus anglicanum, *achieved wider fame in Europe than any other English art-form during the Middle Ages. It was sought after by the greatest potentates for the adornment of their churches and private chapels, but became redundant in England at the Reformation. This chasuble, mutilated at a later date to make it more modern in shape, was safeguarded by an old Yorkshire Catholic family, the Constables, and may correspond to the 'ancient vestment' mentioned in the will of Lady Margaret Constable in 1599. Worked in silver and silver-gilt thread and coloured silks on red velvet and once enriched with pearls, it celebrates the Virgin. The scenes, in ascending order, are: the Annunciation, the Adoration of the Magi, the Coronation of the Virgin.*

Left: *As a result of the Reformation imposed on Ireland in areas under English rule, practically nothing has survived of Irish medieval ecclesiastical art. The alabaster carving discovered in a walled-up niche at 'Black Abbey' Church, Kilkenny, is a rare survival. It depicts God the Father as an old man with the dove and crucifix to represent the Trinity, an image that was anathema to the reformers.*

St Mary's, Binham, Norfolk, was once a great Benedictine priory. All that now remains of it is the west end, which acts as a parish church. The base of its medieval rood screen was cut down, whitewashed and covered with texts from Tyndale's translation of the New Testament, but we can see the original painted decoration reappearing through the texts. At a later date the screen was incorporated into the choir stalls.

Reformation was destined to take the same course as on the mainland. In 1536 the Irish Parliament proclaimed Henry VIII Head of the Church of Ireland and a royal commission suppressed eight monasteries; fourteen more followed in 1537 under the Act of Suppression of Abbeys, and the dissolution of the rest two years later. Their plate, jewels and ornaments were confiscated by the Crown, while the remainder of their contents and their buildings were subjected to the same treatment as in England. Relics were ruthlessly destroyed, the most famous, the Barculus or Staff of Jesus, being publicly burnt in Dublin. A chronicler wrote of his area of the country: 'there was not in Erinn a holy cross or a figure of Mary, or an illustrious image over which their power reached, that wasn't burned'.

The fate of the monastic buildings was similar; new landowners moved in, often converting parts of them into country houses. However, the dissolution was a slow business in Ireland, as it was entirely dependent on the ascendancy of the English

Left: *Hans Holbein's famous portrait of William Wareham, Archbishop of Canterbury, was painted in 1527. It is an exact record of a pre-Reformation prelate with the full panoply of office – his episcopal cross and bejewelled mitre – around him. Within a few years these were to be confiscated by the Crown. Books of devotion, such as that lying open on a cushion, survived into the reign of Edward VI but were then burnt.*

Opposite, left: *A detail showing the archbishop's jewelled mitre. Several pearl-encrusted mitres are listed by Sir John Williams as being received into the King's Jewel-house on the dissolution.*

Opposite, right: *The cross must have been made for Wareham as archbishop, which he became in 1504, since it bears his arms. It is a unique record of the ecclesiastical art being made in England on the eve of the Reformation. The figure of Christ, which is of a noble, classical type rather than late Gothic, indicates that church art was responsive to the new Renaissance influences reaching England through contacts with Italy and through Italian sculptors working here.*

Protestants, so outside the Pale friaries continued to exist into the early seventeenth century.

Scotland, of course, was an independent kingdom until 1603, when James VI succeeded his cousin, Elizabeth, as King of England. The Reformation there and its consequences for buildings and religious artefacts took quite a different and far more violent course. The Stuarts were to remain resolutely Catholic until James was taken from his mother and brought up as a strict Protestant. Like England, Scotland was open to the pressures of the Lutheran reform in the 1520s and 1530s through trade links between Germany and the eastern ports, but during the later years of James V's reign the Scottish Parliament passed Acts attempting to suppress the reform movement. When England

turned Protestant, it became a haven for Scottish reformers, but nothing was to happen until after James's death, when the kingdom passed to his young daughter. Mary Queen of Scots was spirited away to the Valois court to be educated, leaving her mother, Mary of Guise, to rule Scotland under French influence.

Although there had been isolated instances of iconoclasm since the 1530s, it was not until 1559 that it erupted with a decisive fury from below as a result of the alliance between John Knox and the anglophile and ostensibly Protestant opponents of the French regent, known as the Lords of the Congregation. The birth pangs of the Kirk, a form of Protestantism far more extreme than the *via media* of England, owed its origins to John Calvin's Geneva, which was the holy city of the reform at its most extreme. The

turning point was the return of Knox, who had been in exile in England and on the Continent, on 2 May 1559. Nine days later in Perth he preached in the Church of St John attacking the whole apparatus of late medieval Catholicism. After the sermon a priest somewhat foolishly opened a tabernacle filled with relics. Within a short time the whole church interior was smashed to pieces and the mob went on to raze to the ground the houses of the Grey Friars, the Black Friars and the Carthusians.

Knox's progress from Perth to Edinburgh triggered similar outbursts along the route. He preached at Crail and Ansthruther, where 'the hearers were so moved as they fell immediately to the pulling down of altars and images and destroyed all the monuments which were abused to idolatry in that town'. At St Andrews, Stirling and Edinburgh these scenes of violent destruction were repeated and by midsummer the same had occurred in Glasgow.

The noble head of a wooden polychrome crucifix figure, once part of a twelfth-century Romanesque rood. This is the earliest surviving piece of English wood-carving, of exquisite quality, and provides an indication of what vanished during Edward VI's rein. The fragments were discovered at the church of All Hallows, South Cerney, in Gloucestershire.

After the event the whole movement received official status in two documents, *The Book of Discipline* (1560) and an Act of the Privy Council the year after. Spottiswoode in his *History* (1655) writes of the latter:

An Act was passed for the demolishing of Cloisters and abbey-churches, such as were not as yet pulled down ... Thereupon ensued a pitiful vastation of the churches and church-buildings throughout all the parts of the realm ... all the churches were either defaced or pulled to the ground. The holy vessels, and whatsoever else men could make gain of, as timber, lead, and bells, were put to sale. The very sepulchres of the dead were not spared. The registers of the Church and bibliotheques were cast into the fire. In a word all was ruined ...

Even allowing for a degree of exaggeration, the frenzy of destruction in Scotland was far greater than in England, in response to a more extreme form of Protestantism. Demolition often went beyond the monastic sites to include parish churches and even where churches were not destroyed the absence of any means of maintenance led to their ruin and eventual abandonment. Henceforth, this was to be the Scotland of the Kirk. When James's son Charles I attempted to introduce a prayer book of the English kind north of the border, it led to the crisis which precipitated the fall of the monarchy.

In England the Elizabethan religious compromise brought a welcome eighty-year break in the saga of destruction. When mob iconoclasm did occur in the early years of Elizabeth's reign, it met with official revulsion and a fear that such destruction could lead to civil disorder (conservation has always gone hand in hand with the notion that to preserve the artefacts of a society preserves that society itself). The Government issued a royal proclamation 'against breaking or defacing Monuments of Antiquitie, being set up in Churches, or other publike places, for memory, and not for superstition'. Tombs were to be protected from defacement and it ceased to be legal to 'breake downe or deface any image in glasse-windowe in any Church, without consent of the Ordinary'.

Nothing more was to happen until the Tudor system broke down in the next century and England entered the upside-down world of the Civil War and Commonwealth.

CHAPTER FOUR

The Dispersal of Libraries

The Reformation brought with it a holocaust of books as the libraries of the monasteries, great seats of learning throughout the Middle Ages, were dispersed, the university libraries purged of the old scholastic theological works, and successive prayer books introduced under Edward VI to replace their medieval predecessors. The destruction extended beyond public institutions into private houses, as a systematic effort was made to eliminate all evidence of Catholic forms of piety and devotion down to the humblest missal or breviary belonging to the ordinary citizen of Tudor England. Even more so than the visual trappings of medieval Christianity, books embodied a way of thought which was to be wiped out by order of the state.

The holocaust began between 1535 and 1540 with the libraries of the 800 monastic houses that were dissolved. The manuscripts and books housed in the new cathedral priories and minsters were to suffer the same fate. Worcester, for example, had 600 volumes at the time of the dissolution. Of these, only six found their way into the Royal Libraries; the Austin Friars at York had a library of 646 volumes of which only three have ever been traced.

Anthony Powell in his book on John Aubrey, the antiquary, records the consequences of the plundering of Malmesbury.

Opposite: *The Gorleston Psalter must have survived thanks to Sir Thomas Cornwallis, a Catholic and a favourite of Mary I. He lost office on the accession of Elizabeth I and retired to his estates at Brome Hall in Suffolk. By government order this type of manuscript was to be surrendered and destroyed. It came from Norwich Cathedral Priory and is among the most famous of East Anglian manuscripts. The calendar contains the feast of the dedication of the parish church of St Andrew, Gorleston, Suffolk.*

Much of the neighbourhood had been church lands, held of Glastonbury, and there had been a nunnery at Kington, so that many of these manuscripts were still to be found, here and there, throughout the country. They were often used by glovers, that flourishing local trade, to wrap up their wares; and it was also the fashion to save the covers of books by giving them a jacket of parchment that was, more often than not, a medieval document. Music books, account books and copybooks were also bound in this material. Aubrey had noticed these covers at school, and had admired the elegance of the script and the illuminated initial letters. It grieved him that the Rector ... should use the manuscripts he possessed to stop the bung-hole of his barrel of special ale; but the Rector was so far from being persuaded to the contrary that he was accustomed to assert repeatedly that for stopping a bung-hole there was nothing in the world like an ancient parchment manuscript.

John Bale, the Tudor antiquary, also captures the full horror of what happened in the preface he wrote to a book published in 1549, which reflects a certain degree of bravery on his part for it appeared when destruction was at its apogee.

But to destroye all without consyderacyon, is and wyll be vnto Englande for euer, a most horryble infamy amonge the graue senyours of other nacyons. A great nombre of them whych purchased those superstycyous mansyons, reserued of those lybrarye bokes, some to serue theyr jakes, some to scoure candelstyckes, and some to rubbe their bootes. Some they solde to the grossers and sopsellers, and some they sent ouersee to the bokebynders, not in small nombre, but at tymes whole shyppes full, to the wonderynge of the foren nacyons.

In July 1560 he was still bewailing their fate when he wrote to Archbishop Parker, who was to be responsible for stemming the tide:

And as concernynge bookes of antiquitie ... I had great plenty of them, whom I obtayned in tyme of the lamentable spoyle of the libraryes of Englande, throgh much fryndeshypp, labour and expenses. Some I found in stacyoners and bokebynders store howses, some in grosers, sope sellers, taylers, and occupyers shoppes, some in shoppes ready to be caryed over the sea into Flaunders to be solde ...

There is no lack of evidence to support these accounts. Any

This eleventh-century copy of Aelfric's homilies owes its survival to a servant of the fiercely Protestant Francis Russell, second Earl of Bedford. The abbey at Tavistock had passed to the Russell family on the dissolution, and the servant had found the homilies among other manuscripts. He gave them to the earl, who presented them to Matthew Parker, Archbishop of Canterbury, in 1567. Parker tried to stem the further destruction of such material, and collected what he could in his library at Lambeth Palace.

major library today will have among its collection books whose fly leaves or strengthening binding strips are fragments of medieval manuscripts. Many of the account books and forge books of the iron foundry started by Sir William Sidney at Robertsbridge are covered with leaves from the local priory psalter. Pages from the great Bible of c.700 presented by King Offa to Worcester turn up amongst the bindings of the estate

The famous Luttrell Psalter also owes its survival to old Catholic families. In the sixteenth century it had belonged to Lord William Howard, third son of the fourth Duke of Norfolk. It probably came to him from the last Earl of Arundel, another Catholic, whose family owned the manuscript and who had brought Howard up as a boy. He became an antiquary and assembled a large library at Naworth Castle. The psalter was made for Geoffrey Luttrell (1276–1345) and is celebrated above all for its abundance of marginal scenes depicting daily life in early-fourteenth-century England.

papers of Sir Francis Willoughby at Wollaton. Anglo-Saxon manuscripts suffered particularly badly, and only a few leaves of the important heroic poem, *Waldere*, survive in a binding now in the Royal Library, Copenhagen. The university libraries were likewise purged. A letter to Cromwell from two of his most devoted henchmen, Dr London and Dr Layton, catches vividly what happened at Oxford:

The second time we came to New College, after we had declared your injnunctions we found all the great Quadrant Court full of the leaves of Duns [Scotus], the wind blowing them into every corner. And there we found one Mr. Greenfield, a gentleman of Buckinghamshire, gathering up part of the same book leaves, as he said, to make him sewells [scarecrows] or blawnshers [obstructions] to keep the deer within his wood, thereby to have the better cry with his hounds.

Anthony à Wood records in the next century that a cartload of manuscripts was taken from Merton College and destroyed, as well as quantities from Balliol and New College. We can measure the loss from the fact that today only two out of the 300 volumes given to Oxford University between 1411 and 1444 by Duke Humphrey have survived. At Cambridge, of the 175 manuscripts listed at King's College in 1452 only one can now be identified.

Even the Royal Libraries did not escape destruction under Edward VI, when an order was also given to 'deliver the garnyture of the same bookes, being either of golde or silver'. This accounts for the virtual absence of any medieval binding adorned with jewels and metalwork.

Even more vulnerable than the library books were the service books, for they contained the words, ceremonial and music for a forbidden liturgy. Time and again we read entries such as 'Old books in the choir, 6d.' or 'fourteen great books in the choir, 14s.'. The final disaster was the Act of 1550:

Be it therefore enacte . . . that all bookes called antiphoners, missals, grails, processionals, legends, pies, portuises [portable breviaries], primers in Latin or English, couchers [large breviaries kept on a desk or table], journals, ordinals, or other service books or writings whatsoever heretofore used for the service of the Church, written or printed in the English or Latin tongue, other than such as are or shall be set forth by the King's Majesty, shall be by

The Queen Mary Psalter: one of the finest fourteenth-century psalters, it was about to be shipped abroad but was stopped by a London customs' officer, who presented it to Queen Mary I in October 1553.

authority of this present Act clearly and utterly abolished, extinguished, and forbidden for ever to be used or kept in this realm or elsewhere within any of the King's dominions.

All such books had to be surrendered to officials, who passed them on to the archbishop, bishop, chancellor or commissary of

It is likely that we owe the survival of the celebrated Book of Kells to Richard Plunket, the last abbot of St Mary's Abbey, who must have taken it when the house was dissolved on 18 November 1539. An inscription in the manuscript records that it belonged to another member of the family, a 'Geralde Plunket' of Dublin in 1568.

the diocese, to be immediately 'openly burnt or otherways defaced and destroyed'. To appreciate the full impact of this loss to England's artistic heritage, it is important to realize that these books had by far the richest illumination, as we can see if we look at a few of the masterpieces which have survived, such as the Lindisfarne Gospels, the Winchester Bible, the Benedictional of St Aethelwold, the Beaufort Hours, the Luttrell Psalter or the Sherborne Missal.

However, even at the darkest hour, there were those who sought to preserve the old books. The inmates of the religious houses removed and hid what they could. Other volumes were smuggled out of the country and can be found today in various continental libraries. With the accession of Elizabeth in 1558 the worst was over, and measures were taken to stabilize the situation. John Leland, the antiquary, received some sort of royal commission 'to make a search after England's antiquities, and peruse the libraries of all cathedrals, abbies, priories, colleges, &c'. Leland records that Henry VIII had 'built three libraries in his palaces with maximum concern for the preservation of the greatest number of rescued old books'.

A letter from the Privy Council in July 1568 emphasized the queen's interest in preserving ancient records which were now 'in possession of sundry private persons', who were asked to notify the archbishop's deputies of what they possessed. Families loyal to the old faith had been among the most assiduous collectors. For example, Henry FitzAlan, Earl of Arundel, who remained a Catholic, acquired the library of Thomas Cranmer on his fall, one rich in theological works acquired by the archbishop at the time of the Dissolution. On the earl's death in 1579, his collection comprised 1,000 printed books and 150 manuscripts, and was inherited by his son-in-law, another collector, John, Lord Lumley. His library was to run to 7,000 works and pass first to James I's eldest son Henry, Prince of Wales, and then to the Royal Library.

Matthew Parker formed a remarkable library at Lambeth Palace. Soon after his consecration as Archbishop of Canterbury in 1559 he instructed the scholar John Bale to seek out manuscripts from the monastic libraries. On Bale's death he laid claim to his collection in Ireland: 'I have bespoken them, and am promised to have them, if I be not deceived.' Agents scoured the Continent to reclaim books which had been exported. By the 1560s many of them were being viewed in a very different way, as providing material supporting the theological position of the Church of England and feeding the new nationalist myths essential to the Elizabethan state. By 1600 what was left of the medieval inheritance had re-formed itself and become the core of libraries, such as the Royal Library, the Bodleian and that at Corpus Christi in Oxford, which are still there today.

PART TWO

THE COLLAPSE OF THE
CROWN
1603–60

When James I and his family travelled south in 1603 they were overwhelmed by the riches of their inherited patrimony. Their wealth had been created by Henry VIII, but not extended by his daughter Elizabeth, who carefully husbanded the Crown's financial resources and whose reign was remarkable for the total absence of any royal patronage of the arts. This policy was to be reversed under James I and Charles I and their queens, Anne of Denmark and Henrietta Maria. Financial woes contributed to the ruin of the Stuarts, but they did not impede the flourishing of royal patronage. The royal palaces were increased in number: in 1607 James I acquired the great Cecil house of Theobalds and in 1608 Sir Christopher Hatton's even larger mansion of Holdenby. Both Stuart queens transformed Somerset House into a magnificent royal residence, Whitehall Palace underwent substantial alterations culminating in the building of the famous Banqueting House in 1619, and in 1639 another great Cecil property, Wimbledon House, was purchased for Henrietta Maria.

Meanwhile, the first four decades of the seventeenth century saw the Court and the educated classes welcome Renaissance cultural ideals in the visual arts. In this the architect Inigo Jones was the presiding genius. We can recognize him almost everywhere, designing perspective stage machinery and introducing Palladian villas, promoting old master paintings and advocating new fashions in garden design. In the aftermath of peace with Spain in 1604 a wave of artists from abroad brought Britain up to date with developments on the Continent. The peace also enabled people to travel and see the achievements of Renaissance

Opposite: *The 'Ermine Portrait' of 1585 showing Elizabeth I wearing the Three Brothers jewel as part of a jewelled collar.*

civilization for the first time. Charles I and his circle of connoisseurs acquired collections of Italian art and of classical antiquities that also put England at the centre of European cultural developments. The island was no longer marooned. The art they created can, in retrospect, be seen to have far more in common with what was to follow than with what had preceded it. This sudden aesthetic leap, embodied in the painter Van Dyke and the architect Inigo Jones, was revolutionary, not evolutionary.

This cultural jump is important in assessing the iconoclastic mood of the age. It was confined to the few, while the many continued to look at such developments and artefacts with the eyes of the Protestant theologians of the previous century, full of distrust for the visual image. There was an enormous gulf between this fragile, highly sophisticated minority with its elegant, courtly culture and the majority of the population, who resented its Catholic overtones. Queen Henrietta Maria maintained Catholic chapels, while Charles I's chosen form of Anglicanism was highly visual and ritualistic, which was anathema to his Protestant subjects.

It would be an oversimplification to attribute the Civil War to a polarity between these two opposed cultures. The issue is more complex than that, but there is no doubt that a king who openly received gifts of works of art from the Vatican, hung the walls of the royal palaces with pictures whose religious subject-matter would offend the sensibilities of his Puritan subjects and who filled the royal chapels with ordered ritual had no sympathy for reformist scruples about images. Although the king remained firmly Protestant and Anglican to anyone outside his charmed circle, in effect he presided over a court far more receptive to Catholic than Puritan modes of thought. The feelings of distrust and pent-up horror at the dalliance of the Crown with the Antichrist of Rome, whom the Tudors laid low, certainly account for the huge resurgence of iconoclasm triggered by the Civil War. In the sixteenth century the churches had been emptied at the instigation of the Crown. This new wave was an expression of the reverse, an association of the monarchy with a revival of image-making and ritual in the movement of church reform identified with Archbishop Laud.

Few cathedrals or churches were to escape the ravaging hand of the Puritans when the war came and Parliament ordered a renewed cleansing of church buildings from any lingering 'idolatry'. The losses on the secular side during the progress of the war were far more arbitrary, depending on how the campaigns ebbed and flowed across the country. Raglan Castle, seat of the royalist Marquis of Worcester, with its wondrous Renaissance water-gardens and its great library, was destroyed and the family never returned. Lathom, chief seat of the Earls of Derby, vanished; Wardour Castle, seat of the royalist Catholic Arundells, was twice besieged and sacked; the Earl of Chester-field's 'stately home' at Shelford was left a blackened ruin. And so the list runs on but, compared with the devastation of the churches and the royal palaces, there was only one great loss, Basing House, near Basingstoke, seat of the Catholic Marquesses of Winchester. After Parliament had stormed and sacked this treasure-house a hundred trunks were required to carry away the booty. It was also important architecturally, built by the crafts-men who had constructed Longleat with additions, it is thought likely, by Inigo Jones. The Parliamentary army saw that nothing was left 'but bare walls and chimneys in less than twenty-four hours'.

Significantly, the destruction which resulted from the Civil War was turned towards the obliteration of symbols that were secular. Under the Tudors the royal image and its visual presence in portrait and symbol had been built up as a secular liturgy, as powerful in its impact on the public as the old rituals of the pre-Reformation Church. If, as the Stuarts believed, the king was the image of God on earth, artefacts connected with the Crown could take on an almost sacrosanct connotation. Parliament's fury at Charles I's dissolution and sale of the Tudor royal plate and jewels was the reaction of men who saw these things as a tangible heritage from the golden age of the Tudors, when the monarchy had ridden high in popular esteem and led its people to victory against both the pope and Spain. By 1649, when Charles was executed and the country went republican, attitudes to things royal were very different. Just as in the sixteenth century there had been no aesthetic outcry against either the dissolution of the monasteries or the reform of images, so no widespread voice of dismay was raised at the despoliation of the royal palaces, the sale of their contents, the desolation of their gardens and parklands, and, in some instances, their demolition.

CHAPTER FIVE

The Sale of the Royal Jewels and
Plate

On 28 October 1625 one of Charles I's secretaries of state
recorded that he had 'sent towards Harwich all the jewels of value
within in his charge'. A week later a ship set sail for Amsterdam
with forty pieces or sets of gold plate and ten of the richest of the
royal jewels. On 7 December a warrant was issued under the
authority of the Great Seal entrusting this consignment to the
Duke of Buckingham, the king's favourite, and the Earl of Holland, who were designated ambassadors extraordinary to the
States of Holland, with these words: 'The saide Jewells and Plate
are of greate Value, and many of them have longe contynued as
itt were in a continuall Discent for many Years togeather with
the Crowne of England'.

In this way Charles I set about dispersing and destroying some
of the greatest masterpieces of goldsmith's and jeweller's work in
the Royal Collection, in the main an array of treasures created for
the Tudor court, above all by Henry VIII, as a result of the
confiscation of the plate and jewels of the medieval Church.
Although gifts, melting down, theft and damage had made some
incursions during the second half of the sixteenth century, the
collection was remarkably intact when the Stuarts inherited it in
1603. Thereafter the story was to be a very different one.

Within a decade the financial situation of the Crown had so
deteriorated that the king's lawyer, Sir Robert Cotton, oblig-
ingly discovered earlier precedents for pawning the royal jewels –
an extremity not resorted to until 1625. At The Hague, Charles

---

Opposite: *Listed amongst the nineteen 'Cuppes of Christall garnished with golde' in
the inventory of Elizabeth I, this piece, attributed to Hans Holbein, remained part of
the Royal Collection until it was disposed of in the Commonwealth sale. Both the cover
and the foot contain enamelled inscriptions.*

I's consignment became the subject of protracted negotiations between Buckingham's servant, Sackville Crowe, and an Amsterdam merchant, Philip Calandrini. The entire charge of Crowe's stuff amounted to £92,651 10s., securing a loan of £92,400, which was spent in paying English troops involved in the Thirty Years War. For his part in these squalid transactions, Crowe was rewarded with a baronetcy. In August 1629 Calandrini was commissioned to redeem the jewels and plate and sell thirty pieces. Five were sold intact, while the others, tragically, were melted down. Others were disposed of two years later, followed in 1639 by the liquidation of the remaining pieces. The whole saga was a bungled disaster. The items sold in 1629 and 1631 were pledged for £14,000 and were redeemed for the same amount. They were melted down to realize a mere £17,704 13s., which, minus the interest charges, yielded to the Crown little more than £10,000. A contemporary valued the collection at £200,000, but the king was so desperate for money by the close of the 1630s that he had fallen victim to the sharp dealing of the Amsterdam bankers.

What vanished from England in 1625 was the equivalent of what we marvel at today in any of the great European royal or ducal treasuries – in Vienna, Munich, Copenhagen or Stockholm: the fabulous gold plate and jewels from the Renaissance and mannerist periods. This was the Stuart inheritance from the age of Elizabeth I, which by the close of the 1620s had already acquired legendary status, as is evident from Sir John Eliot's dismay at the King's action. On 27 March 1626 he said to the House of Commons:

> Would that such a commission might be granted, if only that we then could search for the treasures and jewels that were left by that ever-blessed princess of never-dying memory, queen Elizabeth! O, those jewels! the pride and glory of this kingdom! which have made it so far shining beyond others! Would they were here, within the compass of these walls, to be viewed and seen by us, to be examined in this place! Their very name and memory have transported me.

In 1574 an inventory had been drawn up of those treasures and jewels. The 1,605 items included 43 jewels of gold, 13 gold cups and bowls, 18 crystal cups mounted in gold, 30 gold salts, 14 gold ewers and 'laires', 224 silver-gilt cups, 103 silver-gilt bowls

Given by Anne Boleyn to Henry VIII as a new year's gift in 1534, this design by Hans Holbein is for a table fountain, which would have stood on a ewer to catch the water spouting from the breasts of the three female figures. This lavish piece was for the performance of ablutions at table during banquets. It escaped the fate of much of the royal plate, being sold off in 1620.

This magnificent cup, designed by Hans Holbein, was presented by Henry VIII to his third queen, Jane Seymour, at about the time of their marriage in 1536. The cup is in gold, with table diamonds and pearls. The rich decoration includes a band with the initials of Henry and Jane entwined with true lovers' knots and, on the base, the queen's motto: Bound to Obey and Serve.

and 94 silver-gilt pots. Only three pieces listed in the inventory
have survived to give us an impression of what disappeared. The
first is the Royal Gold Cup of the Kings of England and France,
which was presented to Charles VI of France by the Duc de Berri
in 1391 and passed into the possession of the English royal house
in the fifteenth century. That escaped because James I presented

*This Royal Tudor Clock Salt was first
recorded in an inventory of the Royal Collection in 1550. An extraordinary con-
fection of silver-gilt, enamel and rock
crystal set with ivory cameos and garnets,
it epitomizes the almost bizarre splendour
of early Tudor display. The piece was
made in France about 1530 and was last
recorded in the Royal Collection in 1649.
It found its way into a country house
collection and remained unidentified until
1968, when it was recognized as one of
three surviving items of the Tudor Royal
Collection.*

The presentation by James I of the Royal Gold Cup of the Kings of France and England to the Constable of Castile in 1604 ensured its survival. It is a unique piece of medieval plate, having been made for the art-loving Jean, Duc de Berri, in Paris about 1380. He probably intended to give it to his brother, but instead it was presented to Charles VI of France and eventually came into the possession of John, Duke of Bedford, in 1434. On his death it passed to his heir, the infant Henry VI, and into the Royal Collection. The enamelled scenes are from the life of St Agnes.

it to the Constable of Castile in 1604. The second is the Royal Tudor Clock Salt, an object of French workmanship composed of silver-gilt, enamel and rock crystal, set with ivory cameos and garnets. This was last recorded in the Upper Jewel-house in August 1649, before being sold to H. Smith on 31 December for £43:

2 Faire large Salts of silvergilt, with a Clocke in it garnisht with 6 Ivory heads about the bottome, & enriched with stones, 8 little gold heads enamelled with a Man upon a Falcon a top of it.

It resurfaced in 1968 when it was sold from Drayton House, Northamptonshire.

The third is attributed to Holbein and is now in the Schatzkammer in Munich. It was purchased probably by a Dutch dealer and passed into the treasury of the Electors Palatine, who later amalgamated with Bavaria. It is listed amongst the 'Cuppes of Christall garnisshed with golde':

Item one Bolle of Christall the foote and bryme garnisshed with golde the foote also sette with thre smale Diamoundes and cartaiyne writinges in thre places upon whyte enamelid upon the brym therof is cartayne Antique worke of gold enamelid wherin is set a goodly Rubie and an Emeraude in collettes of golde being very curiously wrought and garnisshed with fyve roses of Diamoundes and v places written enamelid white the top of the louer being a Christall and golde garnisshed with a Rubie and a Diamounde an Emeraude and thre perles in the top of the same is two pearles in oone and oone great pearle lower set in golde and thre smale pearles perdaunte at the same . . .

This bowl was first recorded in 1550 and was still in the Upper Jewel-house in August 1649, when it was valued at £120.

From these descriptions we can imagine just how magnificent a state banquet at the Tudor court must have been. We also have a design by Holbein for a table fountain given by Anne Boleyn to Henry VIII as a new year's gift in 1534, which was sold off in 1620 as unserviceable. It is listed in the inventory of 1574 as:

item oone Basone of silver guilt the border railed with golde and set with stone and pearle in collettes of golde standing in the same a Fountaine and thre women parte of them being Copper water runnying oute at ther brestes with

The Three Brothers is perhaps the most legendary of all the royal jewels. The 'brothers' were three huge balas rubies. They were grouped around a large central pointed diamond to which were added four pearls, one pendant, to form one splendid jewel. It began its life as one of the treasures of the Dukes of Burgundy, which were seized as booty by Swiss mercenaries in 1476. The Three Brothers next appeared in the hands of the magistrates of the town of Basle, who commissioned the water-colour shown opposite. The jewel was then sold to Jakob Fugger, the banker, in 1504 and he sold it in 1551 to Edward VI. In the detail from the 'Ermine Portrait' of Elizabeth I (1585) shown on the left, it is suspended at the end of a huge collar of diamonds and pearls. James I used the Three Brothers as a hat jewel, as in the portrait below (and detail, left) of c.1615. His son pawned it about ten years later. Still intact in Amsterdam in 1650, it was probably dismembered soon after.

two borders of golde in the Fountaine lacking oone Rose of garnettes in the nethermost border with a plate of golde in the toppe of the Cover with the Quenis Armes and Quene Annes therin ...

Holbein's preliminary design does not include the basin but one can see the spectacular fountain with the imperial crown at the top, its supporting satyrs and the three women standing below around the stem. On the body of the fountain is Anne Boleyn's badge: on the stump of a tree couped and erased, from which spring red and white roses, a crowned falcon holding a sceptre. Such a piece was the height of luxury, being used not for wine but for ablutions at table.

The greatest lost pieces were undoubtedly those made for Henry VIII. There was the gold cup called 'the Dreame of Paris havinge vpon the Cover therof the Image of Paris Jubiter Venus Pallas and Juno Paris horse vpon the cover', every figure jewel-encrusted; a gold looking-glass with two putti supporting the

James I celebrated the formal union of England and Scotland into the 'Empire of Great Britain' in 1604 by commissioning the Mirror of Great Britain, specified by him in 1605 as a royal heirloom. It was largely made from jewels in the old Elizabethan hoard. It consisted of three diamonds and two large pearls with, to the left, a huge ruby taken from a famous Scottish jewel, the 'Letter H of Scotland' or the 'Great Harry'. From the Mirror hung a diamond cut in facets, the famous Sancy Diamond, purchased by James I in 1604. Later in the century it belonged to Louis XIV.

The Feather was another of James I's specially commissioned spectacular hat jewels, put together by dismantling the jewels of Elizabeth I, from which a large table-diamond and twenty-five others were taken.

queen's arms, a clock and a man on horseback on the reverse and four enamelled 'Antique boyes'; 'oone faire large Boll with a Couer having a Crowne in the toppe of the same all of Golde garnisshed with Crownes of golde and Rooses white and red enamelid'; 'oone Laire of golde chasid with large doppes the Spowte a Sarpent garnisshed with Rubies pearles and Flowers enamelid white blewe and red'; and a salt 'called the Morice dawnce' decorated with five morris dancers and a musician, all studded with diamonds and rubies. What a delight that must have been!

Of the pieces of plate that were shipped to Amsterdam in 1625, we have records of only one: the cup Henry VIII gave to his third queen, Jane Seymour, on the occasion of their marriage in 1536. Two designs by Holbein survive. It is described in the Elizabethan inventory as:

Item oone faire standing Cup of golde garnisshed about the Cover with eleuen table Diamoundes and two pointed Diamoundes about the Cup Seuenteene table Diamoundes and thre pearles pendaunte vpon the Cup with this worde bounde to obeye and serve and H and J knitte together in the toppe of the Couer the Quenis Armes and Quene Janes Armes holdone by two boyes vnder a Crowne Imperiall.

Even the parsimonious Elizabeth added to this treasure-house items such as the enamelled gold cup given her by Sir William Cordell on the occasion of her visit to Long Melford in 1578. An even greater loss in terms of British history was the piece commissioned by Lord Burghley and presented to the queen to mark the defeat of the Spanish Armada: a gold plate with the figure of Astronomy on one side and Frobisher's ship, *The Triumph*, on the other.

Parliament had some right to feel aggrieved over these losses to the Crown patrimony and to resent the sale of jewels which James I had declared heirlooms 'to be indyvidually and inseparately for ever hereafter annexed to the Kingdome of this Realme'. The jewels in question were the Feather, the Mirror of Great Britain, and the Three Brothers. All three were worn as hat jewels by James I and may be recognized in the many portraits of him. The first two were made for him and the last was a legendary jewel which he had inherited from Elizabeth.

Over the Feather there is no cause to linger. It is described in an inventory of 1606 as 'one fayre jewell, like a feather of gould, conteyning a fayre table-diamond in the middest, and five-and-twenty diamonds of divers forms made of sondrous other jewells'. It is as well to remember that those 'sondrous other jewells' would doubtless have come from Elizabeth's great collection, of which not one piece survives.

More spectacular was the Mirror of Great Britain, clearly made to commemorate for all time the union of England and Scotland in 1604. This figures in the same inventory as:

Item, a greate and riche jewell of goulde, called the MIRROR OF GREATE BRITTAINE, containing one very faire table diamonde, one very faire table-rubie, two other large diamonds cutt lozengewise, the one of them called the stone of the letter H. of SCOTLANDE, garnished wth small diamonds, two rounde pearles fixed, and one fayre diamonde cut in fawcetts, bought of Sancy.

Again this was made from jewels taken from the Virgin Queen's hoard as well as two jewels famous in their own right. The diamond letter H of Scotland was also known as the 'Great Harry' and it appears in an inventory of 1566 amongst those jewels inalienable from the Crown of Scotland. The 'fayre diamonde cut in fawcetts' which formed the pendant was the legendary Sancy diamond, which was sold by Nicolas Harlay, Sieur de Sancy, to James I in 1604 and worn by the king in his hat for his coronation entry into London in March of that year.

By far the most famous, however, was the Three Brothers, which had been one of the greatest treasures of the Dukes of Burgundy in the fifteenth century. The jewel was called the Brothers on account of the three balas rubies which were remarkably alike in size and weight. These had been set by Duke Philip the Good around a large pointed diamond and adorned with four huge pearls. At the defeat of the Burgundians in 1476 it was part of the booty taken by the Swiss and its appearance when in the possession of the magistrates of Basle is recorded in a watercolour which matches the description exactly. In 1502 the jewel came on to the market and was purchased by the great Augsburg banker, Jakob Fugger, who eventually sold it to Edward VI in 1551, shortly after the last great influx of wealth from ecclesiastical confiscations. Thirty years later we can see Elizabeth I wearing it at the end of a collar of pearls in the famous Ermine Portrait at Hatfield House. James I had it re-set as a hat jewel but in the same form for his son Charles to wear in Spain when wooing the infanta. At that time the jeweller declared the great diamond at its centre to be 'the most complete stone that ever he sawe'. Such was its fame that it was still intact in Amsterdam in 1650, although by then it had come to be called the Three Sisters.

Sir John Eliot's speech to the Parliament of 1626 lamenting the pawning of the royal jewels and plate drew applause but it did not deny the king's right to do so; it was aimed at what the opposition party regarded as the evil influence of the royal favourite, the Duke of Buckingham. That attitude had shifted radically by 1642 when the queen left for Holland, ostensibly to escort her daughter to her marriage, but in reality carrying the pathetic remnants of the royal hoard to raise money for the impending war between the king and Parliament. In June Parliament declared all those who participated in the traffic in Crown Jewels to be enemies of the state, and, for the first time, denied the king the right to dispose of them, 'which by the Law of the Land ought not to be alienated'.

CHAPTER SIX

The Purging of Cathedrals and Churches

The Elizabethan Church had attempted to be comprehensive, keeping within its ample folds the more extreme Protestants. Under the first two Stuarts this was to change as Anglicanism began to be defined both theologically and liturgically to the exclusion of the Puritans. The great revival in church ceremonial and decoration is usually designated as the Laudian movement, after Charles I's archbishop, William Laud. It reached its apogee during the 1630s, under the king's personal rule.

Both churches and cathedrals were in a sad state of repair by the opening years of the seventeenth century, but cathedrals had suffered particularly badly, as no revenues had been provided for the maintenance and renewal of their fabric. The need for repair and restoration went hand in hand with the ideal of order and decency in both the appearance and ritual of the Church of England first propagated by the theologian Richard Hooker and taken up by Lancelot Andrewes, Bishop of Worcester, and John Donne, poet and Dean of St Paul's. Much that was anathema to the Puritans – organs and music, reverence of gesture, the re-ordering of interiors, including placing the communion table where the old altar had stood and railing it off from the congregation – they categorized as 'things indifferent', which allowed for

Opposite: *The systematic smashing of Canterbury's famous stained glass in 1643 was typical of the appalling destruction wreaked on the cathedrals, the seats of the hated episcopacy, by the Puritans. The twelve windows depicting the miracles of St Thomas à Becket, executed between 1213 and 1220, were a major feature of the splendid décor of the shrine. Only seven now survive, rearranged and heavily restored in the Victorian period. Illustrated here is a panel now in the Trinity Chapel. It depicts Audrey of Canterbury, suffering from a fever, drinking from a bowl at St Thomas's tomb.*

A *contemporary view of Canterbury Cathedral from the top of Prior Chillenden's pulpitum, under the Angel Tower or Clock House looking towards the high altar, which has already been demolished. The minor artist Thomas Johnson painted this picture during the Commonwealth in 1657. It shows a Parliamentary Committee at a table apparently supervising the devastation. To the left choir stalls are being hatcheted, while to the right a man has climbed up on a windowsill to smash the stained glass.*

considerable elaboration in church furniture and rituals. The development was piecemeal at the start, affecting certain private chapels and subsequently some churches and cathedrals, but when William Laud became Archbishop of Canterbury in 1633 his aim was to introduce this kind of elaboration into every church in the kingdom.

At St Giles in the Fields in London, for example, a screen was built across the church with statues of St Barnabas, St Paul and St Peter framed by winged cherubim. A lectern near the altar was covered in purple and gold cloth supporting two large books with embroidered covers portraying Christ and the Virgin. The cathedrals took things even further. At Lichfield the bishop introduced a crucifix 'as big and large as any three men'. At Durham, under the aegis of John Cosin, who was to return as bishop in 1660, the clergy officiated in copes, candlesticks were placed on an altar adorned with golden cherubim, and a huge canopy was commissioned to cover the font. This had the Holy Ghost in the form of a dove carved upon it and paintings of Christ, St John and the Four Evangelists. All over the country similar developments began to occur under the influence of the Laudian bishops and clergy, and for a few years there was a brief revival of religious art, but when the Puritans triumphed, their retribution knew no bounds.

More than three hundred and fifty years later virtually every church still bears witness to the actions of the Long Parliament, which met in 1640 and gave vent to the views of the Puritan opposition, committed to obliterating once and for all any lingering vestiges of Catholicism. In December 1640 a petition went to the House of Commons listing ceremonial abuses and expressing

The Italian sculptor Pietro Torrigiani had executed the tombs of Margaret, Countess of Richmond, Henry VII and Elizabeth of York. This altarpiece, commissioned by Henry VIII in 1517, was a masterpiece of Florentine Renaissance sculpture. It stood in Henry VII's chapel, Westminster Abbey, which was ravaged in 1644.

distaste for the revival of religious art: 'the frequent venting of crucifixes and Popish pictures', and 'the turning of the Communion Table altarwise, setting images, crucifixes and conceits over them, and tapers and books upon them'. In January 1641 the House of Commons issued an order directing commissioners to be sent into several counties 'to demolish and remove out of churches and chapels all images, altars, or tables turned altarwise, crucifixes, superstitious pictures, and other monuments and relics of idolatry'. All altar rails were to be removed, the chancels were to be levelled and 'all crucifixes, scandalous pictures of any one or more of the Trinity, and all images of the Virgin Mary shall be taken away and abolished'. It was not, however, until Civil War actually broke out in 1642 that Parliament found a legal way to implement this. In August 1643 all these directives were made official and in May of the following year an ordinance required the removal of all organs, copes, surplices, fonts and screens. To ensure that this happened, regional committees for the demolition of monuments of superstition were set up.

How this was carried out across the country is impossible to chart in detail. Where the forces of Parliament triumphed, the destruction was appalling. Elsewhere it could be minimal. The local reaction also varied: some parishioners hid their church's stained glass; others smashed anything they thought

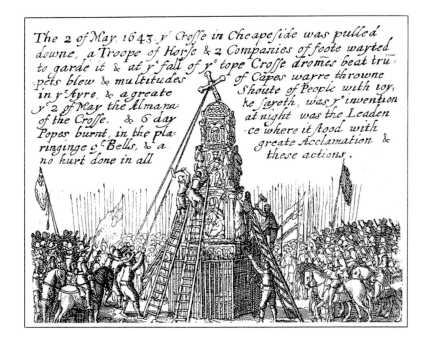

Between 1291 and 1293 Edward I erected twelve crosses marking the resting places of the funeral cortège of his queen, Eleanor of Castile. The two most spectacular of these were at Charing Cross and Cheapside. Both were demolished by the Puritans amidst scenes of rejoicing. Wenceslas Hollar's engraving shows the Parliamentary soldiery about to deface Cheapside Cross in 1643.

East Anglia was stoutly Puritan and the churches suffered accordingly. Defacement centred on representations of any member of the Trinity, but the likenesses of saints and angels were indiscriminately damaged, as in these chancel windows at Great Massingham Parish Church, Norfolk, whose images of saints and the Lamb of God have been defaced.

superstitious before the commissioners arrived. An extreme instance of the activities of the commissioners is the visit paid by Francis Jessup of Beccles to Gorleston in Suffolk:

In the chancel, as it is called, we took up twenty brazen inscriptions, *Ora pro nobis*, &c.; broke twelve apostles, carved in wood, and cherubims, and a lamb with a cross; and took up four superstitious inscriptions in brass, in the north chancel, *Jesu filii Dei miserere mei*, &c.; broke in pieces the rails, and broke

95

down twenty-two popish pictures of angels and saints. We did deface the font and a cross on the font; and took up a brass inscription there, with *Cujus animae propitietur Deus*, and 'Pray for ye soul,' &c.; in English. We took up thirteen superstitious brasses. Ordered Moses with his rod and Aaron with his mitre, to be taken down. Ordered eighteen angels off the roof, and cherubims to be taken down, and nineteen pictures on the windows. The organ I brake; and we brake seven popish pictures in the chancel window, – one of Christ, another of St. Andrew, another of St. James, &c. We ordered the steps to be levelled by the parson of the town; and brake the popish inscription, *My flesh is meat indeed, and my blood is drink indeed.* I gave orders to brake in pieces the carved work, which I have seen done. There were six superstitious pictures, one crucifix, and the Virgin Mary with the infant Jesus in her arms, and Christ lying in a manger, and the three kings coming to Christ with presents, and three bishops with their mitres and crosier staffs, and eighteen Jesuses written in capital letters, which we gave orders to do out. A picture of St. George, and many others which I remember not, with divers pictures in the windows, which we could not reach, neither would they help us to raise ladders; so we left a warrant with the constable to do it in fourteen days. We brake down a pot of holy water, St. Andrew wth his cross, and St. Catherine with her wheel; and we took down the cover of the font, and the four evangelists, and a triangle for the Trinity, a superstitious picture of St. Peter and his keys, an eagle, and a lion with wings.

Jessup was acting on behalf of one William Dowsing, who kept a detailed diary of his progress of destruction through the parishes of Suffolk. It opens on 6 January 1643 and closes on 1 October 1644, during which time he visited more than 150 places in less than fifty days. On one day he went through as many as eleven churches. There are some 500 churches in Suffolk, so huge numbers escaped unscathed. None the less I know of few more chilling documents than this monument to bigotry, made worse by the appreciation today of the sheer quantity and quality of what went. The diary opens with a typical entry:

SUDBURY, Suffolk. *Peter's* Parish. Jan the 9th. 1643. We brake down a picture of God the Father, 2 Crucifix's, and Pictures of Christ, about an hundred in all; and gave order to take down a Cross off the Steeple; and diverse Angels, 20 at the least, on the roof of the Church.

Clare was subject to destruction on a gargantuan scale:

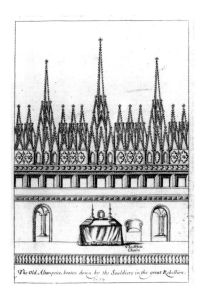

The Old Altarpeice, beaten down by the Souldiers in the great Rebellion.

Cromwell's horsemen broke into Peterborough Cathedral in April 1643 and systematically destroyed its furnishings. The reredos, 'because it bore the name of the High Altar, was pulled down with Ropes, lay'd low and level with the ground'. We owe this record of what vanished to a local antiquary, Simon Gunton, who provides a vivid narrative of the desecration of the church.

We brake down 1000 Picture superstitious; I brake down 200; 3 of God the Father, and 3 of Christ, and the Holy Lamb, and 3 of the Holy Ghost like a Dove with Wings; and the 12 Apostles were carved in Wood, on top of the Roof, which we gave order to take down; and 20 Cherubims to be taken down; and the Sun and Moon in the East Window, by the King's Arms, to be taken down.

Twelve thousand women of Middlesex petitioned Parliament in 1644 'that prophane glass windowes, whose superstitious paint makes many idolaters, may be humbled and dashed in pieces against the ground; for our conscious tell us that they are diabolicall, and the father of Darkness was the inventor of them, being the chief Patron of damnable pride.' In the case of most stained-glass windows the heads of saints were either removed or smashed, as we can see from the windows of York Minster or the parish church at Great Massingham, Norfolk.

Such was the fate of parish churches and of the chapels of the Oxford and Cambridge colleges, which provide an unending litany of desecration. Where Puritan sympathies ran high the market and Eleanor crosses were also demolished. The beautiful Eleanor crosses had been erected by Edward I to mark the route taken by his wife's funeral cortège in 1290. Of the twelve erected only three survive today. In their time they were major innovative monuments in the evolution of the decorated style. Charing Cross was demolished in 1643 amidst scenes of public rejoicing.

The greatest tragedy lay with the cathedrals, which, with the abolition of the episcopacy in the Root and Branch Bill in 1642, were totally redundant. They had been in the Laudian vanguard and the accounts of their fate, above all in areas fought over during the Civil War or where Puritanism was at its strongest, as in East Anglia, make tragic reading. In the west the destruction was less. Wells, although left to rot, only suffered one major incursion of iconoclasts in April 1643, who smashed 'divers pictures and crusifixes in the church and our lady chaple, likewise did plunder the Bishops Pallace and broke all such monumentes and pictures they espied, either of religion antiquity or the kinges of England'. Canterbury experienced a catalogue of disasters. It had been a prime exemplar of Laudian style, with a purple velvet cloth covering the communion table and a hanging behind it richly embroidered with gold and silver rays surrounded the name Jehovah. In 1642 the nave was used as a barracks by Parliament troops, who stripped the lead from the roof, the chapter house and the cloisters, destroyed the organ, tore down the hangings in the choir and overthrew the high altar and its reredos 'richly overlaid with gold'. Worse was to follow the next year when a fanatical priest called Richard Culmer led an attack on the cathedral's legendary stained glass. He climbed up a ladder bearing a pike:

In that window was now a picture of God the Father and of Christ, besides a large Crucifix and the picture of the Holy Ghost, in the form of a Dove, and of the twelve Apostles; and in that window were seven large pictures of the Virgin Marie, in seven several glorious appearances, as of the Angells lifting her into heaven, and the Sun, Moon and Stars under her feet ... Many window-images or pictures in glass were destroyed that day and many idolls of stone, thirteen representing Christ and the twelve Apostles standing over the West door of the Quire were all hewed down and twelve more at the North door of the Quire, which were all cast down headlong, and some fell on their heads and their myters brake their necks ... Many other images were defaced ... several pictures of God the Father, of Crucifixes and men praying to Crucifixes and to the Virgin Mary: and images lay on the tombs with eyes and hands lifted up, and right over them was pictured God the Father, embracing a Crucifix to which the Image seemed to pray ... the last execution against the idols in that Cathedral was done in the Cloysters, divers crucifixes and mitred saints were battered in pieces there.

This was a holocaust of some of the finest stained glass of the thirteenth century. Of the forty-nine single-light windows in the clerestory, all went save five. The fourteen large windows in the side aisles of the choir and the five in the apse were all destroyed bar a few fragments. The great north window was attacked with hatchets and today we see it only in rearranged and restored form.

East Anglia suffered the worst. The Puritans of Great Yarmouth petitioned to demolish Norwich cathedral. The demolition of Ely was considered and abandoned on account of the expense. Those who visit the Lady Chapel, where the head of every figure has been hacked off, can sense exactly what that great building endured at Puritan hands. Peterborough was absolutely wrecked. Everything went including a screen behind the altar which 'was well wrought, painted and gilt, which rose up as high almost as the roof of the church in a row of three lofty spires, with other lesser spires, growing out of each of them'. An engraving of this screen is included in a post-Restoration history of the cathedral. All the tombs were mutilated or hacked down and the glass in the cloisters, acknowledged to be 'most famed of all, for their great art and pleasing variety', vanished. The cloisters, chapter house, bishop's hall and chapel were all demolished. The cathedral itself was granted to Oliver St John, Chief Justice of the

The damage perpetrated by William Dowsing in 1643–4 on his tour of Suffolk churches is chronicled in his diary. On this fifteenth-century screen at the church of St Edmund King and Martyr, Southwold, Suffolk, the faces have been scratched out.

Common Pleas, who gave it to the town as a parish church. The townspeople were too poor to maintain it, so they demolished the Lady Chapel.

Lichfield suffered from being besieged by both sides in the Civil War. In 1643 Lord Brooke attacked it but was himself shot in the battle. When the royalists inside at last surrendered, the great steeple had already been blown up, shattering the roof in several places. The Parliamentary troops then sacked the cathedral, even opening and ransacking the tombs. It was left to become a ruin and after the Restoration it took eight years to restore it to proper use. At Worcester, Essex's troops wreaked damage on the interior, the bell tower was demolished for its materials, and the cloisters for their wood and lead. At Lincoln there is the usual saga of destruction, Evelyn recording seeing barge-loads of metal being taken away from the building. Norwich was subject to horrendous profanities. All that didn't accord with Puritan susceptibilities – organ pipes, vestments and books – was carried to the marketplace and burnt. In Winchester the Parliamentary troops entered the cathedral on horseback to begin their fearful work of retribution on tombs, images and glass. The choir at Exeter was mutilated as what was left of the gorgeous reredos, sedilia and bishop's throne fell prey to the axes and hammers of the Puritans.

In London the same fate befell St Paul's, as I shall discuss later, and Westminster Abbey. In 1643 the abbey was visited by a commission headed by Sir Robert Harley. That summer two companies of soldiers were quartered in the church. During their stay, the new high altar was destroyed and the thirteenth-century tapestries which adorned the choir were sold. Then, in April 1644 Henry VII's Chapel was defaced, which included the 'rassing out of all the painted images', the 'cleaning out of the pictures from the chapel windows' and, most tragically of all, the demolition of Pietro Torrigiani's altar.

We know that this was a major masterpiece of the early Tudor Renaissance from the engraving of it in Sandford's *A Genealogical History of the Kings and Queens of England*. It had been commissioned by Henry VIII in 1517 and was completed three years later. Even though it had lost the terracotta Dead Christ beneath the altar, the rest remained intact – an altar of black marble below a canopy of bronze and white marble. Over the altar was a major bronze relief in the new Renaissance style and above the canopy were the royal arms, flanked by kneeling angels in glazed Della Rubbia ware, supporting symbols of the Passion. Surpassing even Torrigiani's royal tombs, this was the most wholly Italianate work of art in early Tudor England.

In the north, Carlisle and Durham suffered from the incursion of the Scots. Most of Carlisle Cathedral was demolished between 1645 and 1652 by the Scottish troops garrisoned there, while the Scottish covenanting army occupied Durham Cathedral in 1641 and literally tore the interior to pieces. A similar story is repeated in all the great cathedrals. Although the damage was irreparable, most cathedrals are so overlaid with nineteenth-century restoration that it is easy to forget this terrible part of their history – a fate which echoed that suffered by the monasteries in the previous century. For almost two decades the cathedrals were to be fitted out as preaching houses or shut up as useless, to become mere ruins and quarries.

CHAPTER SEVEN

The Fate of the Royal Palaces

Until the Civil War nothing had disturbed the development of the royal palaces since the accession of the Tudors in 1485. Richmond, with its many towers and turrets on the banks of the Thames, was the first Tudor creation, built by Henry VII to symbolize the power and prestige of the new dynasty and to receive Catharine of Aragon as his son's bride in 1501, the triumph of his international diplomacy. Down the river was the manor of Greenwich, which was developed under Henry VII but his son, Henry VIII, turned it into a major palace and the setting for some of his most spectacular feats of romantic chivalry. It was in the 1530s, however, that the Crown's newly acquired ecclesiastical wealth led to the creation of the greatest of the royal palaces. Two came from Henry's fallen first minister, Cardinal Wolsey: Hampton Court with its gracious rose-brick courtyards was rapidly enlarged and surrounded by splendid gardens and a tiltyard with banqueting houses; *Whitehall*, hard by Westminster, was transformed by armies of artists and craftsmen at great speed to receive Anne Boleyn as queen in 1533. Simultaneously the king built a new palace at St James's, complete by 1536. In 1535 he had purchased Oatlands in Surrey, which was vastly enlarged, and in 1538 he embarked on his legendary magical folly of Nonsuch. None of Henry's children added to this majestic list, which only expanded again under the Stuarts.

These buildings were the precious and ill-fated inheritance that fell into the hands of the newly created Commonwealth in

Opposite: *Charles I's inventory records that this picture,* Girl in a Fur, *was 'bought in Spaine by him' on his abortive mission to woo the Infanta. Disposed of after the Civil War, the picture surfaced again in Vienna in 1705, and is now in the city's Kunsthistorisches Museum.*

1649. The initial attack was on the contents. In one sense it was a re-enactment a century on of the fate of the monasteries and churches, whose treasures had been confiscated, defaced or destroyed. But there were no bonfires of royal portraits and no desecration of the symbols of royal power. Instead there was a purging of the idolatrous followed by the sale of what remained or was of no use to the new Government.

What does survive today, such as Hampton Court, is merely a shell. To get a measure of what was dismembered under the Commonwealth we need to quote only one or two descriptions by visitors to the royal palaces as they were seen in the reign of Elizabeth, when they were a wonder to behold indeed. Here is a flavour of Hampton Court in 1598:

We were led into two chambers, called the presence, or chambers of audience, which shone with tapestry of gold and silver and silk of sundry colours: under the canopy of state are the words embroidered in pearl: 'Vivat Henricus Octavus'.

Here is besides a small chapel richly hung with tapestry, where the Queen performs her devotions ... All the other rooms, being very numerous, are adorned with tapestry of gold, silver, and velvet ... there were numbers of cushions ornamented with gold and silver; many counterpanes and coverlids of beds lined with ermine: in short all the walls of the palace shine with gold and silver. Here is besides a certain cabinet called Paradise, where besides that everything glitters so with silver, gold, and jewels, as to dazzle one's eyes, there is a musical instrument made all of glass, except the strings.

The following year, a German describes what was known as the Field Room at Greenwich:

There we saw many fine objects, amongst them a very costly backgammon set, gift of Christian, Elector of Saxony, to the queen. On the pieces were the coloured portraits of great lords and queens in relief covered with pure crystal. The edge or border of the board was encircled and inlaid with ivory and ebony and set with costly jewels ... We were then shown a fine high silver-gilt escritoire on which stood a good clear mirror. Item, another escritoire like a little box, beautifully worked. Next a tall saltcellar like a candlestick was pointed out to us, very tastefully ornamented with a tree made of natural silver material. Another saltcellar was in the shape of a native decked out with fine feathers, on his shoulders was a shell inlaid and set with pearls and precious stones ... On the side-board was a long cover worked in silver and gold showing the queen in a coach driving up to a house ... Further we saw an exceedingly lovely cover of peacock's feathers sewn together into pretty pictures ... Following these came a rich gilt clock; item, two fine large globes of

The Prince's Lodgings at Newmarket, Berkshire, were built between 1618 and 1619 for the future Charles I.

Opposite: *In the preliminary design Inigo Jones is still working within the vocabulary of the Renaissance architect Scamozzi.* Right: *In the later design Jones has freed himself from these constrictions and produced a design which anticipates the classic English country house of the Queen Anne period. Whether any of this design was built is unknown, but the demolition of the building itself under the Commonwealth was a major loss for architectural history.*

The sale by the Commonwealth of the Royal Collection after the execution of Charles I in 1649 dispersed England's greatest assembly of Italian High Renaissance painting. The king's agents had scoured Europe looking for masterpieces and their greatest coup was the acquisition of the collection of the Dukes of Mantua, which included not only world-famous paintings but also classical antiquities. Charles I loved the work of Titian, and no less than twenty-one of his paintings, of which five are illustrated here, adorned the Royal Privy Lodgings at Whitehall Palace.

Left: *Alfonso d'Avalos, Marquis of Vasto, attended by his son, Ferrante, addresses his troops. This was one of the pictures which came to England from Mantua. It reappeared in 1666 in the Spanish royal collection and can be seen today in the Prado, Madrid.*

Opposite: *Pope Alexander II presents Jacopo Pesaro to St Peter. Pesaro was Bishop of Pafo and Commissioner of the Papal Galleys which, together with those of Venice, routed the Turks at Santa Maura in 1502. The picture was sold by a Venetian church and passed to Charles I, later reappearing in the monastery of St Pascal in Madrid. Today it hangs in the Musée Royal des Beaux-Arts, Antwerp.*

heaven and earth. They told us that all these splendid objects were gifts to the queen from the great potentates and lords to whom she showed some favour, for they were aware that Her Royal Highness took pleasure in such strange and lovely curios.

Much may have gone, been altered or added to and enriched by the reign of Charles I, but virtually everything was to be defaced or dispersed in the two decades between the outbreak of the Civil War and the return of the monarchy in 1660.

The erosions to the royal patrimony began soon after the outbreak of the Civil War in 1642 and inevitably focused on the royal chapels, as expressions of Laudian ideals, and, of course, on

Queen Henrietta Maria's Roman Catholic chapels. In 1643 the House of Commons appointed a committee to expel the Capuchin friars from the queen's chapel in Somerset House and to purge it of its altar and all 'other superstitious Pictures and Matters'. On 30 March a band of soldiers 'licentiously rifled' the chapel, one of Inigo Jones's masterpieces, smashing the altar, throwing the Rubens picture out into the Thames and breaking and defacing anything else which might be labelled popish. Attacks then followed on the king's chapels: in December 1643 the Commons ordered the removal of all 'scandalous Monuments and Pictures' from those at Eton and Windsor, and the same fate was meted out to St James's and Whitehall. At the royal chapel in Whitehall the pictures and sculptures were defaced and the stained glass smashed. New white glass was put into the one

Left: *This allegory depicts the happy union of a betrothed or recently married couple attended by the figures of Hope, Faith and Love. The painting passed into the collection of Louis XIV, and is now in the Louvre, Paris.*

Below: *Venus and an Organist, another of the royal pictures which found its way into the Spanish royal collection, where it is first recorded in 1686. It too is now part of the Prado collection.*

'idolatrous' window, some of the walls were white-washed and a number of 'boards' were tidied up after 'the carpenter had planed off the pictures'.

A great deal must have been lost, notably the plate made at the king's behest by van Vianen for the chapel at Windsor. But perhaps the greatest loss was the destruction of Henry VIII's tomb. The tomb at Windsor was unfinished and was the work of the Italian sculptor Benedetto da Ravezzano. It had been commissioned for Cardinal Wolsey but at his death it was adapted for the king. Between 1530 and 1536 Benedetto Giovanni da Maiano and a team of assistants worked at full steam to complete it. By December 1536 it was 'well onward and almost made'. It was a free-standing sarcophagus with columns at each corner, ten feet in height surmounted by bronze capitals and gilded bronze figures. There were also numerous bronze reliefs and figures plus an enclosure of bronze. If it had been completed, it would have far surpassed the tomb of his parents in Westminster Abbey in splendour and magnificence, for the design made brilliant use of the contrasting materials of white marble, black touchstone and gilded bronze. This is what vanished in March 1645 when the Commons ordered that 'the Brass Statue at Windsour Castle, and the Images there defaced, and other broken Pieces of Brass, be forthwith sold to the best advantage of the State . . .'

Meanwhile the rest of the royal plate was liquidated. In 1644 the Commons ordered that the plate in the Tower should be melted down and turned to coin, a move which was rejected by the Lords, who regarded such pieces with veneration on account of the 'Fashion of it, and the Badges upon it' which, they said, made it 'more Worth than the Plate itself'. In November the Commons reiterated the order and its destruction followed.

It was not, however, until after Charles's execution that damage on a huge and irreparable scale was done to the pre-Civil War heritage. On 1 February 1649 a special committee was set up to 'take care' of all the royal goods. On 25 February Parliament ordered that the Council should be responsible for the care of the library, pictures and statues at St James's, with a mandate that they could dispose of them for the 'present service of the State'. A month later the Commons ordered an inventory of the entire contents of all the royal palaces and residences with a view to their sale. The Council was to have first right to choose things for its own use, the use of the Lord Protector, Parliament and ambassadors. This inevitably held up the sale, the process meandering on through the first half of the 1650s. It was recognized that the best prices for many of the items would come from abroad, where such rulers as Louis XIV were assembling magnificent collections.

Looking through the surviving inventories it is less the pictures, a large proportion of which survive, than the furnishings, now scattered to the four winds, that leave one with a sense of desolation: the suites of superb tapestries, the gold bespangled cloths of state, the richly upholstered furniture, the embroidered cushions and curtains, the chairs, stools and beds which made up the legendary interiors of these palaces in their heyday — the backdrop for the lives of the rulers of Tudor and Stuart England. Like Prospero in the masque scene, the Puritans ensured that not a wrack was left behind.

The modern edition of the valuations made for Parliament to facilitate the sales runs to over 400 pages, yet it is far from complete. It makes heady reading, even down to the humblest artefact. The list of embroidered canopies at Somerset House alone is breathtaking in terms of fabrics: 'silver Tynnsell raised with Carnacon Vellvett', 'white Groggan wrought with flowers of gould, siver and silke of sundry cullours' or 'Orring cullord cloth of gold wrought in flowers'. Here is just one carpet, sold for £25, from the same residence:

One very rich Carpet of Needleworke of gould silver and silke wrought very curiously with the Sea and all sorts of Fishes, and Shippes in ye same, all in Waves, And haveing in yt ye Firmament, and all kind of Landworke with Fowles and Beasts wrought therein . . .

Or one of three clocks:

A Clocke made in ye fashion of a coach of Ebboney garnished with silver droune by Two Lyons, The Lyons Wheeles, and 2 personages all of silver having a Clock in the same in a greene woodden Case . . .

Although the pictures survived, what went was a unique and irreplaceable collection of Renaissance art, above all Venetian, the like of which Britain was never to see again. There was no

110

shortage of purchasers. The Spanish ambassador was active in acquiring works of art of the highest value; so too was Cardinal Mazarin's minister, M de Bordeaux, who was sent over 'to traffic in the purchase of the rich goods and jewels of the rifled Crown'.

Purchases were often made from the king's creditors, who received royal goods as a settlement for debts. In 1652 the painter Emmanuel de Critz had no less than three rooms stacked with Charles I's pictures as well as Bernini's celebrated bust of the king. The fate of the collection is encapsulated in what happened to the twenty-one paintings attributed to Titian, the painter Charles admired more than any other, which hung in the royal Privy Lodgings at Whitehall Palace. Some we would no longer accept as being by the artist, and some have not been traced, but of those that have, four are in the Louvre, three in the Prado, one in Vienna, one in Antwerp, two in private collections, leaving only three in the present royal collection. It was indeed a mighty dissolution.

Now to turn to the buildings themselves. In 1649–50 Parliament sold all but seven of the royal palaces. Minor ones such as Eltham, Ampthill, Havering, Grafton and Woodstock were already in ruin or bad repair. These were left to moulder. The tragedy was that among those sold were major architectural monuments whose purchasers simply demolished them, wholly or in part, for the materials. Although Newmarket was never a major palace, it did include one building of crucial importance. James I discovered Newmarket as an ideal resort for the pursuit of the chase and erected a building there of some substance in 1614–15, but it was Inigo Jones's later additions, above all the Prince's Lodging, which were seminal in introducing the Palladian villa ideal in England. We have two splendid designs for the Prince's Lodging, neither of which seems to have been executed, probably because they were considered too ambitious. What was constructed in 1618–19 was similar but on a smaller scale. The Lodging had a tremendous impact on the direction of architectural taste, from the surviving Queen's House at Greenwich to the Palladian revival of Lord Burlington in the next century and his villa at Chiswick.

More of Jones's work vanished with the demolition of Oatlands, where he had added classical gateways, notably the monumental one into the vineyard, for Anne of Denmark, and chimneypieces and a series of cartouches framing views of the queen's residences in the 'lower gallery' for Henrietta Maria. Today the site of Oatlands is covered by a modern housing estate. An even sadder loss was the first great royal Tudor palace, Richmond. The great hall had a massive timber ceiling and between its windows eleven life-size statues of the most famous of England's kings. Its chapel was adorned with a parallel series of kings renowned for their piety. A series of timber-framed galleries enclosed the gardens:

moost faire and pleasaunt ... with ryall knotts aleyed and herbid; many maruelous beasts, as lyons, dragons, and such othre of dyvers kynde, properly fachyoned and coruyd in the grounde ... with many vynys, sedis, and straunge frute ... In the lougher end of this gardeyn beth plesaunt galerys, and housis of pleasure to disporte inn, at chesse, tables, dise, cardes, bylys; bowlyng aleys, butts for archers, and goodly tenes plays; as well to use the seid plays and disports as to behold them so disportyng.

Although not much used by Henry VIII, Richmond was kept in good repair and, indeed, in the Stuart period ranked fourth in terms of upkeep. In 1650 it was dismantled and sold off to Sir Gregory Norton, one of the king's judges, who had to return it to the Crown in 1660. It was assigned to Henrietta Maria but she let it and the palace then began its long descent into decay and piecemeal demolition.

A detail of a portrait of James I's queen, Anne of Denmark, commemorating the erection of Inigo Jones's new classical gateway to the vineyard at Oatlands Palace, Surrey. The view looks north-east across the Privy Garden towards the heart of the old Tudor palace.

Jones's design for the Vineyard Gateway was an innovation in Jacobean England, its rough-cut rustication establishing an intriguing interplay between 'natural' stone and stone tamed by art into architecture that was appropriate to mark the passage from the garden to the park. The gateway survived the Commonwealth and was re-erected in the grounds of the ninth Earl of Lincoln. It was subsequently demolished, although some fragments are in Weybridge Museum, Surrey.

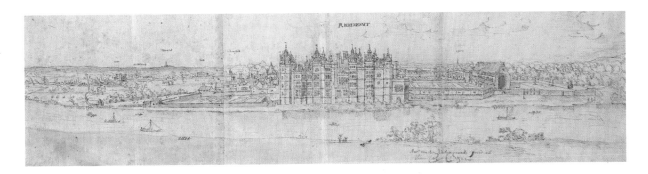

A view of Henry VII's palace at Richmond, Surrey, from across the Thames by the topographical artist A. van den Wyngaerde, c.1558–62. The earliest of the Tudor royal palaces, it was built to celebrate the triumph of the new dynasty. In the central turreted block were the royal apartments, to the left the Great Orchard with kitchen and service areas beyond, to the right a series of covered galleries enclosing the Privy Orchard and Garden. After its contents were sold off by the Commonwealth, the palace was purchased by Sir Gregory Norton, who resided there until it was returned to the Crown in 1660. It was used occasionally thereafter but fell into decay and began to be demolished under Queen Anne.

Shortly after the accession of James I in 1603 the Crown had acquired two great aristocratic houses, Theobalds and Holdenby, which were not only innovative architecturally but were regarded as showplaces of the age. Holdenby in Northamptonshire, purchased in 1608, was built by Elizabeth I's bachelor chancellor, Sir Christopher Hatton. Like Lord Burghley's Theobalds, the house was 'consecrated to Her Majesty', although she never went there. It has been suggested that Hatton saw himself as Lord Burghley's successor (which was not to be, as Hatton died prematurely at the age of fifty-one), and hence built a mansion that was bigger than both the present Chatsworth and Burghley's own house, which was recognized as the most palatial in England. Holdenby measured 352 by 216 feet as against Theobalds' 304 by 188 feet. Both were courtyard houses and Hatton unashamedly modelled his on Lord Burghley's. The latter, on visiting Holdenby in 1579, was loud in its praise:

Approaching the house, being led by a large, long, straight fairway, I found a great magnificence in the front or front pieces of the house, and so every part answerable to other, to allure liking. I found no other thing of greater grace than your stately ascent from your hall to your great chamber, and your chambers answerable with largeness and lightsomeness, that truly a Momus could find no fault.

Holdenby was almost complete in that year, although the date on one of the two surviving gateway arches is 1583. The Parliamentary Survey of 1650 speaks of 'magnificent Towers or Turretts and ... costly and rare chymney peices' as well as of a 'pleasant spacious and faire garden adorned with severall long walks, mounts, arbors and seats'. Mark Girouard's reconstruction, based on John Thorpe's plan of 1606–7, and the surviving

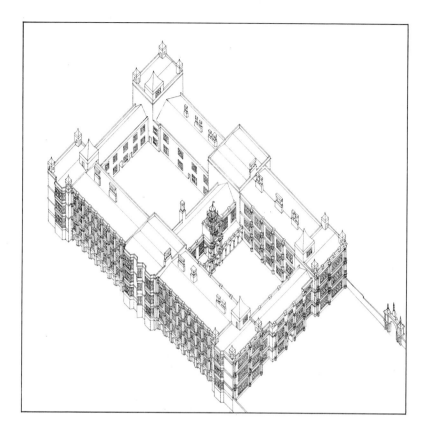

This projection of Holdenby House shows the stupendous scale of the building. In 1608 James I purchased Holdenby, the largest of all the great Elizabethan houses. It was built by Elizabeth I's Lord Chancellor, Sir Christopher Hatton, in the 1570s with a view to receiving the court. If it had survived, the 350-foot south front would have eclipsed by far Hardwick Hall, also conceived as more glass than wall.

drawings of the ruins show a house with towers at its four corners and two great pavilions at the end of the range between the two courtyards. But the remarkable long south front, which contained the state apartments and looked on to splendid gardens, must have been the great 'lantern house' of the age. Holdenby, like most Elizabethan houses, was prominently sited on a hill, and over 350 feet of mullioned window surface, twice as long as that at Hardwick Hall, twinkled and reflected the light across the surrounding countryside. As Girouard writes, 'the south front used glass more daringly than any other house in England, and probably Europe'.

Below this spread the most intricate of knot gardens, laid out on a terrace created by landscaping the hillside on a huge scale. In 1595 John Norden the cartographer tells how Hatton, out of 'a most craggye and unfitable lande', had made

a most pleasante, sweete, and princely place, with divers walks, many ascendings and descendings, replenished also with manie delightful Trees of Fruite, artifically composed Arbors, and a Destilling House on the west end of the same gardens, over which is a Ponde of water, broughte by conduit pypes, out of the feyld adjoyninge on the west, quarter of a myle from the same house.

Holdenby was sold to a Parliamentary soldier, Adam Baynes, for £22,299 6s. 10d. in 1650. He proceeded to demolish it for its materials and made a residence for himself out of its kitchen wing. Thomas Fuller, writing two years after the Restoration, sadly refers to Holdenby's 'beauty and brittleness, short flourishing and soon fading'.

Theobalds was in Hertfordshire, just off the main road from London to Ware and thence to Stamford, where the other great Cecil house, Burghley, stood and indeed still stands. Built between 1564 and 1585 by Elizabeth I's great minister, Lord Burghley, Theobalds had always acted as a royal palace, regularly visited by the queen. Most foreign visitors came here to record its many splendours and marvels. Like Holdenby, it was famous for

All that remains on the site of Holdenby are the two entrance arches which flanked the great forecourt to the east front.

its many turrets. The plan of the house consisted of a succession of courtyards, stretching over a quarter of a mile. Visitors eulogized its interior and its gardens. The Parliamentary Survey describes the Presence Chamber with its roof of beams and 'gilded pendants hanginge downe, settinge forth the roome with greate splendor; as alsoe with verie large windowes, and several coates of armes sett in the same'. The Green Gallery was 109 feet long and 12 feet wide, 'excellently well painted round with the several shires in England, and the armes of the noblemen and gentlemen in the same'. A German visitor in 1600 describes how there was a tree for each of the counties, hung with coats of arms and the 'specialities of any county are included, so if one of them is outstandingly rich in flocks and herds it has them painted here also, and if some fruit or other is particularly abundant, then you find it recorded in the same way'. One room was decorated with busts of the Roman emperors, portraits of foreign princes and of the kings of England; another had a painting of the coronation of Elizabeth I. On the roof of the house there was 'an Astronomer's Walk'. The most extraordinary room of all, however, was referred to as the grotto, whose interior was studded with stones and metallic ore. On either side of the grotto were six artificial fruit trees; it was 'thatched with green grass, and inside can be seen a man and a woman dressed like wild men of the woods, and a number of animals creeping through the bushes. A bronze centaur stands at the base of it'.

The garden was equally marvellous, particularly the Great Garden, which covered two acres and was divided into nine

James I acquired Theobalds, Hertfordshire, from Sir Robert Cecil in 1607 in exchange for the old palace of Hatfield. This vast house was built by Elizabeth I's Lord Treasurer, Lord Burghley, between 1564 and 1585. It was enormously innovative and had a huge influence on other houses. The main axis of the house ran for a quarter of a mile through five courtyards. Its lavish interiors and spectacular gardens were visited and described in detail by many foreigners. Although not sold by the Commonwealth, from 1650 onwards its demolition began. This reconstruction is of Theobalds from the south-west.

116

separate knots. The central knot garden had a white marble fountain, another the royal arms in box, a third was 'planted with choice flowers' and in one of them there seems to have been a maze and mount 'called Venusberg'. Even more strikingly, the garden was enclosed by a canal upon which it was possible to row a boat and on which a miniature, fully rigged ship floated. There was a summer house, too, with yet more Roman emperors, and an ornamental fishpond. Although this wonderful ensemble was not placed on the list for disposal in 1649, from 1650 onwards it was largely demolished.

At the Restoration the main royal palaces that remained were Whitehall, Nonsuch, St James's, Hampton Court, Windsor Castle, Richmond and Greenwich, all virtually emptied. By the close of the century Whitehall had gone up in flames, Nonsuch had been demolished, Hampton Court and Greenwich were rebuilt either wholly or in part by Wren, Windsor Castle was subjected to great alterations within, and Richmond was also to be demolished. All of this only serves to emphasize how very little of the pre-Civil-War heritage has survived into this century.

CHAPTER EIGHT

The Destruction of the Crown Jewels

The emergence of the Commonwealth after the execution of Charles I rendered the Crown Jewels redundant. This was the only time in British history that there was a break in the long series of coronation ceremonies which stretched back to pre-Conquest days. By the Tudor period two sets of regalia existed: that in Westminster Abbey, which was only used for the rite of coronation and was in the custody of the Dean and Chapter, and hence rarely seen; and the state regalia, which came under the care of the master of the Jewel-house and was worn on ceremonial public occasions, such as the State Opening of Parliament. The former is first listed in 1450:

Relics of Holy Confessors, St. Edward, King and Confessor, for the memory of posterity and for the dignity of the royal coronation caused to be preserved in this church all the royal ornaments with which he was crowned namely his tunicle, supertunica, armilla, girdle and embroidered pall, a pair of buskins, a pair of gloves, a golden sceptre, one wooden rod, gilt, another of iron.

The list also includes 'an excellent golden crown, a golden comb and a spoon', 'a crown and two rods for a queen' and 'one chalice of onyx stone with foot rivets and a paten of the best gold'. All of these were designated 'precious relics'. They certainly did not all belong to Edward the Confessor, but probably represent an accumulation of very early items from royal

Opposite: *Great confusion surrounds the identity of the crowns which appear in various royal portraits. This one, in Van Dyck's portrait of Charles I's queen, Henrietta Maria, painted in 1635, may be that listed in 1649 as 'A Small Crowne ... enrich't with Diamonds Rubies Saphires Emrods and pearles', valued at £428 16s. 08d., almost £100 more than the queen's official State Crown.*

tombs, particularly those recovered during the reign of Henry III, when the Confessor's shrine was built in its present form. We can recognize from that list all the items still used in the coronation ceremony, but many other crowns, not worn for the crowning itself, were made for the nine coronations which took place between 1485 and 1625.

There is no doubt that in the minds of the Parliamentarians these were the most tangible objects associated with the monarchy as a sacrosanct institution – holy regal relics used in the solemn rite of coronation, which emphasized the sanctity and semi-divinity of the head that wore the crown. Shortly after the execution of Charles I in January 1649 an order was sent to the clerk of the Jewel-house to surrender the state regalia, but there is a note to the effect that this was 'not obeyed'. In the autumn of that year, however, the Trustees of Parliament actually 'broake into the Jewel-house and took away these three crowns, 2 sept[res], bracelets, globe, &c. and secured all other things'. An order was given that they should be 'totallie broken and defaced', and, to avoid any possibility of the manufacture of royal relics, the metal was to be used for coin.

In this way the historic regalia of the Crown of England was destroyed, so that when Charles II returned in 1660 a completely new set had to be made for his coronation. The records of this act of barbarism are very detailed, as indeed are the inventories of what vanished, although it is difficult to establish the exact appearance of what went, particularly because there are innumerable conflicting representations of parts of the regalia in portraits.

There is, for instance, no certain picture of the most precious and earliest item, the crown of Edward the Confessor, part of the coronation regalia held in Westminster Abbey. Henry V is depicted on his chantry in the Abbey being crowned with St Edward's crown, which, according to one description, was a 'crowne of gould wyer worke sett with slight stones; and two little bells'. In the post-Reformation period it was re-named King Alfred's crown, thus removing any possible context in which it could be regarded as a holy relic. There is no agreement as to the origin of this crown but it is likely that what was destroyed was an Anglo-Saxon burial crown.

Daniel Mytens's portrait of Charles I, painted in 1631, gives one of the certain representations of the king's state regalia. The State Crown was made for either Henry VII or Henry VIII. Although stones were taken from and added to it, the crown remained unchanged until the stones were sold off by Parliament and the gold minted into coin in 1649. On the table are the State Orb and Sceptre, both of which were also converted into coin.

We do, in contrast, know the appearance of the king's State Crown, which appears in a number of portraits of Charles I by Daniel Mytens and by Van Dyck. We do not know when it was made but it first appears in an inventory of 1520, which indicates that it may have been made for Henry VII. It is highly unlikely to have been any later, for in appearance it belongs to the last wave of the Gothic and shows no Renaissance influence. The crown was a circlet of gold adorned with eight balas rubies, eight sapphires and five pointed diamonds, twenty rubies and nineteen pearls. From the circlet arose five crosses alternating with five fleurs-de-lis, each of the latter containing a figure. In Mytens' painting of the crown the facing fleur-de-lis bears the Virgin and Child. On the others were St George, the patron saint of England, and three representations of Christ which, after the Reformation, were referred to as kings. In Van Dyck's portrayal of the crown it is viewed from the back, perhaps to obscure what many of the king's subjects would undoubtedly have considered popish imagery.

These very detailed depictions of the State Crown in the king's portraits make it clear that the small bejewelled crown which appears in some of Van Dyck's portraits of Henrietta Maria, described in inventories as the 'Small Crowne', must be a matching diadem for the queen. This crown had little gold content, only twenty-five ounces, but was composed almost entirely of an unspecified number of diamonds, rubies, sapphires, emeralds and pearls. No identifiable picture exists of the queen's official State Crown, which weighed over three and a half pounds and was set with some twenty-two balas rubies, twenty sapphires and eighty-three pearls.

The coronation regalia in the Abbey must have been a treasure-trove of medieval goldsmiths' work. It is striking that many items which formed part of the regalia were made of silver-gilt or base metals, which lends weight to the argument that such pieces came from royal tombs and were made for burial. The Confessor's crown was complemented by Queen Edith's, valued at only £16, of 'Siluer gilt Enriched with Garnetts foule pearle Saphires and some odd stones'. There were several ancient sceptres and staffs, two with doves on the top and one with a fleur-de-lis, which turned out to be not of gold but of iron silver-gilt, two more sceptres, one of gold set with jewels and the other silver-gilt.

Unlike the state regalia, which was kept in the Tower of London, the coronation regalia was kept in Westminster Abbey for use only at that event, and we have no certain visual records of it. The items used in the ceremony were extremely old and some of them may have been parts of burial regalia. This detail from an illumination of the apotheosis of St Edmund in the thirteenth-century manuscript Miracula Sancti Eadmundi *includes a depiction of what appears to be the Crown of St Edward the Confessor, although the orb and cross on its summit were not part of it.*

The exact origin and date of what became known as the Crown of St Edward the Confessor, used for the coronation ceremony, is not known but it may have belonged to Edward the Confessor or to William I. This relief depicting the coronation of Henry V is one of the most likely representations of it.

There was the ampulla which contained the holy oil for the anointing, listed as 'A doue [actually it was an eagle] of gould sett with stones and pearle'.

Even more interesting must have been the medieval robes with which any king was invested before the crowning. All of this was regarded as so much superstitious rubbish and valued only for any gold or silver content in the textile, or, like the 'old Comb of horne' – probably a carved Anglo-Saxon liturgical comb which was used to arrange the king's hair after his head was anointed – listed as 'worth nothing'. We are left to wonder about the exact age of three of the garments which even the Parliamentarians recognized to be 'very old'. All nine items were sold to a Mr Humphreys for £5 in November 1649.

As no visual record of these items survived, one can understand why Sir Edward Walker, Garter King of Arms, begins his report in 1660 with such a sigh:

And because through the Rapine of the late vnhappy times, all the Royall Ornaments and Regalia heretofore preserved from age to age in the Treasury of the Church of Westminster, were taken away, sold and destroyed, the Committee mett divers times, not only to direct the remaking such Royal Ornaments and Regalia, but even to setle the forme and fashion of each particular.

Nothing on such a dramatic scale was to occur again.

PART THREE

ACCIDENT, AVARICE
AND FASHION
1660–1837

The monarchy returned in 1660, and the Church of England was restored to its former primacy. Neither institution has suffered a reversal since. Never again was the country to be subject to internal conflict or an ideology which espoused destruction. It was not just the king who was restored in 1660 but the physical trappings of the Crown, the royal palaces and their contents. The fount of honour in the form of titles has continued to flow, ensuring the semblance of an unchanging social structure that allows new families to join the existing hierarchy.

Later forces of destruction lacked the cataclysmic effect of the era before the Civil War. Neither the Glorious Revolution of 1688, when the Catholic James II was forced to flee the realm in favour of the Protestant William III and Mary II, nor the accession of George I and the House of Hanover in 1714, resulted in any loss of artefacts. From the second half of the seventeenth century until the advent of the conservation age in the mid-nineteenth century, the greatest threat to British heritage came from changes in taste; and these pressures resulted in the destruction not so much of artefacts, such as furniture and pictures, but of buildings and gardens. It is easy to forget that few houses of any substance date to before the Tudor age, when prosperity allied with political stability led to a building boom, particularly from 1580 to 1620. By 1660 these Tudor and Jacobean houses were radically out of date, not only in their aesthetic style but also in comfort. Huge numbers of new houses were built and gardens laid out but we see a novel phenomenon, the demolition of the past in favour of the present. To some extent this process had

Opposite: *Detail from a painting by Danckert showing Whitehall Palace, from 1533 to 1698 the official residence of the king and court.*

already started before the Civil War. The Elizabethans had re-modelled medieval castles and fortified houses such as Broughton Castle and Haddon Hall. Before 1642 the most spectacular instance of demolition was Lord Pembroke's decision to rebuild Tudor Wilton as a vast Palladian villa in the new classical style.

In the period following 1660 the classical aesthetic became universally accepted and went through its various phases of baroque, Palladian, rococo and neo-classical. Despite periodic set-backs, the prosperity of the country through commercial endeavour and the creation of an empire was set on a long upward curve. The ruling classes shared a cultural base built on a classical education and what became a part of any gentleman's political education, the Grand Tour. This made a lasting impact on the landscape of Britain as houses inspired by the palaces and villas of Italy were built. The next two hundred years also saw the creation in the great country houses of picture and sculpture galleries filled with works purchased on the mainland of Europe. Most of them came from Italy, but the collections were infinitely enriched by the upheavals of the French Revolution and the Napoleonic era, when works of art flooded on to the market.

On the whole people still travelled to view what was new. A radical shift in that perception of the environment only really occurred under Queen Victoria. Celia Fiennes, who voyaged around England at the end of the seventeenth century, was wholly enamoured of the present, noting above all new houses, the insertion of new sash windows, new gardening styles, and referring in a derogatory manner to old timbered houses. By the end of the eighteenth century, under the impact of the anti-quarians and, more particularly, the Romantic movement and the cult of the picturesque, the old began to acquire greater status. Medieval castles and Tudor houses were now viewed not as anti-quated residences which required either demolition or radical mod-ernization but as buildings and interiors whose period flavour needed not only preserving but judiciously heightening. With the publication of Joseph Nash's hugely influential *The Mansions of England in the Olden Time* between 1839 and 1849, the cult of the historic country house had arrived. On the decaying ancient manor houses of England Nash bestowed glamour, hitherto the preserve of the new, which remains unchanged to this day.

These factors conspired to make the chronicle of artistic loss after 1660 and before 1837 a patchwork of accidents and incidents – notably fires, and destruction motivated by sheer greed – in an age before the old had become a cult. No preservation societies existed, and everyone had the right to do what they liked with their own property.

Even more so than in the earlier eras, a survey of such losses must be a personal anthology. The palaces of Whitehall and Westminster together with the City of London epitomize the greatest losses by fire, but the destruction of the early Tudor wall-paintings at Cowdray Park should not go unmentioned.

The Caroline garden at Wilton must symbolize the thousands of formal gardens swept away by the fashion for the new landscape style. Here 'Capability' Brown emerges as a vandal, for he destroyed the three greatest baroque gardens in England: Longleat House in 1757, and Chatsworth and Blenheim in 1760. Parterres, statues, canals, fountains, topiary, stately avenues and walks, all went down before the scythe of the 'improver'.

Somerset House and Nonsuch Palace must stand as monuments to the demands of greed and redevelopment, although one cannot overlook the loss of Elizabethan Chatsworth, Bess of Hardwick's first great house, or the demolition of Wimbledon, built by the Earl of Exeter at the time of the defeat of the Spanish Armada. This splendid house included in its grand approach the earliest English response to Vignola's Caprarola. Vanbrugh's eradication of most of Audley End in Suffolk, the magnificent pile built by the Earl of Suffolk early in the reign of James I; the Duke of Chandos selling off the baroque palace of Cannons in Middlesex for its building materials; George IV's decision to demolish his own masterpiece of palace building and decoration, Henry Holland's Carlton House – all would be considered acts of vandalism today. Had any of these buildings survived, they would be places not only of intense interest to the historian but of wonder to the modern tourist and visitor.

More important in its consequences for the next century were the activities of 'The Destroyer', James Wyatt, in his cathedral 'restorations'. These embraced major demolitions apart from the re-siting of innumerable tombs and artefacts. In the outrage evoked we see the stirrings of what was to become scientific conservation.

CHAPTER NINE

The Great Fire of London

The Great Fire of London was more remarkable in many ways for what did not perish in its flames than for what did. The Fire spread over four days and was, therefore, slow enough to allow the contents of both civic institutions and private houses to be evacuated to places of safety beyond the City walls. In fact by 1666 the City of London was not rich in major public buildings or works of art. The Reformation had taken a savage toll of London's heritage of Gothic art and architecture – Londoners were stoutly Protestant and vigorous in their destruction of any artefact that might remotely be construed as popish. Had the fire continued westwards to engulf the great houses of the aristocracy lining the Strand and the Thames, and the royal palace at White-hall, seat of king and court, many more buildings and works of art would have been lost. Mercifully that did not happen, yet it was a gargantuan tragedy: 100,000 were left homeless and over 13,000 houses were destroyed.

The fire began on Sunday 1 September 1666 in a narrow street leading down to the river near London Bridge, and ended not far from Temple Bar. During those four days the London of Chaucer and of Shakespeare vanished, a city we only know from engravings which show narrow streets and wooden gabled houses, the skyline punctuated by the many spires of the medieval churches and dominated by the cathedral of Old St Paul's on the summit of Ludgate Hill.

Opposite: *A detail from a picture depicting the Great Fire of London as the flames began to engulf the ancient cathedral of Old St Paul's on the evening of Tuesday 4 September, two days after the fire began. The picture is so exact that it was probably painted by an eye-witness on a boat moored close to Tower Wharf. Old London Bridge can be seen on the left.*

The fire changed the focus of the City from the old monastic buildings, albeit dissolved, to one which was wholly commercial. One hundred and nine churches and forty-four company halls were burnt. It is impossible to gauge the importance of these buildings in architectural terms, but clearly there was a huge loss of stained glass and interior church fittings, notably woodwork and tombs. For instance, Dick Whittington's tomb in St Michael Paternoster Royal was burnt. Luckily the contents of many of the company halls were rescued. Holbein's great portrait group of Henry VIII and the Barber-Surgeons was carried to safety, although the scorch marks are visible on it to this day. Some companies were less fortunate. The Watermen lost everything, the Merchant Taylors their plate. More serious was the destruction of Dean Colet's school, including his library of printed books and manuscripts – a crucial collection of material for the study of the early Renaissance in England. Most of the contents of the Royal College of Physicians went too. Although the portraits of Dr Harvey and Dr Fox were cut from their frames and about 140 books rescued, Harvey's library and museum were consumed in the flames.

A German print showing the fire engulfing the City of London from the Tower of London, right, to Barnard's Castle, left. The fire effectively wiped out the London of Chaucer and Shakespeare. John Evelyn, the diarist, summed up its impact: 'God grant mine eyes may never behold the like, who now saw above ten thousand houses all in one flame.'

132

Two buildings, however, represent outstanding losses: the old Royal Exchange and Old St Paul's. The Royal Exchange, the symbol of London's commercial prosperity and the financial independence of the nation, was a place where merchants could meet in convenient surroundings to transact business. It was built between 1566 and 1569 after the site between Cornhill and Threadneedle Street was acquired by the City Corporation and 'given to Sir Thomas Gresham, agent to the queen's highness, thereupon to build a burse … at his owne proper charges'. Its architect was a Fleming, Henri van Paesschen, and the plan of the building closely followed that of the Exchange at Antwerp, only with Gresham's emblem of the grasshopper at its corners. Two handsome engravings record its Netherlandish mannerist appearance shortly after it was completed. One is a view of the exterior from the south and the other shows the inner courtyard

An etching by Wenceslas Hollar of the Royal Exchange, erected between 1566 and 1569 on a site between Cornhill and Threadneedle Street. It was designed by a Flemish architect, Henri van Paesschen, who based his design on the famous Antwerp Exchange, and was a symbol of England's growing strength in foreign trade. The interior courtyard was adorned with statues of the kings of England. With the destruction of the Exchange in the fire, the City lost one of its finest public buildings.

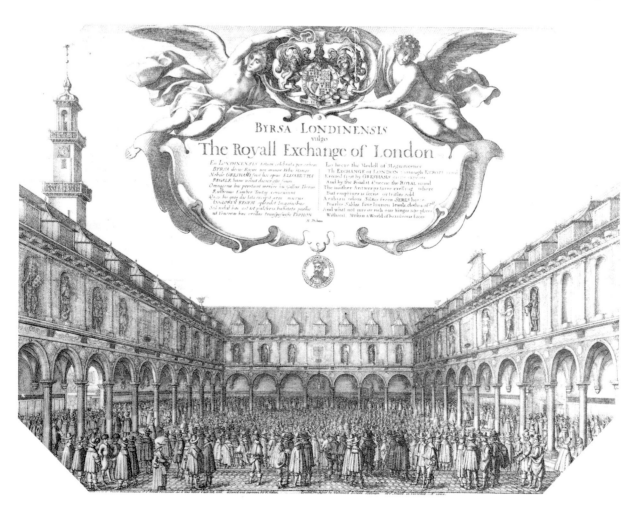

with its statues of the kings of England running all the way around it at the upper level. Even more evocative is Wenceslas Hollar's engraving of 1644 of the courtyard thronged with traders.

Surprisingly, Old St Paul's was less important for its medieval architecture than for its more recent additions. Fortunately we know a great deal about the appearance of the cathedral both within and without, because it was the subject of a major publication by the antiquary Sir William Dugdale eight years before the fire. The story of Old St Paul's in the aftermath of the dissolution is a sorry one. A fire in 1561 destroyed its steeple, thus lessening its impact as the focal point of the London skyline, while the Puritan city fathers and populace had little time for the edifice and its fabric continued to decay throughout the reign of Elizabeth. In July 1608 James I asked the Lord Mayor and the Bishop of London to survey the cathedral and build a new spire. Nothing, however, came of it. Another commission followed in 1620, again with no action being taken, although for the second time Inigo Jones made sketch proposals. It was not until William Laud became Bishop of London in 1628 that a scheme was actually implemented. In 1631 another commission was appointed and Jones was ordered to encase the Romanesque nave and transepts in classical guise. In addition, the west front was to be entirely rebuilt, including a new great portico, the gift of Charles I, the foundation stone of which was laid in July 1635.

We owe to the architectural historian Sir John Summerson the recognition that Jones's work, above all the West Portico, created one of the greatest of all English Renaissance buildings. Sir Christopher Wren was aware of this when he rebuilt the cathedral and it was only with extreme reluctance that he demolished the portico, which became a source of inspiration for his own designs.

Old St Paul's was perhaps the supreme expression of Jones's belief in the value of superimposing classical order on to the architecture of the heroic British past. For Jones, classical architecture was a reassertion of ancient British architecture, just as for Anglican divines the Church of England was the revived and reformed descendant of the ancient British Church, Christianity having been brought hither from the Holy Land by St Joseph of Arimathea. Jones was able to give perfect architectural expression

St Paul's Cathedral began life as a Saxon church. This was burnt down in 1087, and succeeded by a vast Norman church which took a century to build. In the second half of the thirteenth century the choir was extended, making the church almost 600 feet long. After the Reformation it fell into decay until William Laud became Bishop of London. Laud employed Inigo Jones to undertake a huge programme of restoration, which began in 1631 and transformed the cathedral into one of the most remarkable manifestations of Renaissance architectural ideals north of the Alps. We owe our knowledge of it in the main to Wenceslas Hollar's engravings in Sir William Dugdale's The History of St. Paul's Cathedral *(1658).*

Opposite, above: Inigo Jones's West Portico was the gift of the king and the largest in northern Europe. Work began on it in 1635 and it was virtually complete when the Civil War broke out in 1642. It was eventually demolished by Wren in 1687.

Opposite, below: A sketch of one of the ruined transepts after the fire.

to these Caroline Anglican ideals in his 'deliberate quest for the primitive', his choice of a bold, innovative, classical repertory with which to encase the external walls of the Norman nave.

To be suitably regal, the grand West Portico was built in the Corinthian order. It would have stood out more dramatically in the London of Charles II than any tall building does in that of Elizabeth II. It was simply huge, the largest classical portico north of the Alps, some 56 feet in height, as high as the present classical portico and colonnade of the British Museum, but built in the midst of a city of timber-framed houses and narrow streets. The columns which formed the portico were spaced with infinite sensitivity; behind them were three great marble doorways and the ceiling above was coffered, carved and gilded. Adorning the balustrading on the top was a series of over life-size statues of the kings of England, including one of the donor. John Webb, who was the architect's pupil and assistant, records that Inigo Jones 'contracted the envy of all *Christendom* upon our Nation, for a

This engraving shows the Chapter House in the middle of the cloister and Jones's classical re-casing above the arcading. The cloister was built in 1332 in the only available space, a small garden, which accounts for the position of the Chapter House and the use of two storeys. It was one of the earliest instances of Perpendicular architecture.

Piece of Architecture, not to be paralell'd in these last Ages of the World'. Even when it was being built this masterpiece epitomized everything that the Puritan populace of London most abhorred: the beauty of holiness promoted by the Caroline High Church divines. As soon as Civil War broke out, work ceased and the Puritans treated the cathedral shamefully. The statues were toppled and smashed and the great portico was infilled with shops and ramshackle buildings running to several storeys, whose joists were embedded in the stone. In 1660 there was a chance that the great portico and the church itself would be restored to its pre-Civil-War splendour. The fire rendered that hope futile. As a result, we have lost one of our greatest and least-remembered monuments to the English Renaissance.

CHAPTER TEN

The Demolition of Nonsuch Palace

Of all the vanished Tudor royal palaces Nonsuch was undoubtedly the greatest. Hampton Court and Whitehall Palace, which preceded it, were adapted from houses begun by Cardinal Wolsey, whereas Nonsuch was conceived to celebrate Henry VIII at the apogee of his power. It was built during the last decade of the king's reign at enormous speed, and everyone who saw it over the next century and a half acknowledged it to be remarkable. So it was meant to be from its inception, as its name – presumably the king's own personal choice – indicates. There was literally to be 'none such' like it, nor was there; it must have been the most fantastic and magical of all the royal palaces and a supreme expression of the early Tudor renaissance in architecture. All architectural historians acknowledge the enormous influence of its galleries and exotic plaster decoration on the Elizabethan age.

The driving force behind Nonsuch, which was built as the monastic wealth poured into the exchequer, was a passionate desire to emulate the French king Francis I and above all his palace of Fontainebleau. The location chosen was Cuddington in Surrey, a village close to Cheam and Ewell, which was razed to the ground as an army of workmen descended on the site in April 1538. William Camden, the historian and herald, wrote an account of the palace in his *Britannia* (1586) which captures its magnificence. He writes that it was:

Opposite: *A detail of a picture painted about 1620 looking from the north-west across the bowling green towards the main gateway to the Outer Court of Nonsuch Palace. Beyond we can see the second gate surmounted by a clock tower, which led to the celebrated Inner Court, and, on the far right, one of the two fantastic octagonal turrets at the corners of the south front.*

built with so great sumpteousnesse and rare workmanship, that it aspireth to the very top of ostentation for show; so as a man may thinke, that all the skill of Architecture is in this peece of worke bestowed, and heaped up together. So many statues and lively images there are in euery place, so many wonders of absolute workmanship, and workes seeming to contend with Romane antiquities, that most worthily it may have, and maintaine still this name that it hath of Nonsuch.

Loseley House, close to the site of Nonsuch, houses a series of painted arabesque panels that may have come from the palace. They include the devices of Henry VIII and his last queen, Catharine Parr: a maiden's head rising from a Tudor rose. Attributed to an Italian artist working in the king's service, Toto del Nunziata, they represent the earliest response in England to the revival of antique grotesque decoration.

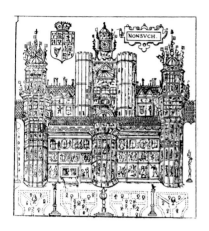

Above: *Speed's* Atlas *of 1610 gives us an aerial view of the south front and of part of the famous gardens created by John, Lord Lumley, who owned Nonsuch during the 1580s. The Privy Garden, looked down upon from the state apartments, consisted of a symmetrical arrangement of knots interspersed with garden ornaments commemorating Lumley and Elizabeth I. Away from the palace there was a wilderness with a grotto – probably the first constructed in England. Speed's engraving also gives some indication of the astonishing plaster relief wall panels.*

By 1586 the palace had passed to John, Lord Lumley, collector and antiquarian, who assembled in it the greatest collection of pictures in the Elizabethan period. Lumley had inherited Nonsuch from his father-in-law, the last Earl of Arundel, but in 1592 the palace was purchased back by the Crown and entered its regal heyday during the last decade of Elizabeth's reign.

The earliest picture we have of the palace, a drawing by Joris Hoefnagel dated 1568, captures the fantasy of the two amazing octagonal towers at each corner of the south-facing façade. They are quite unprecedented structures topped by a forest of pinnacles and onion-shaped domes reminiscent of Eastern Europe. Unlike any other surviving Tudor building, every wall surface that we can see was encrusted with high relief decoration. When John Evelyn, the diarist, visited the palace in 1666, he thought so highly of it that he felt that the panels ought to be removed from the walls and placed in some specially constructed gallery.

Our fullest account of this lost palace comes from the pen of Anthony Watson, a cleric writing in the 1580s. With him as our guide we are able to stroll through the courtyards and re-live some of its splendours. The approach to Nonsuch was from the north to the great gateways which led to the Outer Court. This was reached by a tree-lined road and across a bowling green laid out directly before the gate.

Right: *In 1590 Lord Lumley had an illustrated inventory compiled. These three examples of his garden ornaments are identifiable in the Speed engraving: the obelisk to the left, one of two marble columns bearing the Lumley cognizance of the popinjay, which stood on either side of the fountain of Diana, a tribute to the Virgin Queen, who was often celebrated as the moon goddess.*

This gatehouse ... is adorned with the double support of a stone window, bearing the insignia of the king and kingdom with exquisite art ... On entering the house itself, one sees long paths of smooth stone, and everywhere else is paved with rougher stones. Notice the size of the rooms, the splendid windows, the manifestly royal style of the building, the high pinnacles, which at the bottom are held up by small animals and at the top have dogs, griffins and lions resting on decorated shields.

The fountain in the Inner Court consisted of two circular basins from which masks and griffins spouted water into a square basin below. This drawing is from the illustrated inventory of 1590.

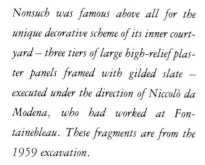

Nonsuch was famous above all for the unique decorative scheme of its inner courtyard – three tiers of large high-relief plaster panels framed with gilded slate – executed under the direction of Niccolò da Modena, who had worked at Fontainebleau. These fragments are from the 1959 excavation.

This first courtyard cannot have been so very different in feel from what we can still see at Hampton Court, a typical late Gothic building in red brick with stone finishings and with a roofline peppered with pinnacles bearing the royal beasts in polychrome. What set Nonsuch apart and made its loss such a major tragedy was the Inner Court. Watson continues:

An entrance leads, by the ascent of eight steps, to the royal court. In the middle gatehouse (which outdoes the first gatehouse by a tower, a clock, chimes and six golden horoscopes), the projecting windows might be thought to have been hewn from the heart of the rock ... The quadrangular spaces ... [have] nowhere anything that displeases; its fountain gives much delight and is the very perfection of art ... everywhere there are kings, caesars, sciences, gods. Since the whole edifice is royal, it is divided into a king's side and a queen's side, on either wise of the square. The king's wing is guarded night and day by Scipio, clothed in bronze garments, and the queen's by warlike Penthesilia.

This astonishing tableau is no late Gothic sunset but a Renaissance sunrise. We have no detailed picture of the inside of this courtyard (except for the fountain), but we get a glimpse in the bird's-eye-view from the south in John Speed's map of 1610. It gives an indication of the huge decorated surfaces with large figures, which, according to both Speed and Hoefnagel, adorned the external walls of the Inner Court, although the inner ones were undoubtedly considered the more remarkable. No other English sixteenth-century building has a similar form of decoration, but perhaps the frieze in the High Great Chamber at Hardwick is a distant echo of the exterior of Nonsuch.

The Inner Court was built of timber and plasterwork, and it was the areas between the timber framing that supported these alto-relievo plaster sculptures. They were arranged in three tiers, the lowest depicting the arts and the virtues, and one of the upper tiers on the king's side portrayed the Labours of Hercules (presumably identified with Henry) and gods and goddesses intermingled with floral panels and royal insignia. At the top, running all round the courtyard, were about thirty three-quarter life-size sculptures of Roman Emperors, probably busts. The panels were painted white and framed in slate carved with birds, fruit, scrolls and a guilloche pattern with gilded highlights. The focal point was a statue of Henry VIII with his son, Edward, below or near a balcony opposite the central gateway in the south wall. As John Dent has written, the 'Nonsuch stuccoes were unique and priceless treasures, as a colossal three-tiered decorative scheme covering at least 900 ft. of wall'.

Again, the driving force behind this spectacular sculptural ensemble was the wish to emulate Francis I. The man who designed, supervised and executed at least part of it was an Italian, Niccolò da Modena, who had worked on the *Grande Galerie* at Fontainebleau. The plasterwork there still survives, a major monument to French Renaissance culture. The originality of using these decorative panels on the outside of a building, as at Nonsuch, was never repeated. With their bold relief, their new-fangled classical form and glistening highlights, they must have looked sensational.

Watson sums up the whole schema when he writes:

Can harm befall the body politic when its most sagacious king, wielding the sceptre, is protected, on the right, by the arts and virtues and avenging goddesses, on the left by the feats of Hercules and the tender care of the gods; that he may act always in affairs without danger, in leisure with dignity.

We know very little about the palace interior but there is a drawing, almost certainly by Modena himself, for one half of an

Catharine Parr's device appears in this design, attributed to Niccolò da Modena, for the left-hand wall of a gallery, the right-hand section of which would have been a mirror image. Possibly intended for Nonsuch, it hints at the quality of design of the relief panels in the Inner Court.

interior wall with wainscotting below, bearing the badges of Henry's last queen, Catharine Parr, which dates it to 1543–7. Whether it is an unexecuted design or, indeed, intended for another palace, which is unlikely, its upper section evokes exactly those Inner Court alto-relievo sculptures. In addition we have a series of interior decorative panels at nearby Loseley House, which are said to have come from Nonsuch. These again include Catharine Parr's badge. In delicate pastel colours on a white ground, they are the earliest example in England of grotesque decoration, only a few years after Raphael's use of it in the Vatican *loggie*.

During the 1580s John, Lord Lumley, made Nonsuch remarkable for something else: the earliest Italianate garden in sixteenth-century England. Lumley had visited Italy in the 1560s and seen the revolutionary new architectural garden style, which

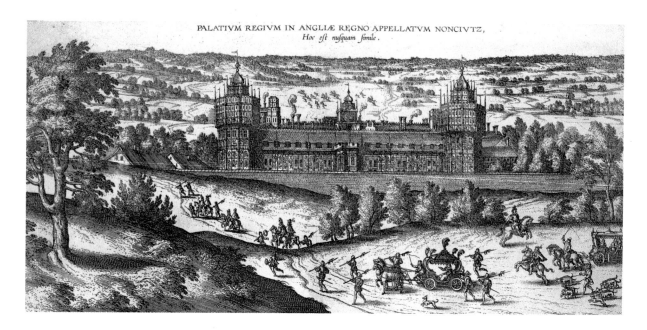

PALATIVM REGIVM IN ANGLIÆ REGNO APPELLATVM NONCIVTZ,
Hoc est nusquam simile.

united villa and garden by ordering the surrounding space through the imposition of geometry and sculpting the terrain into levels. The use of perspective, built features, sculpture, topiary and water contributed to an integrated new art form. Under Lumley's aegis some of those elements were brought to Elizabethan England. The Privy Garden, part of which is shown in a Jacobean engraving, was arranged around symmetrically placed heraldic sculpture. Even more Italianate was the creation of a *bosco* nearby: paths ending in built features and meeting points were cut through the woods, which also boasted a pyramid, a banqueting house, an archway and the earliest recorded English grotto, in which Diana, the chaste goddess of the hunt – a homage to the Virgin Queen – confronted Actaeon.

The garden is described by a whole series of visitors in the late Elizabethan period, and the ornaments were depicted in an inventory ordered by Lord Lumley in 1590. This includes pictures of the various fountains (including the one in the Inner Court) and obelisks in the Privy Garden but not the grotto. The garden survived until the outbreak of Civil War in 1642.

After Elizabeth's death in 1603 Nonsuch was never to enjoy royal favour again. It was assigned by Charles I to his queen, who seems rarely, if ever, to have gone there. After the king's execution in 1649 it was sold by order of Parliament to one of Cromwell's generals, Major General John Lambert, after its contents

Joris Hoefnagel's drawing of 1568 of the south front differs markedly from that in Speed's Atlas *some forty years later. The artist probably worked up this view, which captures the fantasy of the palace, on his return to the Continent, from material collected during his visit to England.*

had been sold off and most of its trees felled for shipbuilding. In 1660 it returned to the Crown, which allowed it to continue to decay until, in 1670, Charles II gave it to one of his most extravagant and unprincipled mistresses, Lady Castlemaine, later Duchess of Cleveland. She never lived there and, being short of cash, must have viewed it as an unnecessary drain on her resources. She disliked the keeper of the palace, George, Lord Berkeley, but in 1682 they reached an agreement whereby he would demolish it for building materials in return for the sum of £1,800. The execution of this barbarous decision must have taken some time, as a drawing dated 1702 shows at least one of its famous towers still standing.

There is a final twist to the story, for Berkeley used the materials from the Inner Court to build his own house. John Evelyn in his *An account of architects and architecture* (1697) states that his lordship had the famous stuccoes 'translated, and ornamently placed ... at his delicious villa, Durdans'. Tragically, that house too was demolished, but an early eighteenth-century picture of it shows an unmistakable row of Tudor heraldic royal beasts from Nonsuch across the front.

CHAPTER ELEVEN

The Burning of Whitehall Palace

On the afternoon of 4 January 1698 a Dutch maidservant lit a charcoal fire in a gentleman's lodging in the vicinity of Whitehall Palace in order to facilitate the drying of laundry. Within a few hours 'merciless and devouring flames' swept through one of the most famous of all the Tudor and Stuart royal palaces. From 1533 until this disastrous fire, Whitehall had been the official London residence of the king and court. The fire raged throughout the night, unabated by the work of fire engines or the blowing up of some twenty houses in the hope of blocking its path. When it was finally extinguished at eight o'clock the following morning, the whole palace between King Street and the Thames had vanished save the Banqueting House, which still stood, blackened and begrimed. 'To conclude', a contemporary wrote, 'it is a dismal sight to behold such a glorious, famous, and much renowned palace reduced to a heap of rubbish and ashes, which the day before might justly contend with any palace in the world for riches, nobility, honour and grandeur'.

With the destruction of Whitehall England lost its equivalent of the Louvre in Paris. It was not, however, its equivalent in the quality of its architecture, for the palace had always presented a rambling, haphazard aspect to its many visitors. In 1664 one visitor described it as 'nothing more than an assemblage of several

---

Opposite: The ceiling panel in Charles II's Bedchamber was the work of Michael Wright. It was salvaged from the fire and was later recorded at Windsor Castle and Somerset House, after which it disappeared from the Royal Collection. The subject is an allegory of the Restoration of Charles II, in which the Golden Age, personified by Astraea or the Maiden Justice, enthroned above, returns to earth again. Below the flying figure bearing the legend Terras Astraea revisit *floats the Boscobel oak, which had hidden the king during his flight after the Battle of Worcester in 1651.*

houses, badly built at different times', reserving praise only for Inigo Jones's Banqueting House. That reflects the taste of the time, but today what would we not give to have this ramshackle accumulation of some 2,000 rooms, the setting in which some of Shakespeare's greatest plays were performed?

Whitehall began its life as the London residence of the arch-bishops of York and from 1514 Cardinal Wolsey began to rebuild and remodel the medieval residence on a grand and palatial scale until it was appropriated by Henry VIII in 1529. Under Wolsey the great hall and the chapel were built, which must have resembled the rooms which still survive at Hampton Court. The king decided to expand it into a major palace, which was built with great speed in order to receive Anne Boleyn as queen there in 1533. Large tracts of land were purchased to the west and old buildings demolished, but Henry was never able to suppress the public right of way from Charing Cross to Westminster. This became King Street and was straddled by two of the palace's most famous showpieces, its gateways, which were to survive the fire. Wolsey's nucleus was greatly extended by the creation of suites of rooms for the king and the queen. The king's suite included his Privy Chamber, which in 1537 was adorned by Hans Holbein with his famous wall-painting celebrating the Tudor dynasty. Whitehall was also famous for its galleries: the Privy Gallery was a re-erection of Cardinal Wolsey's gallery at Esher, the demolition of which 'byfore my lordes face', his servant Cavendish wrote, 'was to hyme a corrysife'. The richness of the interior decoration struck every visitor, 'the ceiling being marvellously wrought in stone with gold, and the wainscot of carved wood representing a thousand beautiful figures'. One feature of the outside was so extraordinary that it was still remarked upon in 1658: 'As for *Grotesco* or (as we say) *Antique-worke*, it takes my fancy, though in forms of different Natures, or *Sexes, Sirenes, Centaures*, and such like, as the outward walls of *White-Hall* . . .' On the other side of King Street lay a unique leisure complex including a tennis court, cockpit and tiltyard.

The old Tudor palace survived virtually unchanged into the seventeenth century – the only significant addition made by the Stuarts was the Banqueting House with its ceiling by Rubens – which was probably due more to the Stuarts' lack of money than to any respect for the building, for there were numerous schemes

The so-called 'Agas' map of London shows Whitehall Palace between 1561 and 1570. The view is looking north up King Street towards Charing Cross. To the left lie a jumble of buildings which included the Tennis Court, the Cockpit and the Tiltyard, while to the right stretches the Privy Garden, with a fountain in the middle, and a medley of buildings which made up the galleries, privy lodgings, chapel and hall of the main palace.

150

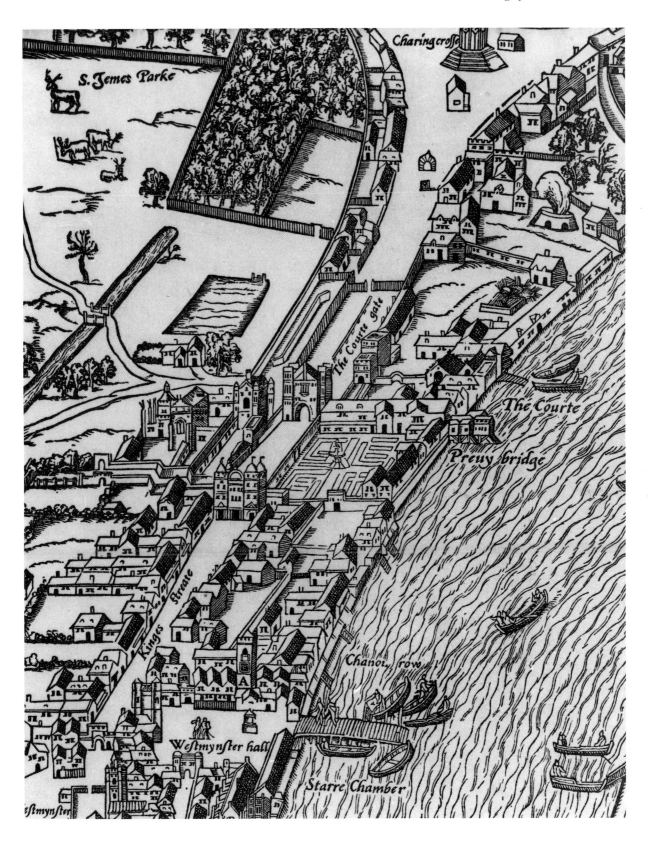

to demolish it and replace it with one in the symmetrical classical style. Only under James II was anything resembling a substantial remodelling initiated. James called upon Wren to modernize sections of the palace. These became known as the New Building, which, had it survived, we would recognize as being in the manner of Kensington Palace. It had one lavish addition, a Roman Catholic chapel with a huge altarpiece designed by Wren with sculptures by Grinling Gibbons and Arnold Quellinus. John Evelyn, the diarist, noted in 1686 that 'nothing can be finer than the magnificent marblework and architecture at the end, where are four statues, representing St John, St Peter, St Paul, and the Church, in white marble, the work of Mr Gibbons, with all the carving and pillars of exquisite art and cost'. He 'could not have believ'd I should ever seene such things in the King of England's Palace'. The chapel was consumed in the fire of 1698 but the altarpiece had already been dismantled by William III and put in store at Hampton Court. Queen Anne gave it to Westminster Abbey in 1708.

Like the Great Fire of London, the Whitehall fire was as remarkable for what was not destroyed as for what was. Thanks to

Opposite: Bernini's great bust of Charles I, executed in the summer of 1636, perished in the fire through negligence. This copy, attributed to Thomas Adye, is thought to have been made from a plaster cast in the possession of the sculptor Francis Bird.

Below: A view of Whitehall from St James's Park, looking towards Inigo Jones's Banqueting House on the left, the stairs leading to the old Tilt Gallery and thence over the 'Holbein Gate' to the Privy Gallery, and, to the right, the octagonal roof of the Cockpit, which Jones converted into a theatre in the reign of Charles I.

On his accession in 1685 James II commissioned Sir Christopher Wren to create a Roman Catholic chapel in Whitehall Palace. Although small in scale, the chapel was decorated in the full-blown baroque style, including allegorical paintings by Antonio Verrio and a huge altarpiece designed by Wren, with sculpted figures by Grinling Gibbons and these reliefs by Arnold Quellinus. During the Glorious Revolution of 1688 the altarpiece was dismantled and began a chequered history. Four statues in a weathered condition are now in the Canons' Garden at Westminster Abbey and four reliefs of cherubs can be seen in Burnham Church, Somerset.

the prompt action of the Deputy Chamberlain, Sir John Stanley, who was on the spot soon after the fire broke out, the rooms of the palace were cleared so well that there was 'not so much as a Curtain or stool missing'. Stanley blamed Sir Christopher Wren for the destruction of the greatest moveable work of art, Bernini's bust of Charles I. Stanley had gone to Wren at the outbreak of the fire and suggested that his workmen take care of its evacuation together with that of the other statuary. Wren had told Stanley, 'Take you care of what you are concerned in, and leave the rest to me.' It took five to six hours for the fire to reach the part of the palace which contained the bust – plenty of time in which to move it – but perish it did.

This was a major loss, for the bust was a portrait of the greatest connoisseur king ever to sit on the English throne by the greatest of all baroque sculptors. It was commissioned by the queen as a present to her husband and Pope Urban VIII had to give his permission to Bernini to execute it. On 13 June 1635 the Pope's special envoy wrote from England that 'the King is extremely satisfied about the papal permission given to Bernini to execute this bust'. Van Dyck painted his celebrated triple portrait of Charles I to enable the sculptor to proceed in the summer of 1636. By the April of the following year the bust was complete and on 17 July it was presented to the king and queen at Oatlands, where it was much admired 'nott only for the exquisitenesse of the worke but the likenesse and nere resemblaunce it had to the King['s] countenaunce'.

By 1698 the bust had already assumed a legendary status. John Evelyn in his *Numismata* (1697) records that when Bernini saw the Van Dyck portrait he commented upon 'something of the funest and unhappy, which the Countenance of that Excellent Prince foreboded'. This was embroidery after the event, for at the time no one read impending doom in the king's features, nor is there a trace of it in the bust as we know it – we have the copy probably made by one Thomas Adye in the mid-eighteenth century from a plaster cast of the original. On the contrary, one is struck by the monarch's bravura and assurance.

The other major loss was Holbein's monumental wall-painting of the Tudor dynasty in the Privy Chamber. So famous was it that after the fire ways were sought to move the wall on which it was painted, 'but all proved ineffectual' and it perished. The 160-

Overleaf: Leonard Knyff's panorama of Whitehall Palace and St James's Park was made shortly before the fire. It gives an idea of the rambling sprawl of the palace, even after considerable rebuilding by Wren in the classical style. From left to right we can see: the Privy Garden laid out in formal grass 'plats'; the rebuilt Privy Gallery and Council Chamber by Wren; his lodgings for Queen Mary, with her garden jutting out into the Thames; the palace entrance courtyard with its statue of James II by Grinling Gibbons silhouetted against Inigo Jones's Banqueting House. Beyond the Privy Garden runs the horizontal axis of King Street, bridged by the two Tudor gateways.

year-old painting had fared well. Evelyn, reporting on the state of the palace under the Commonwealth, 'was glad to find, they had not much defac'd that rare piece'. William Sanderson had commented on its remarkable state of preservation twenty years earlier. After lamenting the havoc wrought by damp, he tells us that it had been saved from decay because Holbein had painted it in oil, it had been indoors in the warm, and the wall had been 'prim'd with a very thick Compost of Playster, and some other mixture fixed, to preserve the work'. Evelyn, a connoisseur, had no doubts that it was a major masterpiece.

It is more difficult to imagine what was lost than in the case of the Holbein. We know that the wall-painting was executed in 1537 (it was dated) in the room that by 1600 had become the sovereign's Privy Chamber. Sited between the public presence chamber and the royal bedchamber it was close to the hall and chapel, in the area between the Thames and the entrance court to the palace. The Privy Chamber would have been on the first floor, but unfortunately we only have a plan of the ground floor in 1670, which affords few clues. At the close of Elizabeth's reign we have a description of someone being received by the queen here, coming along a 'passage somewhat dark' and into 'this chamber . . . which resembles somewhat a closet'. This confirms that the painting cannot have been large. Its dimensions were recorded as 12 feet wide by 9 feet high, but confusingly, a Frenchman in 1671 describes it as being painted 'on the gable of the window'. We can deduce from this that it would seem to have been painted above the wainscot in the usual early Tudor manner and possibly around an upper window.

We know what the composition looked like because Charles I commissioned a copy in 1667 from an artist called Remigius, or Remée, van Leemput. The copy shows us that what vanished was the English equivalent of Mantegna's celebrated *Camera degli Sposi* at Mantua, with its portraits of members of the Gonzaga family, although the informality of that group contrasts with the stateliness of Whitehall's homage to the Tudor family. Against a background of an ornate gilded room in the early Renaissance style stand Henry VII with Elizabeth of York, and Henry VIII with his third queen, Jane Seymour. They appear to float on a dais covered by a carpet and they flank a stone 'altar' bearing a Latin poem. The verses celebrate the achievements of both Henry

Grinling Gibbons' statue of James II, executed in 1686 for the courtyard of Whitehall Palace, today stands in front of the National Gallery in Trafalgar Square.

VII and Henry VIII, above all the latter for his 'unerring virtue', to which 'the presumption of popes has yielded': the painting was a commemoration of Henry VIII's historic defeat in 1537 of the one serious rebellion against his rule, the Pilgrimage of Grace. The poem was certainly part of the original composition, for a visitor transcribed it in 1600, but some scholars argue that it may have been elsewhere in the room and that the monolith was added by the copyist in the place of the window.

The outstanding quality of Holbein's masterpiece, a unique manifestation in England of Renaissance illusionistic wall painting, is captured by the surviving cartoon for the left-hand part,

In the Privy Chamber on the piano nobile *was one of Holbein's great masterpieces, his wall-painting celebrating the Tudor dynasty. The composition was 12 × 9 feet and was painted in oil on plaster; even after the fire its condition was such that it could have been moved had the technical knowledge been available.*

Left: *Charles II commissioned this copy of the wall-painting from Remigius van Leemput, which is a testament to its importance. Scholars now argue about how this copy should be interpreted – whether, for instance, it implies that the original ran from floor to ceiling or above a panelled wainscot, whether the 'altar' in the middle was part of the original composition or was introduced in the place of a royal chair or a window. Henry VII, the founder of the dynasty, and his wife, Elizabeth of York, stand behind Henry VIII and his third queen, Jane Seymour, who gave birth to Edward VI in 1537, the year that this was painted.*

Right: *The most precious testament to the supreme quality of the finished wall-painting is this cartoon composed of sheets of paper bearing the individual figures cut out and mounted on to a backing sheet. Thousands of pin-pricks follow each line of the drawing. Through these chalk was rubbed to transfer the design to the surface of the wall. Holbein made a significant alteration to the composition while he was executing it: in the cartoon the king looks to the right, whereas in the final version he looks directly at the spectator.*

now in the National Portrait Gallery. This cartoon also establishes that changes were made to the composition as it was being executed, notably the decision to turn the king's face towards the onlooker.

After Whitehall was ravaged by the fire of 1698, the remaining buildings included the so-called 'Holbein' and King Street gateways, as well as the old tennis court and cockpit. The King Street Gate, an extraordinary expression of the new classical ideals that had recently reached England, was built not long before Somerset House, probably around 1545. In terms of the history of art it was by far the most important of the two gates, with its classically inspired side entrances crowned with pediments, its Ionic pilasters above and its busts *à l'antique* used as decoration. Oddly enough, no one in the eighteenth century recognized its significance, and when there was a demand for improved means of communication with the Houses of Parliament in 1723, a royal warrant was issued for its demolition.

The 'Holbein' gateway at the north end of King Street was much more highly prized and therefore survived longer. It was not so very different in style to what we see at Hampton Court – a rectangular building with octagonal turrets of chequered stone and flint with mullioned windows and crenellation. Both faces of the gate were similar, each with four terracotta roundels of Roman emperors set into the walls. The gate was first threatened with destruction in 1719 but was saved by the architect Sir John Vanbrugh, who expressed surprise that people should consider demolishing 'one of the greatest curiositys there is in London' merely to facilitate traffic. In this way the gate gained a thirty-year reprieve, but in 1755 it was taken down. Its re-erection was planned but never happened, so the Duke of Cumberland petitioned for the materials with a view to transferring it to the end of the Long Walk in Windsor Great Park. That plan also proved to be abortive, and we are told that the materials were used up in various buildings around the park.

The remaining buildings to the west vanished piecemeal during the next century as the government offices we know today gradually arose. The odd Tudor window is still visible in the Treasury and the tennis court did not disappear until 1809. Today the Banqueting House stands alone along Whitehall, a fragment, albeit a magnificent one, to remind us of the acres which have gone. Without its context and re-cased by Sir John Soane in 1829–37, it can easily be passed by as just another neo-classical government office rather than the solitary survivor of 'glorious Whitehall'.

Anna Crisacria Foannes
Mori Sponsa anno · 15.

Thomas Morus an=
no · 50

Foannes Morus pater
anno · 76.

CHAPTER TWELVE

Three Famous Holbeins Lost

No other painter has suffered such important losses as Hans Holbein the Younger. The destruction in 1698 of his great wall-painting in the palace of Whitehall was followed half a century later by the loss, again by fire, of three other monumental works which he executed during his two periods in England. In 1752 at Kremsier in what is now Czechoslovakia there vanished *The Family of Sir Thomas More*, together with two huge decorative paintings, *The Triumph of Riches* and *The Triumph of Poverty*.

The first of these, arguably the greatest and most innovative work of his English period, had of course been commissioned by More himself, soon after the artist arrived in England in 1527 with a letter of introduction from Erasmus. The life-scale family group was executed in the fragile medium of distemper during the second half of that year. Something of its supreme quality is evoked by Holbein's sketch, made while he was still working on the painting, although it differs from the final composition. This we know because Sir Thomas More's grandson, Thomas More II, commissioned three copies from a minor Elizabethan artist, Rowland Lockey, in 1590. One is likely to be an exact copy and is now at Nostell Priory. The second copy omitted certain figures and inserted More II's own generation. This is now in the National Portrait Gallery. The third was a miniature, now in the Victoria and Albert Museum, which is close to the second but includes a view of More's Chelsea garden.

How the original ended up in eighteenth-century Bohemia can

Opposite: *Detail from an exact copy by Rowland Lockey of Hans Holbein's lost group* The Family of Sir Thomas More. *Shown here are, left to right: More's father, Sir John, and Sir Thomas himself with his daughter-in-law, Anne Cresacre, standing behind.*

only be conjectured, but the picture's history appears to have been as follows. On More's execution in 1535 it should have been forfeit to the Crown but we know nothing certain about its whereabouts until the Elizabethan period when it was recorded as being in the collection in London of a Flemish merchant called Andreas de Loo. On his death in 1590 it was apparently purchased back by Thomas More II not because it was a great work of art but out of family piety (More II remained faithful to the Catholic faith). It next reappears in the possession of Thomas Howard, Earl of Arundel, who may have either inherited it or purchased it from the estate of his uncle, John, Lord Lumley. When Civil War came in 1642 Arundel sent most of his great collection abroad but on his death it was sold and dispersed. We next hear of the picture in the possession of two brothers who lived in Cologne. From them it passed to the Cardinal Bishop of Olmutz and Kremsier in 1670, in whose palace it was burnt.

Opposite, below: *Lockey's copy of* The Family of Sir Thomas More. *Here we can see a section of a room in Sir Thomas's Chelsea house with a still life of flowers and musical instruments in the background.*

Right: *A sketch made by Holbein during his painting of the More family. He was to make several changes to the composition, some of which are indicated in the notes on the sketch. Holbein took this drawing to Erasmus, Sir Thomas More's friend, who wrote to him: 'I cannot put into words the deep pleasure I felt when the painter Holbein gave me the picture of your whole family which is so completely successful that I should scarcely be able to see you better if I were with you.'*

The Family of Sir Thomas More was the earliest portrait conversation piece in English painting, at least a century ahead of its time; besides being a unique evocation of a great humanist, man of affairs and ultimately saint. His household is portrayed as a small academy of letters, in which the women took an equal part. We see Sir Thomas seated alongside his father, Sir John, on a bench in a room of his house in Chelsea. Behind the two seated figures is More's daughter-in-law, Anne Cresacre, while to Sir John's right stand Margaret Giggs, More's adopted daughter and his daughter Elizabeth, wife of William Dauncey. To Sir Thomas's left is his son and heir, John, with Henry Patenson, More's fool, standing near the doorway. The three seated women are More's wife, Dame Alice, More's youngest daughter, Cecily Heron, and his daughter, Margaret Roper, with a book on her lap.

The informality of the picture, showing the sitters in their own home, was so innovative that such treatment had to await the eighteenth century to become a genre, as in the work of Hogarth, Devis and Zoffany. The originality of its composition also made it a masterpiece: Holbein was drawing upon the tradition of the 'disputa', in which scholars were shown debating and affirming the truths of the Faith; on memories of Andrea Mantegna's informal portrayal of the Gonzaga family in the *Camera degli Sposi* at Mantua; and on traditions of depicting the

Holy Family. Although we know that the painting had suffered some damage by the Elizabethan period, its destruction means we lost the greatest single visual artefact to epitomize the aims and ideals of the early Renaissance in England.

The same importance cannot be attached to the two other works which also perished in the 1752 fire. The *Triumph*s were painted in 1532–3, early in Holbein's second English period, for the Great Hall of the merchants of the German Steelyard in Blackfriars. There these two large canvases remained until the reign of James I, when they appear to have been presented to his eldest son, Prince Henry, on whose early death in 1612 they

The Triumph of Riches *and* The Triumph of Poverty, *in tempera and watercolour on canvas, were commissioned by the merchants of the German Steelyard in London on Holbein's return to England in 1532. Although a number of copies were made of the pictures, the two attributed to Lucas Vorsterman the Elder (early seventeenth century) probably best catch the spirit and colour tonality of the originals.*

Opposite, above: *In* The Triumph of Riches *twenty-two named allegorical personages attend Plutus, God of Riches, whose graceful chariot is drawn by elegant horses; his escort includes the famous rich of classical antiquity. The size of the original was 20'3" × 8'.*

Opposite, below: The Triumph of Poverty *contains nineteen figures in all. Poverty is a hag in rags and her chariot a cart drawn by mules, with a canopy of straw. The size of the original was 9'10½" × 7'3½".*

passed to the future Charles I. He then exchanged them for other pictures in the Earl of Arundel's collection and they arrived in the bishop's palace at Kremsier by the same route as the More group.

As in the case of the family portrait we only know these paintings through one preparatory sketch by Holbein and later copies – drawings with wash and body colour attributed to Lucas Vorsterman the Elder. Both pictures were carried out in another fragile medium, tempera and watercolour, with the figures in grisaille, the flesh tones tinted, the foliage rendered green, the background azure and with inscriptions in gold lettering. Nothing like them had been seen in England nor, indeed, was to be seen until well into the next century. Once again there are debts to Mantegna, for these triumphs belong not to the fading world of the late Gothic but to northern Renaissance art as it responded to his *Triumph of Caesar*. Both are allegorical compositions considered suitable for these sixteenth-century 'tycoons', and their source was the classical texts of Aristophanes and Lucian. In *The Triumph of Riches* Plutus, the aged god of wealth, rides on a chariot escorted by the rich of antiquity. Virtues bridle the horses, which symbolize various vices, such as avarice, consequent upon wealth unless it is tempered by moderation. *The Triumph of Poverty*, represented by ill-clad women, has indigent craftsmen being handed the tools whereby, through their industry, they may engender wealth, but they, too, are warned of the vices which will beset their path and the virtues which they should cultivate.

The fact that these three huge compositions have failed to survive has radically affected our perception of Holbein. They also highlight the massive dispersal of works of art throughout Europe as a result of the break-up of both the royal and the Arundel collections. Today there is hardly a great gallery on the Continent that does not count amongst its greatest treasures items which were once, for a time at least, in pre-Civil War England.

169

CHAPTER THIRTEEN

The End of Wilton's Garden

Of all the ephemeral forms of the visual arts, gardening must surely rank among the highest. It is not only inherently dependent on the whims of fashion but on a far more elementary foe, nature itself, for plants are forever growing and dying and, therefore, changing the original composition. In the relentless march of stylistic change gardens are infinitely more vulnerable than buildings – they are easier and cheaper to demolish and remodel than a house. Time and again in the history of our royal palaces and great country houses it was the garden which was changed first to follow the latest mode. And never was this more true than during the greatest garden revolution, the landscape movement of William Kent, 'Capability' Brown and Humphrey Repton. *Le jardin anglais* swept away two centuries of garden heritage, the masterpieces of the Renaissance and baroque ages, which included a garden that was famous throughout Europe: the garden of Wilton House, Wiltshire, created by the Huguenot architect, garden designer and hydraulic engineer Isaac de Caus during the halcyon days of the personal rule of Charles I, before the outbreak of Civil War in 1642.

We can stand today by the great south façade of the house, a monument to Renaissance ideals in classical architecture, and re-create in our mind's eye what was designed as its perfect horticultural complement. We are able to do so thanks to a series of engravings entitled *Le Jardin de Wilton*, issued about 1645, which record in remarkable detail every aspect of the garden,

Opposite: Wilton's celebrated grotto was the most elaborate ever constructed in pre-Civil-War England. The four bas-reliefs on the walls of the main grotto are now incorporated into a summer house in the Italian garden. Shown here are: a triton blowing a conch shell and nereid; and Venus on a scallop shell attended by Cupid.

from its groundplan to the interior rooms of its famous grotto. Such engravings were exceptionally rare at that period and indicate the importance attached to the garden. John Aubrey, the antiquary, records that 'King Charles the first did love Wilton above all places and came thither every summer. It was he that did put Philip first Earle of Pembroke upon making this magnificent garden and grotto.' Aubrey is a little muddled in his enthusiasm and the earl in question was not the first but the fourth, one of the two brothers to whom Shakespeare's *First Folio* was dedicated. Wilton had been a cradle of English Renaissance civilization since its creation but above all during the life of the earl's mother, Mary, Countess of Pembroke, sister of Sir Philip Sidney. That tradition was sustained by the fourth earl, who made the house and gardens the supreme expression of the ideals of the court of Charles I and its great architect, Inigo Jones.

Philip inherited the property in 1630 and, although wealthy, became even wealthier by marrying in the same year a great heiress and a formidable woman in her own right, the Lady Anne Clifford, only daughter of George, Third Earl of Cumberland, widow of the Earl of Dorset. Shortly after the marriage, with their combined resources they set about remodelling the house and garden on a stupendous scale – if the whole plan had been carried out, Wilton would have been regal rather than aristocratic. In the event the grand scheme for the house was abandoned – the façade we see today is only half that intended – perhaps because of the break-up of the marriage in 1637. The plan for the garden, however, was carried out *in toto*.

The garden was to be the width of the façade of the state rooms, 400 feet, and 1,000 feet in length. This huge rectangle covering some nine and a half acres was enclosed by a wall and divided by a broad central path running down the whole length. The garden was a strictly symmetrical, formal design, but de Caus had one major problem, the fact that the River Nadder wended its way across the middle of it. Undeterred by this, he reversed the garden sequence typical of the period and sited what was known as the wilderness in the middle to conceal the river, building bridges across it where necessary. But the river provided him with an abundance of water for the spectacular hydraulic displays which were to be one of the garden's most distinguishing features.

Leonard Knyff's bird's-eye view of the house and garden with a double frieze of details below shows the state of the garden c.1700. Although alterations have been made, the enclosing walls, central axis and tripartite division of the space is still intact. The radiating allées on the hillside converged on a statue of Marcus Aurelius atop a wooden triumphal arch. The latter may have been part of the 1630s scheme and today the statue stands on the entrance arch to Wilton. In the top frieze of details we see, left to right: the truncated house as it was finally built, with the de Caus embroidered parterres replaced by grass 'plats' and a central fountain; the stables, which still exist today; the Banqueting House, which terminated the great central walk and also survives, re-erected on the bowling green to the east of the house. The bottom frieze shows: an unlocated feature, the earliest known cascade constructed in England, with the figure of Pegasus at the top of it; the main room of the grotto; and the grotto façade.

172

From the *piano nobile* of the house the state rooms looked down on four formal parterres with elaborate patterns of box and a fountain in the middle adorned with plants in containers. Here, too, was some of the earliest garden statuary carved in this country: four female figures famous in the annals of both love and chastity by Nicholas Stone, who was responsible, it seems, for the whole sculptural content, for which he was 'well paide'. The *parterres de broderie* were also a novelty in England, following a format evolved in France in the late-sixteenth century. Pembroke must have been inspired by the dramatic new example at the Luxembourg Palace on his visit to France in 1625 to escort the new queen, Henrietta Maria, back to England.

Beyond the parterres was the wilderness, which was very different from anything we would today categorize as a wild garden. It was a plantation of evergreens divided by geometric walks which converged on two statues, one of Flora and the other of

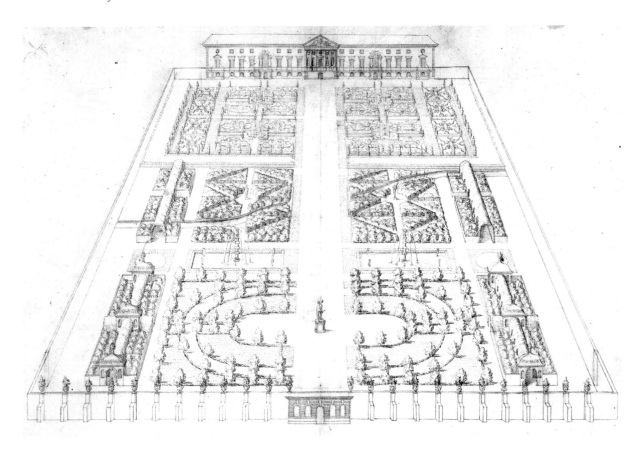

Above: *A drawing by Isaac de Caus of the garden from the hillside beyond, looking towards the house as it was initially conceived. In fact, only the right-hand half of the house was built. The design reveals Renaissance principles, applied on a large scale for the first time in England: the integrated relationship of house and garden, the harmonic orchestration of space, and the use of cross axes and vistas.*

Left: *Below the windows of the house stretched a series of box* parterres de broderie, *focusing on four fountains. This type of parterre had been developed in France by Claude Mollet, gardener to Henry IV, at the close of the sixteenth century, and these were the first designs ever published in England.*

The four main parterres contained fountains with statues of female figures, among them Cleopatra and Venus which still survives. The sculptor was Nicholas Stone, whose limitations are only too apparent in his response to this highly demanding commission. Venus is shown removing a thorn from her foot, the legendary source of the red rose, a white one being tinctured by her blood.

Bacchus. Emerging from this the visitor was confronted by two rectangular ponds, each with a column surmounted by a golden coronet in the middle. Beyond them lay a circus composed of oval walks prettily bordered by flowering cherry trees with, in the middle, a handsome cast in bronze of a famous antique statue, the Borghese Gladiator. This was by the French sculptor Hubert Le Sueur, who had been sent to Rome by Charles I to make such casts for the royal gardens.

The Wilton garden epitomized the new ideals of garden making and design as they had evolved in Renaissance Italy: the relationship of the house to the garden, the imposition of symmetry, the use of pattern, of sculpture in the antique manner, the deployment of water both static and moving, the application of a programme of symbolic meaning, all combined with an assault upon the senses of sight, smell and hearing. Had this survived, it would be England's equivalent of the Villa Lante at Bagnaia or of Hellbrunn outside Salzburg, supreme expressions of Renaissance man's subjection of the earth to the powers of art.

The garden had one feature which was admired above all the others, its grotto, 'the most famous in this kind this Kingdom affords'. At the end of the great walk there was a banqueting house in the new classical style, through which one walked to the grotto. Celia Fiennes, that indefatigable traveller, provides a wonderful description of it half a century on:

About 2 yards off the doore is severall pipes in a line that with a sluce spoutts water up to wett the Strangers; in the middle roome is a round table, a large pipe in the midst, on which they put a crown or a branch, and so it spouts the water through the carvings and poynts all round the roome at the Artists pleasure to wet the Company; there are figures at each corner of the roome that can weep water on the beholders, and by a straight pipe on the table they force up the water into the hollow carving of the rooff like a crown or coronet to appearance, but is hollow within to retaine the water forced into it in great quantetyes, that disperses in the hollow cavity over the roome and descends in a shower of raine about the roome; on each side is two little roomes which by the turning their wires the water runnes in the rockes you see and hear it, and also it is so contrived in one room that it makes the melody of Nightingerlls and all sorts of birds which engaged the curiousity of the Strangers to go in to see, but at the entrance off each room, is a line of pipes that appear not till by a sluce moved it washes the spectators, designed for diversion. The Grottoe is leaded on the top where are fish ponds, and just without the grottoe is a wooden bridge over the river, the barristers [i.e. balusters] are set out with Lyons set thick on either side with their mouths open and by a sluce spout out water each to other in a perfect arch the length of the bridge.

The engravings in *Le Jardin de Wilton* provide pictures of other features which we cannot site with certainty, such as the earliest water parterre ever constructed in this country, and a hillside sculpted like a Roman amphitheatre. A painting of about 1700 shows further features which were either part of the original scheme or added shortly after: a cascade with Pegasus, and a statue of the Emperor Marcus Aurelius, copied from that on the Campidoglio in Rome, atop a triumphal arch crowning the hill beyond the garden and linked to it by a great avenue of trees.

The destruction of this unique expression of Renaissance gardening ideals was piecemeal at first. By about 1700 the elaborate parterres had been banished in favour of a central fountain and grass *plats*, the Banqueting House had been re-erected as a pavilion for the bowling green to the east of the house, while the grotto turns up as a feature in a new garden to the west. By the 1720s Marcus Aurelius and the coronet columns were

Above: *A surviving statue, perhaps of Venus with a dolphin.*

Opposite, above: *Two sections of the garden were flanked by elaborate arbours, each 300-foot long; the arcades afforded shade in summer and some shelter in inclement weather. These were traditional features of Elizabethan gardens.*

Opposite, below: *We do not know the location of the Water Parterre, the first of its kind in England. It is likely to have been inspired by the French palace at St Germain-en-Laye or the Palatine garden in Heidelberg, although the most famous Renaissance exemplar was at the Villa Lante, Bagnaia, constructed in the 1560s.*

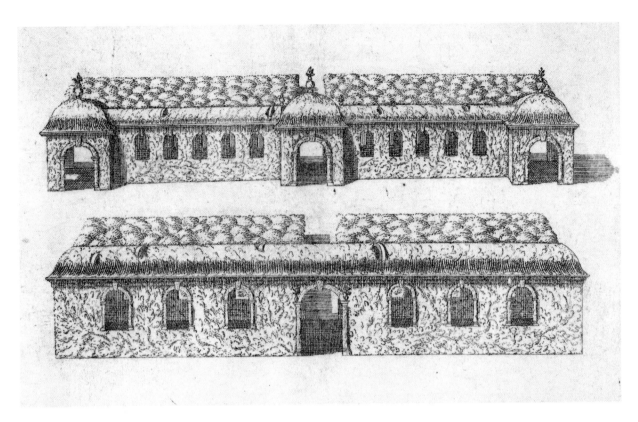

Opposite, above: *The location of the Amphitheatre is uncertain, but it was probably cut out of the hillside beyond the garden. Such architectural sculpturing of the terrain was Italianate in origin and the ascent is punctuated by a staircase found in Serlio's* Architettura (1544).

Opposite, below: *The de Caus garden which survived, although with alterations, into the early eighteenth century, was finally swept away by Henry, ninth Earl of Pembroke. As a friend of Lord Burlington, he responded to the new landscape style of William Kent, composing the scene we see today and designing and erecting in 1736–7, with the assistance of Roger Morris, the famous Palladian bridge.*

incorporated into a new grand entrance to the house. In spite of these depredations, the bones of the de Caus garden remained intact until the 1730s, when the ninth earl dammed the River Nadder and created the present lake. 'The present Earl of Pembroke,' it was recorded at the time, '... has made a further Improvement with regard to Prospect ... throwing down the Walls of the Garden, and making, instead of them Haw-haw Walls, which afford a boundless View all around the Country from every Quarter.' In 1736–7 the Earl, in conjunction with the architect Roger Morris, designed and built the celebrated Palladian bridge, thus creating one of the most glorious of all English country house landscape ensembles, so potent in its appeal that everyone has forgotten the importance of what preceded it.

It is an extraordinary fact that most of the garden sculpture still survives, nearly all of it re-sited somewhere in the grounds, the one missing piece being the Gladiator, a gift which stands at the bottom of the staircase at Houghton, Norfolk. Three of the statues for the parterres now stand in the forecourt in the new garden made in memory of the last earl. A fourth in the same location was once part of the water parterre. The rusticated columns from the coronet fountains are sited to the west of the house. Flora and Bacchus, once presiding over the Wilderness, were incorporated in 1826 into the bridge over the River Wylye. Four fine bas-reliefs from the grotto are inset into the loggia of the present Italian Garden and the grotto façade now forms that of the Park School House to the south-east.

Beneath the smooth verdant lawns of Wilton lies one of garden archaeology's most exciting sites, for it would be possible to restore the 1630s garden just as the Dutch have recreated the baroque glories of William III's Het Loo. Such a proposal, however, would involve 'desecrating' a now famous scene, for the eighteenth-century bridge and lake would have to be re-sited. Under the banner of restoration we accept that the rooms of a country house should be put back to the date of creation and all later accretions removed. In England no one has yet applied this to a garden, but the arguments in favour of doing so are potent, for Wilton's garden and house were conceived as a single artistic unity, and together epitomized the aesthetic aspirations of the court of Charles I.

CHAPTER FOURTEEN

Somerset House Destroyed

Somerset House today is such a splendid monument to the architectural genius of Sir William Chambers that it successfully masks the fact that it replaced the grandest of all Tudor aristocratic London houses. From its completion it passed to the Crown and for a century was the residence of three queens, Anne of Denmark, Henrietta Maria and Catherine of Braganza. Under their aegis it was transformed into a royal palace that was the height of luxury and sophistication. Sir John Summerson has described it as 'a treasury of English architectural genius over three centuries'.

Somerset House was built by Edward VI's Protector, Edward Seymour, Duke of Somerset, between 1547 and 1552, the year of his execution on Tower Hill. It was a typical product of confiscated monastic wealth and Somerset incurred odium by demolishing three episcopal residences and a church to create his site, which had a river frontage of 600 feet and a depth of 500 back to the Strand. Even worse, the materials for its construction were appropriated from forfeited ecclesiastical buildings in the City, thereby destroying one of the sights of medieval London, St Paul's cloister 'with the dance of Powles [the Dance of Death],

Opposite: *Detail of old Somerset House from the Thames from a picture by Canaletto, who painted several versions of this scene during his visits to England between 1746 and 1756. By then Somerset House was used as a residence for visiting foreign ambassadors, but for most of the seventeenth century it had been the London palace of the Stuart queens. The central block by John Webb was erected after the Restoration for Henrietta Maria, Queen Dowager. To the right there are the additions of Anne of Denmark, including the Cross Gallery leading to Inigo Jones's New Cabinet Room at the far end, perhaps his* chef d'oeuvre *of pre-Civil-War interior decoration.*

Charles I assigned Somerset House to Henrietta Maria in 1626 and Inigo Jones was called upon to carry out major alterations, including the addition of a Catholic chapel. When the queen returned after 1660 she employed Jones's pupil, John Webb, to design the new south front. Left: The Catholic chapel which Jones designed was built by 1635. Although it is inadequately documented, it is recognized as one of his most considered projects. This engraving of c.1731 by Isaac Ware is a precious record of a lost masterpiece. The blank space over the altar is where a Rubens canvas hung; it was flung into the Thames when the chapel was sacked in 1643.

Opposite: *Jones's interiors for Queen Henrietta Maria were of the utmost elegance and sophistication. This presentation drawing, which reflects the luxurious style of French interior decoration, was possibly intended for either the New Cabinet Room or the Queen's Bedchamber.*

about the same cloister, costly and cunningly wrought . . . ' Protestant Somerset would have seen this as simply another step in the elimination of popery.

In all the phases of its building Somerset House was architecturally distinguished and innovatory. It began as a typical early-sixteenth-century courtyard house but its most distinctive feature, which was to remain unaltered until its demolition, was its street façade. The great central entrance was designed like a classical triumphal arch with superimposed orders of columns and bays flanking the east and west ends with paired windows united by pillars and a pediment. This façade was the most emphatic statement yet made of the new Renaissance ideals filtering through to England and a startling contrast to Tudor London. Its construction was supervised by the Lord Protector's steward, John Thynne, whose great house at Longleat still stands as a fine example of how the vocabulary of the old Somerset House was developed. Another member of Somerset's household was William Cecil, later Lord Burghley, who also drew on his knowledge of the house when building Burghley House,

Cambridgeshire: in the inner courtyard, the entrance façade has a triumphal arch directly inspired by Somerset House.

On Somerset's attainder the newly finished house passed to the Crown, but it was not to enter another phase of development until early in the following century when James I assigned it to his queen, Anne of Denmark. Between 1609 and 1612 she spent no less than £34,500, excluding what she lavished on the interior decoration. On the river front to the east two sides of a three-sided courtyard were erected, incorporating galleries and a whole suite of rooms for the queen's use. These were in the lavish and ornate style of the Jacobean age, with strapwork ceilings adorned with pendants, knobs, roses and marigolds, magnificent wainscotting and huge, ornate marble fireplaces such as we can still see at Hatfield House, and everything elaborately painted and gilded. A remarkable garden, which included statuary, a fountain and a grotto, was also laid out.

Anne took up residence in 1617, re-naming the house Denmark House, but died two years later. In 1615 Inigo Jones had been appointed Surveyor of the King's Works and at the instigation of the new queen, Henrietta Maria, to whom Charles I assigned the house in 1626, Somerset House was to acquire some of Jones's greatest works. From 1627 to 1636 Jones was engaged in transforming the building to meet the ideals and standards of elegance and comfort associated with a Palladian villa along the Brenta.

His masterpiece of interior decoration was the queen's New Cabinet Room at the end of the Cross Gallery. Here he transformed an existing room into an interior of rare glamour and sophistication – the Cabinet Room at Ham House, which was painted by the same artist, may be a pale reflection of it. The room had a balcony overlooking the river and Jones designed a new ceiling, doorcase, architrave, frieze and pediment. The ceiling was 'a faire skie; among the cloudes are exprest in personages, in proper colours, Architecture, Painting, Musique and Poesie', while the walls had a frieze 'of Angells, Flowers, *Impresas*, *Grotesco*, and such like'. These were executed by Francis Cleyn, while Matthew Goodrich, who was later to work at Wilton, gilded the plaster foliage on the ceiling and painted, marbled and gilded the panelling and chimneypiece. Everything was white and gold with a few touches of blue. The painted decoration, of

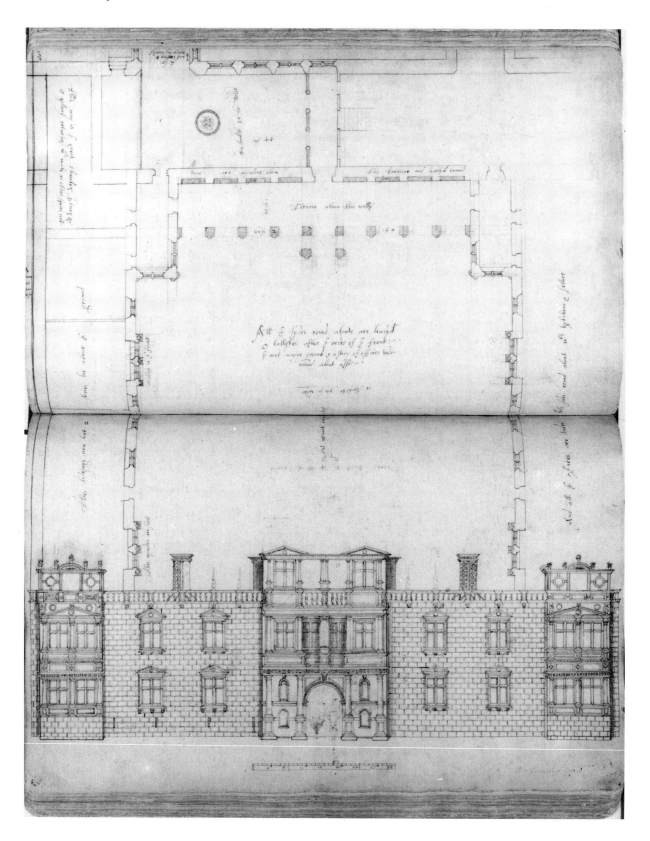

which no instance survives, made this room a supreme expression of Jones's court style, and must have had a seminal influence on country house interiors through the century.

Just as remarkable was the queen's new chapel, a double-cube 30 by 60 feet, built on the site of the old tennis court. It was constructed between 1630 and 1635 and the interior was also acknowledged to be one of Jones's finest works. We know what some of it looked like both from original designs and from engravings made at the beginning of the eighteenth century. One of its most spectacular features was the carved screen which supported the Queen's Closet, whose interior was sumptuously grained and gilded. The Puritans were to wreak their vengeance on the chapel in 1643.

Henrietta Maria returned to Somerset House at the Restoration and added an even more distinctive feature, designed by Jones's assistant John Webb, which was erected in 1661–2. This was the magnificent frontispiece facing the river, which was superimposed on the old Tudor façade. It had a rusticated arcade supporting a storey with five windows divided by pilasters. Sir William Chambers, who believed the frontispiece was by Jones,

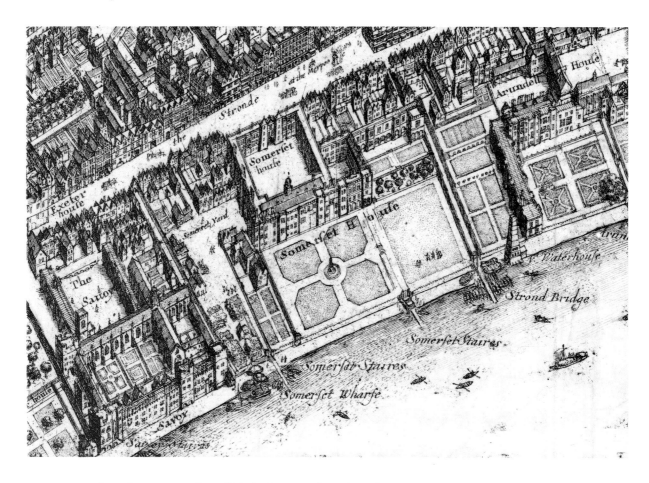

was extremely reluctant to demolish it; he was forced to do so, but he adapted its principles in his design for the huge building which replaced it.

With the demolition of Somerset House in 1776 the key document in the history of Tudor classicism vanished, along with two of Jones's finest achievements. What is so appalling is that both were recognized as such by the connoisseurs of the century which destroyed them. As the author of *A Critical View of Public Buildings* (1734) wrote,

I am extremely pleased with the front of the first court of Somerset House, next the Strand, as it affords us a view of the first dawning of taste in England, this being the only fabric that I know of which deviates from the Gothic and imitates the manner of the ancients.

Someone who accompanied Chambers in exploring the palace provides us with a wonderful word picture of its faded glories as

Hollar's bird's-eye view of Somerset House, c.1658, shows its position as one of the great palaces along the Thames, flanked by the Savoy and Arundel House. The major reconstruction undertaken for Anne of Denmark between 1609 and 1617 included the ranges to the east: the Privy Gallery, the Cross Gallery and the Privy Lodgings.

the party threw open long-sealed doors and wandered through its dusty rooms. He describes how at last they came to

a pair of doors near the eastern extremity, with difficulty opened, [which] gave access to an appartment ... which was unquestionably the work of Inigo Jones. This ... had more the appearance of a small temple than a room; it was of an octagonal form, and the ceiling rose in a dome from a beautiful cornice. There appeared such an elegant simplicity in the architecture, and such a truly Attic grace in the ornaments, that Sir William Chambers exceedingly regretted the necessity there was for its demolition. The figures painted upon the panels were in fresco; the ornaments under the subcase were, in their heights, touched with gold. The four articles of furniture that remained here were in the antique style ...

The age of preservation had yet to come; by the close of the next century such a room would have been dismantled and re-erected in the Victoria and Albert Museum.

FONTHILL ABBEY.

Plate 9

Drawn by C.F. Porden, Arch.   Engraved by John Cleghorn.

SECTION OF THE GRAND SALOON, VESTIBULES, NUNNERIES, &c.

Looking East.

CHAPTER FIFTEEN

The Fall of Fonthill

Fonthill Abbey represents perhaps the most fantastic episode in British architectural history. It arose brashly out of the Wiltshire landscape as a huge gesture of revenge against a society which had condemned its creator to social obloquy. The late eighteenth century was remarkably tolerant in terms of its sexual mores but nineteen-year-old William Beckford's passion for the sixteen-year-old William Courtney of Powderham Castle exceeded the boundaries of what was considered permissible even within the closed world of the established classes of Georgian England.

Beckford came from a background of entrenched privilege. The only child of a millionaire sugar-planter, he was extraordinarily rich and precociously gifted: he was taught music by Mozart and drawing and architecture by Sir William Chambers and Alexander Cozens. Talented, spoilt and self-willed, he was drawn instinctively to anything irregular, odd, exotic or fantastic. His passion for the Orient was expressed in *Vathek* (1787), his enduring literary monument. But he was also a brilliant linguist and became an obsessive collector, one of the greatest connoisseurs Britain has ever produced. Fonthill was to house the extraordinary collection of books, manuscripts, prints, pictures, furniture and other objects which he amassed during his years on the Continent. His response to art was charged with emotion, almost a kind of frenzy. In 1780 he wrote to Cozens from Florence:

Opposite: A section through the Octagon saloon which acted as a central drawing-room or saloon of quite extraordinary proportions. Situated beneath the tower, the ceiling was a vault 120 feet high. Behind the upper arcading were further rooms and bedrooms which were called the 'nunneries'.

I thought I should have gone wild upon my first setting my feet in the [Uffizi] Gallery, and when I beheld such ranks of Statues, such treasures of gems and bronzes – I fell into a delightful delirium – which none but Souls like ours experience, and, unable to check my rapture, flew madly from Bust to Bust and Cabinet to Cabinet like a Butterfly bewildered in a Universe of Flowers.

Beckford as a young man depicted in romantic, melancholic solitude by Romney. The haunting mourning figures on the pedestal on which he leans evoke the strange, private fantasy world of the mind which conceived Fonthill.

Although firmly married off to the daughter of an aristocratic family, such was society's ostracism of Beckford that he went into exile abroad, first in Switzerland, where his wife died, and later in France and Portugal. The Napoleonic Wars finally led to his return in 1796. Even before his arrival work had begun on the Fonthill estate, which he enclosed with a twelve-foot-high perimeter wall some seven miles long. Beckford despised his neighbours and loathed bloodsports: 'I never suffer an animal to be killed but through necessity. In early life I gave up shooting, because I consider we have no right to murder animals for sport.' The wall prevented not just the hunt but practically everyone else from entering Fonthill.

In the early months of 1796 Beckford had been in correspondence with the architect James Wyatt about his plan to erect a tower on the highest point of the estate, but that was abandoned in favour of developing an artificial ruin. Beckford asked Wyatt to design a ruined convent with a tower and a suite of rooms which could be occupied for a day or so but not permanently lived in. By the close of the year, however, the folly had escalated into a house of nightmare proportions centred around a tower and spire designed to eclipse that of nearby Salisbury Cathedral. Its inspiration was the monastery of the Grande Chartreuse in Switzerland, set amidst fir-clad mountains, where Beckford had been kindly received.

In choosing Wyatt for his architect Beckford had found a man whose Gothick style was midway between the rococo fantasy of the early part of the century and the archaeological exactitude of the Victorian age. Wyatt's knowledge of Gothic architecture was certainly deeper than that of his precursors, for he had been employed to restore and re-order the interiors of several major cathedrals, besides being appointed Surveyor General of the Works in succession to Sir William Chambers, which was to give him detailed insight into the construction of Windsor Castle. Wyatt's output was nothing if not prodigious and

Opposite: The plan catches the extraordinary eccentricity of the house, which consisted less of a sequence of rooms than of vast passages.

190

FONTHILL ABBEY.

PLAN OF THE PRINCIPAL STORY.

The dotted lines represent the Ornamented Ceilings, Groining, &c.

included a whole series of Gothick houses. The trouble with him was that he was dishonest, a drunk, and, worse still, lacked staying power. This meant that his site visits were infrequent, which could result in appalling structural defects. In the case of Fonthill, this is the reason why the legendary house has not survived although the speed with which it was built and the materials – wood and cement rather than stone for most of it – can hardly have added to its permanence. Beckford nick-named Wyatt 'Bagasse' Whoremonger, which says much, but, in spite of periodic wrangling and recrimination, the combination of these two quite impossible people gave birth to the most bizarre and original building in Western Europe at the time.

Once the work had begun Beckford became utterly obsessed by it, gloating with delight over the armies of workmen, up to 500 at any one time, slaving both night and day:

It is really stupendous the spectacle here at night, the number of people at work, lit up by lads, the innumerable torches suspended everywhere, the immense and endless spaces, the gulph below, above the gigantic spider's web of scaffolding – especially when, standing under the finished and numberless arches of the galleries, I listen to the reverberating voices of the night, and see immense buckets of plaster and water ascending, as if they were drawn up from the bowels of a mine, amid shouts from subterranean depths, oaths from Hell itself . . .

In letters like these the act of building itself becomes an expression of the Romantic imagination. The construction went on relentlessly, apart from brief interludes through lack of finance or the tower collapsing, which it did twice. By 1808 it was nearing completion but in 1812 a new phase was started, the eastern transept, which was destined to be left unfinished when Beckford was forced to sell the abbey in 1822. But the evolution of the abbey is more complicated than that, as plans were changed and modified over the years. For Beckford the whole phantasmagoria was a rehabilitation of himself and a celebration of his ancestry through art. It is what one might describe as the 'idea' of Fonthill that sets it apart, for it was to be not only a house but also a mausoleum and a church. John Farington in his Diary records in 1798 the

View through the Great West Hall to the main entrance whose doors were usually opened by Beckford's dwarf to emphasize their height. The landscape was orchestrated to continue the perspective of the architecture and the light of common day was deliberately contrasted to the mystery and shadowed gloom of the interior.

New building to be called Fonthill Abbey – the Spire to be 17 feet higher than the top of St. Peter's at Rome. The Abbey to be endowed, & Cathedral service to be performed in the most splendid manner that the Protestant religion will admit. A Gallery leading from the top of the Church to be decorated with paintings the work of English artists. Beckford's own tomb to be placed at the end of this Gallery – as having been an encourager of art.

Fonthill was a collector's house: it amounted to a gigantic stage-set for Beckford's quite staggering accumulation of works of art, books and manuscripts. Both colour and lighting were orchestrated to achieve a highly theatrical effect. It was a house of mystery and wonder in Regency England, although not to everyone's taste, as William Hazlitt's scathing comments reveal: 'It is a desert of magnificence, a glittering waste of laborious idleness, a cathedral turned into a toyshop, an immense museum of all that is most curious and costly and at the same time most worthless, in the productions of art and nature.'

Left above: *Interior of King Edward's Gallery. In the middle stands a* pietre dure *table from the Borghese Palace in Rome, now at Charlecote Park. The cabinets to the left were made for Beckford 'in the ancient taste of the reign of Queen Elizabeth', probably the earliest Elizabethan-revival furniture ever made.*

Left below: *The south end of St Michael's Gallery.*

194

A view of St Michael's Gallery, with the Octagon and King Edward's Gallery beyond. St Michael's Gallery was so named 'because the proprietor intended to have its windows painted with the knights of that Order, from whom he traces his descent'. It was 112 feet long with a ceiling based on the fan-vaulting of Henry VII's Chapel in Westminster Abbey. The windows were filled with painted glass and the walls lined with ebony cabinets. This room was the scene of the only major event ever held at the abbey: the visit of Lord Nelson and Lady Hamilton in December 1800, when the gallery was just finished: 'all was in monastic taste, with shrines, reliquaries, and religious sculptures, the whole illuminated with wax candles in candlesticks of silver'.

The landscape park around the house was transformed at the same time. The conservatory and the flower garden close to the house were already under way in November 1796, while Beckford wrote to his mother that 'My walk, which you will recollect is, according to the Plan, to be carried considerably more than twenty Miles thro' and round the Woods ... has already proceeded to nearly the length of nine Miles'. That year more than a million trees were planted. There was a huge artificial lake with wildfowl, a Norwegian lawn with a pinetum and firs and an American plantation rich in azaleas and rhododendrons. Everything was done on a stupendous scale.

Fonthill, had it survived intact, would have been England's

supreme example of the Romantic imagination expressed through architecture and interior decoration. That there are innumerable prints of the abbey and its interior, notably the series issued with the official guide by John Rutter, shows to what extent Fonthill captured the imagination of a whole generation. It was not just built on a gargantuan scale and of the utmost splendour within; above all it remained a mystery house, a place where a forbidden person, a forlorn pederast, kept court over a motley crew of servants and a handful of friends. The mention of Fonthill always went hand-in-hand with a sense of excitement. The society that had banished Beckford avidly sought any details about the house and the life led there, as this letter by Lady Bessborough recounting a visit by Samuel Rogers reveals. It is a measure of the intense curiosity surrounding the place that she should have devoted a long letter to a second-hand account she had heard at a dinner party. She writes:

He was received by a dwarf who, like a crowd of servants thro' whom he passed, was covered with gold and embroidery. Mr. Beckford received him very courteously, and led him thro' numberless apartments all fitted up most splendidly, one with Minerals, including precious stones; another the finest pictures; another Italian bronzes, china, etc., etc., till they came to a Gallery that surpass'd all the rest from the richness and variety of its ornaments. It seem'd clos'd by a crimson drapery held by a bronze statue, but on Mr. B's stamping and saying, 'Open!' the Statue flew back, and the Gallery was seen extending 350 feet long. At the end an open Arch with a massive balustrade opened to a vast Octagon Hall, from which a window shew'd a fine view of the Park. On approaching this it proved to be the entrance of the famous tower – higher than Salisbury Cathedral: this is not finish'd, but great part is done. The doors, of which there are many, are violet velvet covered over with purple and Gold embroidery. They pass'd from thence to a Chapel, where on the altar were heaped Golden Candlesticks, Vases, and Chalices studded over with jewels; and from there into a great musick room ... They went on to what is called the refectory, a large room built on the model of Henry 7 Chapel, only the ornaments gilt, where a Verdantique table was loaded with gilt plate fill'd with every luxury invention could collect ...

Rogers was pressed to return the following day, which he did, and was taken on a tour of Beckford's private apartments, 'fill'd with fine medals, gems, enamell'd miniatures, drawings old and

Beckford commissioned Turner to paint a series of five views of the Abbey at different times of day. These were exhibited at the Royal Academy in 1800. Turner stayed at Fonthill to gather material for three weeks during August 1799, making numerous pencil and watercolour sketches of the house, which was still under construction. This is a sketch by Turner for a sixth view of the abbey, from the south-east, which was never executed. These views by Turner of Fonthill, it has been suggested, reflect the impact of the works of Claude Lorrain, which the artist saw in Beckford's collection. Nothing captures so well the almost hallucinatory quality of the house as it loomed above the landscape.

modern, curios, prints and Manuscripts, and lastly a fine and well furnish'd library, all the books richly bound and the best Editions, etc., etc.'

Lady Bessborough's letter captures the somewhat ghoulish atmosphere of Fonthill, which makes it seem like a set for a Gothick horror film. The fact that all but a small section of the house was virtually uninhabitable was part of the stupendous folly of it. From the outset it was to be a domain not of sunshine but of shadows. Its plan was without precedent, adapting the cruciform of a medieval cathedral to create a series of rooms of parade. The most spectacular vista stretched along the north–south axis, from St Michael's Gallery through the great central Octagon beneath the tower, through King Edward's Gallery to

the Oratory. At night these great galleries were deliberately sparsely lit to heighten the theatrical effect: only a handful of candles relieved oceans of gloom while at the far end in the Oratory stood a statue of St Anthony beneath a golden lamp surrounded by banks of silver gilt candlesticks and torcheres, whose flickering flames caught the gold tracery of the fan vaulting above.

The fan-vaulted roof of St Michael's Gallery was supported by angels bearing shields, while the floor was carpeted in crimson patterned with white cinquefoils. Either side windows alternated with cabinets standing on ebony tables and bookcases curtained in crimson and deep blue. The colour scheme was carried through the Octagon, whose eight arches, 80 feet in height, were curtained alternately in blue and crimson. King Edward's Gallery beyond was all crimson wallpaper and curtains, beneath a flat hammer-beamed roof. In the centre on a solitary table of inlaid marble stood three superb objects, one of which was by Benvenuto Cellini. The gallery's decoration, celebrating the seventy-two knights, including King Edward III, from whom Beckford claimed descent, hints at his obsession with genealogy. Two of his four attendants were heralds who aided him in his researches, the results of which flooded across the abbey walls, ceilings and stained-glass windows. One unbuilt project was the grand 'Baronial Hall', which was to be part of the upper floor of the eastern transept, where Beckford intended to demonstrate his descent from all of the barons who had signed Magna Carta.

The main entrance to the house was through the Great West Hall whose massive doors were heaved open by Beckford's dwarf to accentuate their enormous height. The visitor must have been further unnerved to see a continuation of the avenue through the park, on the same massive scale as the trees. This led to a grand staircase:

Beckford was forced to sell Fonthill in 1822 and three years later the tower collapsed, demolishing most of the western hall. In this way, by accident, the abbey became what Beckford had initially intended: a ruined convent in the middle of a wood. In 1823 its dramatic fate was foretold by C. F. Porden: 'Would to God it were more substantially built! But, as it is, its ruins will tell a tale of wonder.'

The majestic descent of the broad steps, and their arched parapets; the lofty wainscoting and the pointed arches of the walls, filled with the most beautiful glazing, or hidden by crimson draperies, or retiring into a recess which sculpture has dignified with the effigy of a great man (his father, Alderman Beckford); the darkly coloured and elaborately framed roof, displaying shields of a distinguished ancestry, with all its minutest and most common parts moulded, and arranged into ornamental forms; the massive piers of the Great portal pierced to give light and access to the staircase within them; and the

grand contour of the noble archway, which the gigantic doors seem waiting to close up forever, – all contrast powerfully with the light, the freshness, and the depth of the 'marble stair' and the delicate colouring and simple outline of the external scene.

Thus wrote one of the official chroniclers of the abbey, who then points out to the visitor that 'the masterly arrangement of the chiaroscuro, the atmosphere of the coloured light, and the solemn brilliance of the windows, produces an effect very little removed from the sublime'. And, indeed, Fonthill was one of the earliest manifestations of the aesthetic theory of the sublime, with its emphasis on sensory responses, its fascination with awe and terror, darkness and Stygian gloom, and the impact on a human being of sheer vastness of scale. These were the impulses formulated by the builder which ensured the abbey's enormous influence, not just as an expression of the sublime but later as an archetype of the picturesque aesthetic, as expounded in the writings of Richard Payne Knight and Uvedale Price only two years before Fonthill was begun.

The Octagon saloon beneath the tower, like all the other rooms, was an expression of these new ideals which banished Palladianism; with its ceiling a vault 120 feet high, and the transepts and nave stretching out from it, it must have felt as though part of a medieval cathedral had been turned into a drawing-room. To the east there was a grand suite of reception rooms – the Cabinet Room, the Crimson and the Grand Drawing-Rooms – arranged as an enfilade and picture gallery, containing such masterpieces as Gerard Dou's *The Poulterer's Shop* and Lodovico Caracci's *Sybil*. It also had magnificent pieces of furniture, including the Riesener secretaire, now in the Wallace Collection, and an abundance of *objets d'art* such as bouquets of ivory vases by Fiamingo.

Beckford's own rooms were off St Michael's Gallery to the west, overlooking the Fountain Court and Cloister. His dining-room, known as the Brown or the Oak Parlour, was hung with tapestries and the glass windows celebrated his descent from royalty. On two huge tables of Siena marble stood tableaux of silver-gilt plate and the rarest Dresden and Sèvres porcelain. On the second floor he slept in a simple truckle bed in the Gallery Cabinet, which led to another series of rooms: the so-called

'Board of Works', which housed his collections of books and prints on the fine arts; the book-lined gilded Cedar Boudoir; the Vaulted Library; and the Chintz Boudoir, decorated in yellow, on whose walls hung Van Eyck's *Virgin and Child* and Benjamin West's *Apocalypse*.

In its latter phases Fonthill was built against a backcloth of economic depression. Beckford was particularly affected because in 1815 the sugar trade entered a sharp decline from which it never recovered. In 1817 he was forced to sell some of his books and the contents of his London house, although building at the abbey continued. By 1821 he was heavily in debt and in 1822 he was forced to sell Fonthill for £300,000 to an eccentric millionaire, John Farquhar. The following year Phillips auctioned off the majority of its legendary contents at a sale which drew the fashionable world in droves. Beckford moved to Bath, along with the best of his collection, where he was to die in 1844, seven years into Victoria's reign.

On 21 December 1825 the great tower of Fonthill Abbey fell down for the third and last time. It collapsed on to the Fountain Court, ruining not only the great Octagon but all the buildings to the south and west except the Great West Hall. This ruin was left open to the elements, presided over by the statue of the builder's father, Alderman Beckford. All that remains today is a truncated fragment, the Sanctuary and the Oratory, while the contents of Fonthill are scattered through the great museums and private collections of the world.

Never has a man more truly said, 'Some people drink to forget their unhappiness. I do not drink, I build.'

CHAPTER SIXTEEN

Westminster in Flames

In October 1834 fire deprived England of one of its most ancient buildings, the royal palace of Westminster, a huge rambling complex along the Thames between the Abbey and Whitehall which included the House of Lords and the House of Commons as well as numerous government departments. A unique assembly of buildings dating back to the eleventh century, it had been the main palace of the medieval kings of England, from William I to Richard III, and was abandoned only when Henry VIII moved to Whitehall Palace in the 1530s. In addition, since the twelfth century it had been the seat of government, accommodating both the legal and financial offices of the Crown.

The fire originated, as far as can be ascertained, in a chimney that over-heated due to the burning of thousands of wooden Exchequer tally sticks. Within hours the London skyline was engulfed in flames which drew such large crowds of sightseers that the army was called in to assist the police in maintaining order. Not all was lost for, mercifully, the wind changed direction, thus saving Westminster Hall. Built at the end of the eleventh century, in its day it was the greatest hall in Western Europe. The roof of the House of Lords, however, fell in with a crash so deafening, it was reported, that onlookers 'involuntarily (and from no bad feeling) clapped their hands as though they had been present at the closing scene of some dramatic spectacle'. Unlike previous disasters, this one took place in the age of the antiquarian, and although the loss was certainly grievous, the prevailing preoccupation with recording the artefacts of the past

Opposite: *In this picture by Peter Tillemans, painted c.1708–1714, Queen Anne sits enthroned in the House of Lords with the Armada tapestries adorning the walls and Inigo Jones's* trompe l'oeil *barrel vault above.*

A mid-Tudor panorama of Westminster Palace from the Thames, with Westminster Abbey in the background. In front of the Abbey is the roof of Westminster Hall, which still exists, and, to its left, the soaring clerestory of St Stephen's Chapel, which was removed by Wren in 1692.

ensured that we know far more about what disappeared than in the great Whitehall holocaust of 1698.

No sooner were the flames extinguished than the archaeologists were on the site making sketches and measured drawings. The Government set up a commission empowered to record every available detail about the palace, which reflected the evolution of English central government from the Angevins onwards. It had embraced within its walls the Chancery, the Exchequer, the Star Chamber, the King's Bench, the Court of Augmentations and the Court of Wards. Many of England's greatest medieval craftsmen and artists had added wall-paintings and sculptural decoration over the centuries. When it came to be rebuilt by the architect Sir Charles Barry in the form we know today, only three of its ancient buildings were retained: the Great Hall, the crypt of St Stephen's Chapel, and its adjoining cloister. Even these now seem just part of a huge Victorian building.

The blaze destroyed three supreme works of art, England's equivalents of the Sainte Chapelle, the frescoes by Giotto in the Arena Chapel at Padua, and the Valois Tapestries now in the Uffizi in Florence. Having said that, St Stephen's Chapel had been ravaged by the depredations of previous generations. It was begun by Edward I at the close of the thirteenth century

Opposite: *St Stephen's Chapel. The old royal chapel of the medieval kings of England was initiated by Edward I. Designed to outshine its French counterpart, the Sainte Chapelle in Paris, both the architecture and the interior decoration were of an astonishing richness. In 1548 the chapel was handed over to the Commons by Edward VI and a long series of depredations followed, ending with the fire of 1834. This elevation of the south side of St Stephen's shows the original two-tiered arcading. Above this a clerestory was added in the early 1320s. The design of the chapel is recognized to have been highly influential in many ways; one innovation is the lower tracery superimposed over the practical Gothic windows.*

South Elevation

deliberately to rival the Sainte Chapelle in Paris, a veritable jewel-box of a royal chapel. Its architect was Michael of Canterbury, the designer of the exquisitely elegant crosses which marked the progress of the remains of Eleanor of Acquitaine. In St Stephen's Chapel he developed the use of the most complex and delicate arcading on an unprecedented scale, purely for decorative effect rather than for structural necessity. Recent commentators believe that 'there is remarkably little in early-fourteenth-century English architecture that did not stem directly or indirectly from St Stephen's or Michael of Canterbury's other work'. Financial and other pressures meant that the chapel was not completed until 1348 (work stopped entirely between 1297 and 1320), by

The spectacular programme of decoration carried out during the reign of Edward III covered the entire interior of the chapel, including all of the architecture. Illustrated here are fragments of the wall-painting showing scenes from the Book of Job.

The high altar was framed with murals depicting Edward III and his family in adoration of the Virgin and St George. This copy of what survived of the left-hand section, made in 1800, shows the lower arcading with the male members of the royal family headed by St George. From left to right: Thomas of Woodstock, Duke of Gloucester; Edmund, Duke of York; John of Gaunt, Duke of Lancaster; Lionel, Duke of Clarence; Edward, Prince of Wales; and Edward III. Above there is an Adoration of the Magi.

which time revisions had been made to its original design, including the unfortunate addition of a clerestory.

During the Reformation Edward VI handed St Stephen's over to the Commons as its meeting place. Ironically the unnecessary clerestory was removed in 1692 by Wren, thus restoring the chapel to its original appearance, until it was devastated by 'restoration' at the hands of the architect James Wyatt between 1795 and 1800. Under Wyatt, what remained of the medieval painted wall decoration, the most magnificent carried out in fourteenth-century England, vanished. A few surviving fragments now in the British Museum give some impression of the quality of the work. Every surface was painted and gilded and the walls were embellished with a complete cycle of scenes, including biblical narratives, angels holding draperies and warrior saints, executed by a small army of painters under Master Hugh of St Albans between 1350 and 1360. The antiquarian Richard Smirke made a life-size copy of what we would probably regard as the most important mural, that around the high altar. To the north of the altar St George, the patron saint of England, presented the male members of the royal family to the Virgin: Edward III; Edward, Prince of Wales; Lionel, Duke of Clarence; John of Gaunt, Duke of Lancaster; Edmund, Duke of York; and Thomas of Woodstock, Duke of Gloucester. Each figure was set within a Gothic niche echoing the architecture of the chapel. Opposite

By the early fourteenth century the Painted Chamber was considered one of the wonders of medieval Europe. The main living-room of the medieval kings of England, it was enriched by remarkable painted decoration, first under Henry III and then under Edward I.

Left: *This watercolour of the chamber was painted by William Capon in 1799, a year before the medieval wall-paintings, which had been hidden by overpainting and tapestries, were discovered. The enclosure with the royal bed was at the far end, while visitors entered through the door to the right. The Virtues on the splays of the windows to the left were thus designed to be seen by every visitor as they approached the royal presence.*

Opposite, above: *A copy made in 1819 of the painting above Henry III's bed depicting the coronation of the royal saint, Edward the Confessor, whose shrine the king had rebuilt in Westminster Abbey.*

knelt Queen Philippa and her daughters, while above the two groups was an Adoration of the Magi. The copy gives a clear impression of the immense richness and sophistication of this composition, with its luminous oil-based colour and embossed gilding.

The wall-paintings of the Painted Chamber were even older and are recorded as being amongst the great sights of medieval Europe by two friars who journeyed from Ireland to the Holy Land in the 1320s:

... the celebrated palace of the kings of England, in which is that famous chamber on whose walls all the warlike stories of the whole Bible are painted with wonderful skill, and explained by a complete series of texts accurately written in French to the great admiration of the beholder and with the greatest royal magnificence.

208

Right: *At the close of the thirteenth century the chamber was further enriched with several hundred feet of wall-paintings depicting scenes of Old Testament chivalry. The effect is more that of a brilliant pastel-coloured pageant evoking life at the court of Edward I than of Old Testament warfare. Henceforth the room became known as the* camera picta. *Shown here is the Miracles of Elisha.*

Two watercolours by William Capon show this room as it was in 1799: the paintings were still hidden by layers of whitewash, probably applied during the Reformation, and the walls were covered with tapestries depicting the siege of Troy. This gives no impression of the status of this room during the Middle Ages as the main living-room of the king. It ranked next in importance to the two halls, and in the twelfth century was connected with the Lesser Hall. The royal bed, elaborately curtained off, stood at the far end and both formal and informal occasions, from feasts to diplomatic exchanges, took place here.

By the early fourteenth century this room was referred to as the *camera depicta* or *camera Regis depicta*. Two major series of wall-paintings had been added, the first during the reign of Henry III and the second under Edward I. There can have been no other secular room in medieval England decorated with such splendour. That we know so much about these paintings is due to the excitement engendered by their discovery in 1799–1800, after which, surprisingly, they were papered over, and by their rediscovery in 1818–19. On both occasions antiquarians copied them remarkably accurately.

The first series of paintings is likely to have been executed after 1263, although the documentation is unclear, under the aegis of the art-loving Henry III. The subject matter reflected his concept of the role of the virtuous and just king. The tester of the royal bed, which, enclosed by curtains, formed a room within a room, had over it the coronation of Edward the Confessor (for whom the king had constructed a new shrine in Westminster Abbey), with two life-size knights representing the Guardians of Solomon's Bed. Opposite were the figures of St Edward the Confessor and St John, while in the voussoirs of the windows elegant elongated figures of virtues with crowns on their heads trod underfoot their opposing vices. These took the scheme across the room and their faces were turned towards visitors, reminding them of the king's role in the practice of virtue and the suppression of vice. Much use was made of raised gilt work on the crowns, croziers and armour, which would have added to the richness of the effect, animating the subdued colour palette of crimson, green and blue.

The Edwardian series, probably begun about 1292–7, was on a huge scale, adding several hundred feet of narrative ranked in registers above the dado. It was these paintings that made the room one of the wonders of fourteenth-century Europe. Both their subject matter and their style were adventurous: the stories of the warlike kings of the Old Testament were portrayed as a living pageant embodying Edward I's idea of the monarchy as well as the chivalrous preoccupations of his court. These scenes of Gothic romantic chivalry, with medieval castles and forays of armoured knights, were the fount of a whole new imagery which was to dominate late medieval society. The use of toy-town wooden Gothic architecture with which to frame and hold the scenes was also quite new when it was painted. The palette, too, was very different from that of the first series, prettier in its use of

Henry III's scheme of decoration for the Painted Chamber, executed at the end of the thirteenth century, included a series of eight elegant figures of Virtues vanquishing Vices sited on the splays of the windows. Copies made before their destruction in 1834 survive. Depicted here is Largesce *(Generosity) vanquishing* Covoitise *(Covetousness).*

pink, lilac and pale blues. The elegance, sophistication and the innovative design of the Painted Chamber made it a masterpiece of its period.

As well as the Painted Chamber, a series of artefacts commemorating that great moment in England's history, the defeat of the Spanish Armada in 1588, perished in the fire of 1834. The ten great tapestries that told the story of the battle had been selected by Cromwell in 1650 from the Royal Collection before its dissolution to adorn the walls of the House of Lords. In John Singleton Copley's great canvas *The Death of the Earl of Chatham* (1778) they form a luminous backdrop. They were already recognized as national treasures in 1739, when John Pine produced his remarkable publication *The Tapestry Hangings in the House of Lords representing the several Engagements between the English and the Spanish Fleets.* Pine had been moved to make these handsome, large, exact engravings 'because Time, or Accident, or Moths may deface these valuable Shadows'.

Debonereté *(Tranquillity) conquering* Ira (Anger). *This and the Virtue shown opposite were both sited on the window opposite the royal bed.*

Copley's picture captures the beautiful subtlety of the tapestries' colours, a symphony of shades of blue and green tipped with white for the sea, the ships in gradations of brown, with red, orange and yellow accents on the clothing of the mariners. In any other country these would have been a royal commission, but Elizabeth I was noted for her parsimony, so it was left to the admiral who commanded the English fleet, Charles Howard, Lord Howard of Effingham, later Earl of Nottingham, to commission them from the Brussels weaver Francis Aertsz Spierincx. Initially Spierincx had wanted Carel van Mander to design them, but Van Mander said that his knowledge of maritime matters was insufficient and took him to see Hendrik C. Vroom, who was to become the most famous marine artist of the day.

Vroom made the cartoons from a series of charts which had been drawn up shortly after the event by Robert Adam under Howard's supervision. These showed the successive engagements of the Spanish and English fleets in the Channel, from the first appearance of the Spanish ships thirty miles south-west of the Lizard to their final defeat off Gravelines near Calais and their storm-tossed retreat around the rocky coasts of Scotland and Ireland. Vroom transformed these charts into wonderfully evocative panoramic views and seascapes. It almost looks as though a television camera were sweeping up the Channel during the

encounter. This combination of panoramic seascapes with accurately recorded moments of an historical event was unique. Each tapestry was enclosed within a decorative border of fruits, flowers, cornucopias, putti, monkeys and birds supporting a series of oval medallions with portraits of the naval commanders of the fleet.

In 1595 the tapestries were at last delivered to the admiral, at a cost of £1,582, and were hung in his house, Chelsea Manor. In 1602 Howard moved to Arundel House and took them with him. The queen came to visit and it was rumoured that she hoped he would present them to her. He did not, and it was not until 1616 that financial pressure led him to sell them to James I. So prejudiced is our own century in favour of pictures that we have forgotten that during the Renaissance tapestries were more highly valued in northern Europe, where the damp climate was inimical to the survival of wall-paintings.

There is a footnote to the destruction of the tapestries. A few weeks after the fire in 1834 an antique dealer wrote to the Privy Council offering one of them for sale, stating that it was 'very much worn, and almost reduced to threads, having been used as a carpet'. It emerged that in 1831 this tapestry, which had hung opposite the throne, had been taken down and stored during the

The ten great Armada tapestries were commissioned by Charles Howard, Lord Howard of Effingham, later Earl of Nottingham, to commemorate the defeat of the Spanish Armada in 1588. Designed by the Dutch marine artist Cornelius Vroom and based on contemporary charts and accounts of the encounter, they were woven in Brussels and delivered to England in 1595. In 1616 Lord Howard sold the tapestries to King James I. When the Royal Collection was dispersed in 1650 Oliver Cromwell transferred them to the House of Lords. Shown above is the Spanish fleet to the right in the form of a half-moon being pursued by the English fleet.

construction of the Strangers' Gallery. It must have been removed from the palace and somehow came into the possession of this dealer, who asked the Privy Council more than £100 for it – a huge price at the time. The offer was declined, so the possibility remains that one day a battered survivor of the Armada Tapestries may come to light.

The burning of the palace of Westminster is the only occasion when the loss of so many masterpieces can be offset by the creation of two new ones. Turner, who was obsessed with the theme of cataclysmic disaster, rushed to the scene of the fire and recorded his impressions of it in his sketchbooks. These he transmuted into two of his greatest canvases, both entitled *The Burning of the House of Lords and Commons, 16th October, 1834*. He portrays the event from two different vantage points in an explosion of colour whose radiant intensity turns the loss of the ancient palace of England's medieval kings into a golden apocalyptic glory.

The Triumph of the Past?

With the reign of Queen Victoria a new story begins. I have called it the triumph of the past, albeit with a question-mark, for at no stage in our history has there been such a sustained upward curve of thought and action aimed at preserving our heritage. Before this, what survived was purely arbitrary.

The earliest suggestion that there should be some form of official organized preservation came from John Ruskin in 1854. He suggested to the Society of Antiquaries that an 'inventory of buildings of interest threatened by demolition or bad restoration' be compiled. During the mid-Victorian period churches were subject to alterations as radical as those of the Reformation, only in reverse, for the leaders of the Oxford Movement demanded a revival of ritual and the use of visual aids in religion. Ruskin's enunciation of a philosophy of preservation and protection was quite revolutionary:

I must not leave the truth unstated that it is no question of expediency or feeling whether we shall preserve the buildings of past times or not. We have no right whatever to touch them. They are not ours. They belong partly to those that built them, and partly to all generations of mankind who are to follow us.

The simple idea of compiling a catalogue of buildings which should remain untouched was the acorn from which sprang a

---

Opposite: *A detail from Turner's* The Burning of the House of Lords and Commons, 16th October 1834 *which was exhibited at the Royal Academy in 1835, where it caused a great stir. Although critics pointed out factual mistakes, it was overwhelmingly agreed that this orchestration of artificial light encapsulated the horror of the event.*

mighty tree whose branches spread in every direction for the next century. Ruskin could hardly have foreseen the eventual consequences of his suggestion. At the time of writing no less than 500 buildings a year are being added to the list of those to be preserved, and whole tracts of the landscape as well as the interiors of houses are being reduced to the level of time capsules.

None of this could have been predicted in 1854, only three years on from the Great Exhibition which proclaimed to the civilized world the commercial and industrial dominance of Britain and her empire. This dazzling celebration was the fruit of the Industrial Revolution, which had created a huge new middle class as well as teeming thousands of office and factory workers in the expanding towns. The middle classes campaigned and got what they most wanted – access to political power through the vote – as a succession of bills from 1832 onwards extended the franchise. But the reconfiguration of society on such a scale needed an ideological unity of purpose which would not defy the ideals of the old aristocratic system but extend it across the population.

The Victorian age saw the creation of a national 'Old England' mythology. This cult had a huge impact on people's perception of the buildings and artefacts of the past, for they became the visible and tangible evidence of the country's emergence to nationhood, empire and democratic institutions.

The engendering of collective reverence for the past was one of the driving forces behind the establishment of state-funded museums. Their purpose was to house and display artefacts in such a way as to instil patriotic pride in such things as the famous figures in British history (The National Portrait Gallery, 1856); the arts of design and manufacture (The Victoria & Albert Museum, 1837 onwards); the British School in art (The Tate Gallery, 1897). Through these and other freely accessible public institutions the mass of the population could share in the pleasure of seeing artefacts from the past which had hitherto been the preserve of the privileged. And they were to be viewed not as expressions of historical inequalities of wealth and social structure but as art and history and therefore part of a heritage epitomizing common values and shared achievements.

This apotheosis of the British past was heightened by the advent of the temporary exhibition, allowing items not in public galleries but assembled from the great country houses, colleges and old foundations to be displayed to a huge public. During the 1860s the South Kensington Museum played host to a series of gigantic exhibitions of works of art, miniatures and British portraits. At the close of the century the New Gallery staged a series of exhibitions on the royal houses of Tudor, Stuart and Hanover. At the same time British art history emerged as worthy of study. Major pioneering works appeared, such as Chamberlain's *Hans Holbein* (1913) and Sir Walter Armstrong's *Thomas Gainsborough* (1898), and in 1909 the Walpole Society was founded, dedicated to publishing the documentary history of British art.

In the nineteenth century history became the stuff of bestsellers. Thomas Babington Macaulay's *History of England* (1849–61) sold by the thousand and was devoured by the new literate middle classes. With the Education Act of 1870 that enthusiasm began to extend further down the social scale to the working classes. The type of history that was taught was an overwhelmingly Whig view of the past: a tale in which heroes and heroines and dramatic tableaux such as Magna Carta, the Civil War and the Glorious Revolution of 1688 had their place. Pictures of the triumphs and tragedies of such figures as King Alfred, Mary Queen of Scots, Charles I and Oliver Cromwell were rarely absent from the walls of the Royal Academy, and through cheap mass reproduction they became familiar in the average home.

By the end of the nineteenth century the prevailing literary climate had endowed historic buildings and artefacts with a network of associations and attitudes that would have amazed previous ages. I have already pointed out the importance of Joseph Nash in the emergence of a widespread popular cult of the old manor house. But Nash drew his ideas from literature, from the historical novels which had pioneered the peopling of surviving historic buildings and ruins. Harrison Ainsworth's novels *The Tower of London* (1840), *Old St Paul's* (1841), and *Windsor Castle* (1843) are examples, although the writings of Sir Walter Scott were, of course, seminal. His novel *Kenilworth* (1821), for instance, must have entirely changed everyone's perception of the ruined medieval castle. Henceforth it would be seen as the setting for a story of love and perfidy in the Elizabethan age during the Earl of Leicester's famous 'Princely Pleasures'. In a nationalistic age the artefacts of the past, whether houses, castles, churches or furnishings, came to have the same status as images and relics in the ages of faith. They were there to be visited, revered and above all preserved. The British past became sacred, and to a large extent remains so today.

This trend gathered momentum in the 1870s, when the state legislated for the first time on the preservation of antiquities *in situ*. Such an incursion into private-property rights did not go unopposed, for the milieu from which these ideas sprang was linked with early socialism. Much of the work of the pioneers of preservation was concerned with access to landscape and above all common land, which was still being enclosed by landowners and taken away from ordinary villagers in the mid-Victorian period. Octavia Hill and Hardwicke Rawnsley, two of the driving forces behind the foundation of the National Trust in 1895, were socialists, concerned with the conditions of the poor, their housing and amenities, including access to good fresh air for factory workers. The Trust's concern with aristocratic country houses came much later, only really beginning in 1939.

The first National Monuments Preservation Bill was rejected on its second reading in 1875 and similar bills in 1878 and 1879 suffered the same fate. Meanwhile, in 1877, under the auspices of William Morris and as a result of a threat to 'restore' Tewkesbury Abbey, the Society for the Protection of Ancient Buildings was formed. This helped to engender an atmosphere in favour of preservation, and in 1882 an Ancient Monuments Protection Act was at last passed. This was the first of a series of Acts of Parliament down to the National Heritage Act of 1980 which signalled the intervention of the state in ensuring the preservation of the past.

In retrospect there is a telling inverse relationship between the upward graph of the preservation of the past and the downward curve in the country's political and economic fortunes. Very little was to happen until 1932, when the Town and Country Planning Act extended to local authorities the ability to make preservation orders on any building of special or historic interest. The 1930s also saw the introduction of a control system to prevent an increasing number of major works of art leaving the country, and the foundation of the Georgian Society to promote the appreciation and preservation of all things eighteenth-century. It was not until after the Second World War, however, that the role of government was accelerated. The post-war Socialist Government passed the 1947 Town and Country Planning Act. This repealed all its predecessors, embraced the statutory listing of all buildings of architectural or historic interest according to a grade system established in the 1944 Town and Country Planning Act, and introduced building preservation orders. This Government also commissioned Sir Ernest Gowers' report on the future of country houses. Published in 1950, it was acted upon by the National Trust, which began its long series of acquisitions that now run to well over a hundred. At the same time the owners of country houses began opening on a commercial basis and when petrol rationing was finally abolished the pursuit of the past could be exploited on a tremendous scale. Meanwhile, the Historic Buildings and Ancient Monuments Act of 1953 established the Historic Buildings Councils for England, Wales and Scotland. Their role was to advise on the allocation of State grants to preserve, maintain and restore historic buildings.

The attitude of Socialist governments to this cult of the physical fabric of the past was always ambiguous. In the case of country houses, for instance, preservation certainly did not extend to the owners. Death duties were designed slowly to eliminate them, enabling the major contents to pass to the state in lieu of tax and the building to become redundant, be demolished or given over to a wider social use. By the early 1970s this slow erosion through taxation was beginning to have a dramatic cumulative effect.

New factors emerged to fuel the public interest in preserving the past. One was the emergence of art history as an academic discipline within the universities. British art, mainly as a result of the activities of American collectors such as Paul Mellon, was 'discovered' by a wider audience than ever before. Figures such as Turner and Constable began to be seen not as peripheral but as central and mainstream. In addition, the worship of old buildings was accorded its *vade mecum* in the long series of county-by-county architectural studies entitled *The Buildings of England* edited by Sir Nikolaus Pevsner. Major historians of British art appeared, such as Sir Ellis Waterhouse on painting and Sir John Summerson on architecture.

During the 1960s the Victorian Society was founded to

promote the appreciation and preservation of a period of art that had been a subject for popular ridicule in the immediate post-war era. Declining congregations were making increasing numbers of churches redundant, while concern for the country house and its contents was reactivated in 1973 by a new report by John Cornforth, commissioned by the Historic Houses Committee of the British Tourist Authority, together with an exhibition emotively entitled *The Destruction of the Country House* at the Victoria & Albert Museum. These were a response to the Labour Party's proposed wealth tax and the crisis over the demise of the great Rothschild house, Mentmore Towers.

Interestingly the emergence of the most powerful and widely connected protest lobby on behalf of preservation we have ever seen coincided with the economic recession that followed the 1973 oil crisis, when the fortunes of the country sank low and the social order was drifting towards anarchy. In the 1970s the past offered the only intellectual comfort as Britain slowly slipped downwards. Exhibitions at the V & A went on to tell the sorry tale of the fate of the nation's great gardens (1979) and churches (1977), while two vociferous new protest groups, Heritage in Danger (1974) and SAVE (1979), emerged. The passing of the National Heritage Act in 1980 marked the end of that era. The Act began its life under Labour and was passed by the incoming Thatcher government, whose attitude to the past was to be quite different. 'Heritage', as it was now endlessly called, seemed to rise above party politics and provide myths upon which both the right and the left could draw.

Today there are indications that our long obsession with the past might be beginning to wither. Two generations have grown up since the British Empire vanished and to them even the Commonwealth means little. Their focus is Europe and their attitude to the objects of the past might well be as evidence of a common European cultural heritage rather than as symbols of an inviolate island kingdom. The mainstay of the heritage cult is a generation which saw Britain fall in the world, for whom the pride that was left expressed itself through the cult of artefacts which symbolized past glories or those living embodiments of it, the royal family. Looking across the globe, the post-war generations in Britain must feel a sense of betrayal: in every other civilized country the state seems to show a confidence in things new and to support contemporary artists in great acts of government patronage. The cities of Western Europe and the United States are building those cathedrals of our century, magnificent new opera houses and art galleries expressing a pride in the role of culture in their society. In England, in stark contrast, there is nothing but an endless litany of appeals to preserve and restore. With the twenty-first century only a decade away, the British people are denied any vision that is theirs. In Britain not a single institution is being created by the state to act as an inspiration and a symbol.

It has been forgotten that the definition of the word heritage embraces 'that which has been or may be inherited' and that it includes the material culture of our own time. Our pious concern with preservation can be seen to cloak what is in effect an era of creative stagnation. Looking back at our saga of destruction, I am surprised to find that in retrospect there is something to be said for wiping the slate clean from time to time, so as to enable new initiatives relevant to the age to take off, uncircumscribed by the burdens of yesterday. Preservation has escalated to such a scale that its consequences rise far above the laments of present-day medievalists who have to write their history with a great deal of the evidence missing, or the members of the heritage lobby anxious for the next media fracas about some treasure about to leave these shores. The real pivot of this book is the fact that two apparent opposites, destruction and creation, are in reality indissolubly linked. In any society which has a future, a fair balance between them is necessary.

Have we achieved such a balance or have we tipped the scales too far in one direction for too long? Much of what we most prize as part of our heritage would never have been created without the holocausts of the past. Out of the ruined abbeys of the Reformation arose our great country houses. Out of the rejection of images came, it can be argued, a vigorous culture whose prime expression was to be the word. The loss of our baroque formal gardens made way for the genius of the landscape park. Even the destruction of the old Palace of Westminster gave us the magnificence of Sir Charles Barry's Houses of Parliament. Today we have swung so far to the other extreme that if anything is destroyed we timidly replace it with a facsimile. The last time that a major building was replaced by something totally new was Coventry

Cathedral after it had been bombed in the last war. In retrospect we realize that it is the only ecclesiastical building of any consequence to have been erected in the country in the second half of the twentieth century, the richer for its masterpieces by Epstein, Sutherland and Piper. By contrast, the Wren churches either remained ruined, for lack of funds, or were rebuilt as copies. After the recent York Minster, Hampton Court and Uppark fires, the only alternative considered was putting back a copy of what had been there. This decision would have astonished our ancestors. They would have been equally transfixed by our policy of hanging on to old façades as skins for totally new buildings erected within.

In many ways the last war did not destroy enough, compared with the devastation in Germany, where although certain buildings were reconstructed in facsimile, the cult of the new was taken up with vigour. Nor were we helped by the fact that what we did build in the 1950s and 1960s was so bad that it simply fuelled the conservationist lobby and led in the 1980s to a cry for the restoration of the classical orders. To that we can add a chaotic system of piecemeal planning control that has failed to sort out with any clarity what should and should not be conserved. This appalling state of affairs has been summed up by Mrs Thatcher in one memorable phrase when she alluded to Britain as 'the museum society'. She has certainly done nothing to conceal her distaste for the museums themselves. Her attitude signals what may be the end of the preservation age, for the years of the Thatcher revolution have also been notable for an ambiguity towards the past. Instead of being seen as essential for holding the nation together, it has come to be seen as holding it back, and worse, as having contributed to our economic and political decline by feeding us with the bread and circuses of empty pageantry and the stage scenery of a power which no longer exists. But this ideological leap, which should have signalled a golden age of the present, has been accompanied by the revival of a hard-nosed philistinism against contemporary creativity, unseen since the reaction of the establishment classes following the trial of Oscar Wilde. Where creation can occur it is so circumscribed as to be blunted.

The plight of our churches illustrates well our creative paralysis. The Victorian period was the last age when these buildings could respond to the resurgence of faith expressed in the Oxford Movement. We may view with regret some of the resulting losses and alterations, but we cannot deny that they expressed a vigorous living faith. Churches were cheerfully torn apart as they ceased to be preaching boxes and became altar-orientated. It was a return of images, of mystery, colour and spectacle. That response could not happen in our own day. The heritage lobby has contributed to the death of the Church of England, its members devoting much of their time to maintaining and restoring buildings to be visited as tourists by the 97.5 per cent who do not attend services.

A century and more on, museums present us with a very similar problem. These immovable and ever-growing accumulations of the past demand increasing human and financial resources. The very word 'de-accessioning' produces mass hysteria, but any projection of the resources needed to maintain our national collections into the middle of the next century cannot but be cause for utter dismay.

The British today have all the problems of living in an old country *in extremis*. Unlike the countries on the Continent, which were subjected to a never-ending succession of struggles – the Thirty Years War, the wars of Louis XIV and of the Spanish Succession, the Napoleonic Wars, as well as the two cataclysms of 1914 and 1939 – no hand of destruction has swept through the land for centuries. Apart from the Blitz, little has ruffled the surface of the British Isles since the Civil War three centuries ago. Nor have we endured a great revolution since the Commonwealth, if we except the Industrial Revolution. Families have, of course, risen and fallen, land and houses have changed hands, but by dint of purchase and not by means of pillage or confiscation. We have enjoyed a remarkable and enviable stability but we are in danger of being remembered for saving and preserving the treasures of our forebears, at the tremendous price of not creating ones of our own age. In so doing we have as much betrayed our forebears, whose confidence was always in tomorrow. We need to regain their forward-looking spirit if we are not to be dismissed by future generations as a culture manacled to the corpse of the past. At least those ages had treasures to lose; we have yet to create ours before the dawn of the twenty-first century.

laudabo eum

Qui astitit a dextris pauperis:
ut saluam faceret a persequentibz
animam meam.
Gloria patri
Dñs Galfridus louterell me fieri
fecit

Select Bibliography

Abbreviations

Chivalry: *Age of Chivalry: Art in Plantagenet England 1200–1400*, ed. Jonathan Alexander and Paul Binski, London, Royal Academy, 1987.

King's Works, III: H. M. Colvin, D. R. Ransome and John Summerson, *The History of the King's Works*, III, Part I, 1485–1660, London, HMSO, 1975.

King's Works, IV: H. M. Colvin, John Summerson, Martin Biddle, J. R. Hale and Marcus Merriman, *The History of the King's Works*, IV, Part II, 1485–1660, London, HMSO, 1982.

Briggs, *Goths and Vandals*: Martin S. Briggs, *Goths and Vandals: A Study of the Destruction, Neglect and Preservation of Historical Buildings in England*, London, 1952.

Harris and Higgott, *Inigo Jones*: John Harris and Gordon Higgott, *Inigo Jones: Complete Architectural Drawings*, London, The Drawing Centre, 1989.

Phillips, *Images*: John R. Phillips: *The Reformation of Images: Destruction of Art in England, 1535–1669*, University of California Press, 1974.

Introduction

For the history of the antiquarian movement and the Society of Antiquaries see T. D. Kendrick, *British Antiquity*, London, 1950; David C. Douglas, *English Scholars 1660–1730*, London, 1951; Joan Evans, *A History of the Society of Antiquaries*, Oxford, 1956. For the 1560 proclamation see Phillips, *Images*, pp. 117–18. For James I and the royal jewels as heirlooms, A. J. Collins, *Jewels and Plate of Queen Elizabeth I*, London, 1955, pp. 168–9. On the emergence of the 'virtuoso', W. E. Houghton, 'The English Virtuoso in the Seventeenth Century', *Journal of the History of Ideas*, III, 1942, pp. 51–73, 190–219; F. J. Levy, 'Henry Peacham and the Art of Drawing', *Journal of the Warburg and Courtauld Institutes*, XXXVII, 1974, pp. 174–90. For Inigo Jones and the 'Holbein' porch at Wilton see John Bold with John Reeves, *Wilton House and English Palladianism*, Royal Commission on Historical Monuments, 1988, p. 32. For Vanbrugh and conservation, Kerry Downes, *Sir John Vanbrugh*, London, 1987, pp. 347–9. For the Gothick see Michael McCarthy, *The Origins of the Gothick Revival*, Yale University Press, 1987, pp. 278 ff. For the Romantic Interior, Clive Wainwright, *The Romantic Interior: The British Collector at Home 1750–1850*, Yale University Press, 1989, chs. 1 and 4. On the revival of chivalry, Mark

Girouard, *The Return to Camelot: Chivalry and the English Gentleman*, Yale University Press, 1981.

PART ONE: REVOLUTION AND REFORM
1529–1603

These facts are covered in any history of the period but on the effects of the Reformation on English art and the escalation of the cult of the Crown see Roy Strong, *The English Icon: Elizabethan and Jacobean Portraiture*, London, 1969, pp. 1–3; Strong, *The Cult of Elizabeth: Elizabethan Portraiture and Pageantry*, London, 1977; and Phillips, *Images*.

Chapter One: The Destruction of Shrines and Relics

Generally see J. C. Wall, *Shrines of British Saints*, London, 1905; Abbot Gasquet, *The Greater Abbeys of England*, London, 1905; G. H. Cook, *Letters to Cromwell and Others on the Suppression of the Monasteries*, London, 1965; G. W. O. Woodward, *The Dissolution of the Monasteries*, London, 1966, pp. 51–4, Phillips, *Images*, pp. 71–9. Virtually all the works cited in Chapter 2 on the dissolution of the monasteries deal with shrines in more or less detail. For particular shrines see *Chivalry*, (19) St Albans, (20) St Werburgh, (87) St Thomas à Becket, (380) St Edward the Confessor. All histories and guides to cathedrals which formerly housed shrines contain material, but for Canterbury and Durham see C. Eveleigh Woodruff and W. Danks, *Memorials of the Cathedral and Priory of Christ in Canterbury*, London, 1912, pp. 272–86; *A Description or Breife Declaration of all the Ancient Monuments, Rites, and Customes belonginge or beinge within the Monastical Church of Durham before the Suppression. Written in 1593*, Surtees Society, XV, 1844. For the public parade and burning of relics, Sydney Anglo, *Spectacle: Pageantry and Early Tudor Policy*, Oxford, 1969, pp. 273–4.

Chapter Two: The Dissolution of the Monasteries

There is an enormous literature on this subject but little variation in the accounts of the physical destruction of the monasteries; see Francis A.

Opposite: *A detail from the fourteenth-century manuscript the Luttrell Psalter.*

Gasquet, *Henry VIII and the English Monasteries*, fifth ed., London, 1893, pp. 387–439; Dom David Knowles, *The Religious Orders in England*, III, *The Tudor Age*, Cambridge, 1959, pp. 383–92; G. H. Cook, *Letters to Cromwell and Others on the Suppression of the Monasteries*, London, 1965; G. W. O. Woodward, *The Dissolution of the Monasteries*, London, 1966, pp. 125–30; J. Youings, *The Dissolution of the Monasteries*, London, 1973; Brian de Breffny and George Mott, *The Churches and Abbeys of Ireland*, London, 1973; Lionel Butler and Chris Given-Wilson, *Medieval Monasteries of Great Britain*, London, 1979. For the architecture see Briggs, *Goths and Vandals*, pp. 16–30. For moveables that went to the Crown see Sir John Williams, *Account of the Monastic Treasures confiscated at the Dissolution of the Various Houses in England*, ed. W. B. Turnbull, Abbotsford Club, Edinburgh, 1836. For retrospective nostalgia see Margaret Aston, 'English Ruins and English History: The Dissolution and the Sense of the Past', *Journal of the Warburg and Courtauld Institutes*, XXXVI, 1973, pp. 231–55.

Chapter Three: The Reformation of Images

The only account is in Phillips, *Images*, especially ch. 4. Recently the legislation has been published: Margaret Aston, *England's Iconoclasts*, I, *Laws Against Images*, Oxford, 1989. See also Roy Strong, 'Edward VI and the Pope: a Tudor anti-papal allegory and its setting', *Journal of the Warburg and Courtauld Institutes*, XXIII, 1960, pp. 311–313; R. Whiting, 'Abominable images: image and image-breaking under Henry VIII', *Journal of Ecclesiastical History*, XXXIII, 1982, pp. 30–47. For Scotland see David Hay Fleming, *The Reformation in Scotland*, London, 1910, pp. 356–63, 374–5. The physical impact on churches is recorded in numberless histories and guides but see J. Charles Cox and C. B. Ford, *The Parish Churches of England*, London, 1935, pp. 16–19; H. Munro Cautley, *Suffolk Churches and their Treasures*, London, 1937, pp. 18–29; G. H. Cook, *The English Cathedral through the Centuries*, London, 1960, pp. 312–19; Francis W. Cheetham, *Medieval English Alabaster Carvings in the Castle Museum Nottingham*, 1973 ed., pp. 16–17. On particular objects reproduced here see *Chivalry* (99), (290), (564), (577) and (711).

Chapter Four: The Dispersal of Libraries

The fundamental work is C. E. Wright, 'The Dispersal of Libraries in the Sixteenth Century' in *The English Library before 1700*, ed. F. Wormald and C. E. Wright, London, 1958, pp. 148–71. For Aubrey see Anthony Powell, *John Aubrey and His Friends*, London, 1963 ed., p. 37. See also James P. Carley, 'John Leland and the Foundations of the Royal Library: The Westminster Inventory of 1542', *Bulletin of the Society of Renaissance Studies*, VII, i, October 1989, pp. 13–22; Carley, 'John Leland and the contents of the English Pre-Dissolution Libraries: Glastonbury Abbey', *Scriptorium*, 40, 1986, pp. 107–20. For the Gorleston and Luttrell Psalters see *Chivalry*, (574–75).

PART TWO: THE COLLAPSE OF THE CROWN
1603–60

On the milieu of court culture before the Civil War see Graham Parry, *The Golden Age Restor'd: The Culture of the Stuart Court, 1603–42*, Manchester, 1981; R. Malcolm Smuts, *Court Culture and the Origins of a Royalist Tradition in Early Stuart England*, Pennsylvania, 1987. On the destruction of houses and castles, A. L. Rowse, *Reflections on the Puritan Revolution*, London, 1986, ch. 3.

Chapter Five: The Sale of the Royal Jewels and Plate

See A. J. Collins, *Jewels and Plate of Queen Elizabeth I*, London, 1955, ch. 4; John Hayward, 'A Rock Crystal Bowl from the Treasury of Henry VIII', *Burlington Magazine*, C, 1958, pp. 120–24; Hayward, 'The Restoration of the Royal Tudor Clock-Salt', *Goldsmiths' Company Review*, 1969–70. For Holbein's drawings of lost plate, A. B. Chamberlain, *Hans Holbein the Younger*, London, 1913, II, p. 273 ff. For the royal hat jewels, Roy Strong, 'Three Royal Jewels: The Three Brothers, the Mirror of Great Britain and the Feather', *Burlington Magazine*, CVIII, 1968, pp. 350–52.

Chapter Six: The Purging of Cathedrals and Churches

Generally see Briggs, *Goths and Vandals*, pp. 50–78: G. H. Cook, *The English Cathedral through the Centuries*, London, 1960, pp. 321–5; Phillips, *Images*, chs. 8 and 9; A. L. Rowse, *Reflections on the Puritan Revolution*, London, 1986, chs. 1 and 2. For stained glass see Christopher Woodforde, *The Norwich School of Glass-Painting in the Fifteenth Century*, Oxford, 1950, pp. 202–13; Woodforde, *English Stained and Painted Glass*, Oxford, 1954, pp. 44–6. For Dowsing, *The Journal of William Dowsing*, ed. C. H. Evelyn White, Proceedings of the Suffolk Institute of Archaeology and Natural History, VI, 1888, pp. 276–90. Most histories and guides to both cathedrals and churches relate the woes of the Commonwealth years but for two accounts see C. Eveleigh Woodruff and W. Danks, *Memorials of the Cathedral and Priory of Christ in Canterbury*, London, 1912, p. 318 ff.; Frederick Bussby, *Winchester Cathedral 1079–1979*, Paul Cave, 1979, pp. 137–41. For the Torrigiani altar in Westminster Abbey see *King's Works*, III, pp. 221–2. For the Johnson picture of the iconoclasts in Canterbury Cathedral, O. Millar, *The Age of Charles I*, Tate Gallery, 1972 (177).

Chapter Seven: The Fate of the Royal Palaces

For accounts by foreigners of the palaces in pre-Civil-War England see W. B. Rye, *England as seen by Foreigners in the Days of Elizabeth and James the First*, London, 1865; Paul Hentzner, *Travels in England*, London, 1889; Clare Williams, *Thomas Platter's Travels in England 1599*, London, 1937; G. W. Roos, *The Diary of Baron Waldstein*, London, 1981. For Henry VIII's tomb see Margaret Mitchell, 'Works of Art from Rome for Henry VIII', *Journal of the Warburg and Courtauld Institutes*, XXXIII, 1971, pp. 178–203. For the fate of the royal plate, A. J. Collins, *Jewels and Plate of Queen Elizabeth I*, London, 1955, p. 82 ff. For the sale of the royal goods and chattels see *The Inventories and Valuations of the King's Goods 1649–51*, ed. O. Millar, Walpole Society, XLIII, 1972. For Charles I's Titians see *Abraham van der Doort's Catalogue of the Collections of Charles I*, ed. O. Millar, Walpole Society, XXXVII, 1960, p. 14 ff. For the fate of the various royal palaces see *King's Works*, IV, pp. 175–9 (Newmarket), 205–17 (Oatlands), 153–4 (Holdenby), 273–98 (Theobalds); J. Summerson, 'The Building of Theobalds, 1564–1585', *Archaeologia*, XCVII, 1979, pp. 107–26; Mark Girouard, 'Elizabethan Holdenby', *Country Life*, 1979, 18 and 25 October; Mrs

Arthur Bell, *The Royal Manor of Richmond*, London, 1907, pp. 14–37; Harris and Higgott, *Inigo Jones*, pp. 74–83 (Oatlands), 100–107 (Newmarket), 193–215 (Somerset House).

Chapter Eight: The Destruction of the Crown Jewels

See Martin Holmes, 'The Crowns of England', *Archaeologia*, LXXXVI, 1937, pp. 73–90; A. J. Collins, *Jewels and Plate of Queen Elizabeth I*, London, 1955, p. 190 ff.; Martin Holmes, 'New Light on St. Edward's Crown', *Archaeologia*, XCVII, 1959, pp. 213–23; Lord Twining, *A History of the Crown Jewels of Europe*, London, 1960, p. 99 ff., especially pp. 131–51.

PART THREE: ACCIDENT, AVARICE AND FASHION
1660–1837

For the Cowdray wall-paintings see Sir William H. St John Hope, *Cowdray and Easebourne Priory . . .*, London, 1919, pp. 36–65. For the loss of the great formal gardens of Longleat, Chatsworth and Blenheim see David Green, *Gardener to Queen Anne: Henry Wise (1653–1738) and the Formal Garden*, Oxford, 1956, pp. 9–12, 33–8, 96–121; Dorothy Stroud, *Capability Brown*, London, 1975, pp. 85–6, 104–105, 129–32. For Elizabethan Chatsworth see Mark Girouard, *Robert Smythson and the Elizabethan Country House*, Yale University Press, 1983 ed., pp. 115–17. For Wimbledon, C. S. Higham, *Wimbledon Manor and the Cecils*, London, 1962. For Audley End see Kerry Downes, *Sir John Vanbrugh*, London, 1987, pp. 331–3. For Canons see John Summerson, *Architecture in Britain 1530 to 1830*, London, 1963 ed., pp. 42–3, 206. For Carlton House, 'The History of the Royal Residence of Carlton-House' in *The Royal Residences*, London, 1819; H. Clifford Smith, *Buckingham Palace*, London, 1931, ch. 4; Dorothy Stroud, *Henry Holland: His Life and Architecture*, London, 1966, pp. 63–85. For Wyatt see Briggs, *Goths and Vandals*, pp. 136–46, and for other demolitions and 'restorations', *ibid.*, p. 154 ff.

Chapter Nine: The Great Fire of London

Generally see Walter George Bell, *The Great Fire of London in 1666*, London, 1923 ed. On the Royal Exchange see John William Burgon, *The Life and Times of Sir Thomas Gresham*, II, London, 1839, pp. 107–21, 344–9. On St Paul's see John Summerson, *Inigo Jones*, London, 1966, pp. 97–106; Harris and Higgott, *Inigo Jones*, pp. 238–47. On the medieval cloister, *Chivalry* (386).

Chapter Ten: The Demolition of Nonsuch Palace

John Dent, *The Quest for Nonsuch*, London, 1962; *King's Works*, IV, ii, pp. 179–205; Roy Strong, *The Renaissance Garden in England*, London, 1979, pp. 63–9. For the Nonsuch grotesque panels see E. Croft-Murray, *Decorative Painting in England 1537–1837*, London, 1962, I, p. 165.

Chapter Eleven: The Burning of Whitehall Palace

On the history of the palace see Ernest Sheppard, *The Old Royal Palace of Whitehall*, London, 1902; *London County Council Survey of London*, ed. M. H. Cox and P. Norman, X–XIII, The Parish of St. Margaret, Westminster, parts I, II, III, London, 1926, 1930 and 1931; *The Royal Palaces of Winchester, Whitehall, Kensington and St. James's*, Wren Society, 1930, pp. 71–134; Per Palme, *Triumph of Peace: A Study of the Whitehall Banqueting House*, London, 1957; *King's Works*, IV, pp. 300–43. For the Bernini bust of Charles I see O. Millar, *The Tudor, Stuart and Early Georgian Pictures in the Collection of H. M. The Queen*, London, 1963, p. 97 (146); Rudolf Wittkower, *Gian Lorenzo Bernini*, London, 1966, pp. 16–17, 207–208 (39). For the Holbein wall-painting, Roy Strong, *Holbein and Henry VIII*, London, 1967; John Rowlands, *Holbein*, London, 1985, pp. 113–14, 224–6 (1. 24). For the Wright ceiling painting see Sara Stevenson and Duncan Thomson, *John Michael Wright: The King's Painter*, Scottish National Portrait Gallery, 1982 (14).

Chapter Twelve: Three Famous Holbeins Lost

See Paul Ganz, *The Paintings of Holbein*, London, 1950, pp. 280–8 (175–7); Roy Strong, *Tudor and Jacobean Portraits*, London, 1969, I, pp. 345–7 and bibliography; John Rowlands, *Holbein*, London, 1985, pp. 69–71, 83–5, 222–4.

Chapter Thirteen: The End of Wilton's Garden

Roy Strong, *The Renaissance Garden in England*, London, 1979, pp. 147–64; John Dixon Hunt, *Garden and Grove: The Italian Renaissance Garden in the English Imagination 1600–1750*, London, 1986, pp. 139–42; John Bold with John Reeves, *Wilton House and English Palladianism*, Royal Commission on Historical Monuments, 1988, pp. 80–90.

Chapter Fourteen: Somerset House Destroyed

See R. Needham and A. Webster, *Somerset House Past and Present*, London, 1905; John Summerson, *Architecture in Britain 1530 to 1830*, London, 1963 ed., pp. 16–17, 111, 256; E. Croft-Murray, *Decorative Painting in England 1537–1837*, London, 1962, pp. 203–204; *The Book of Architecture of John Thorpe*, ed. John Summerson, Walpole Society, XL, 1966 (T 87); *King's Works*, III, p. 252 ff.; Harris and Higgott, *Inigo Jones*, pp. 193–215. For the Canaletto view see *London and the Thames: Paintings of Three Centuries*, Department of the Environment Exhibition, Somerset House, 1977 (12).

Chapter Fifteen: The Fall of Fonthill

See J. W. Oliver, *The Life of William Beckford*, London, 1932; Boyd Alexander, *England's Wealthiest Son: A Study of William Beckford*, London, 1962; Terence Davis, *The Gothick Taste*, London, 1974, pp. 103–22; John Martin Robinson, *The Wyatts: An Architectural Dynasty*, Oxford, 1979, pp. 63, 77–8; John Wilton-Ely, 'The Genesis and Evolution of Fonthill Abbey', *Architectural History*, XXIII, 1980, pp. 40–51; Clive Wainwright, *The Romantic Interior: The British Collector at Home 1750–1850*, Yale University Press, 1989, ch. 5. For Turner and

Fonthill see *Turner 1775–1851*, Tate Gallery, 1974 (38–9); *J. M. W. Turner*, British Council, Grand Palais, Paris, 1983–4 (90).

Chapter Sixteen: Westminster in Flames

The most important accumulation of material is in H. M. Colvin, 'Views of the Old Palace of Westminster', *Architectural History*, IX, 1966, pp. 23–184. See also R. J. B. Walker, 'The Palace of Westminster after the Fire of 1834', *Walpole Society*, XLIV, 1974, pp. 94–122. For the history of the palace in the Middle Ages see H. M. Colvin, *The History of the King's Works in the Middle Ages*, London, 1963, I, p. 491 ff. For the Painted Chamber see P. Binski, *The Painted Chamber at Westminster*, Society of Antiquaries of London Occasional Papers, n.s., IX, 1986. For the Armada tapestries see M. Russell, *Visions of the Sea: Hendrick C. Vroom and the Origins of Dutch Marine Painting*, London, 1983, part II, ch. 2; Phillis Rogers, 'The Armada Tapestries in the House of Lords', *Journal of the Royal Society of Arts*, CXXXV, 5386, September 1988, pp. 731–5. For Turner's paintings of the conflagration, Martin Butlin and Evelyn Joll, *The Paintings of J. M. W. Turner*, Yale University Press, 1977, I, pp. 189–90 (359).

Conclusion: The Triumph of the Past?

For Ruskin's proposal for the preservation of medieval buildings see Joan Evans, *A History of the Society of Antiquaries*, Oxford, 1956, p. 309 ff. For a synopsis of preservation legislation see Briggs, *Goths and Vandals*, p. 220 ff; Patrick Cormack, *Heritage in Danger*, Quartet Books, 1978, ch. 1. For further manifestations and histories of the preservation movement in this century see Roy Strong, Marcus Binney and John Harris, *The Destruction of the Country House*, London, 1974; Marcus Binney and Peter Burman, *Change and Decay: The Future of our Churches*, London, 1977; Marcus Binney, *Our Vanishing Heritage*, London, 1984. For an iconoclastic view see Patrick Wright, *On Living in an Old Country: The National Past in Contemporary Britain*, London, 1985. For the whole subject and the dialogue with the past, David Lowenthal, *The Past is a Foreign Country*, Cambridge University Press, 1985.

Index

Index